THE DUKE'S SABER

The Duke's Guard Series, Book Seven

C.H. Admirand

Dragonblade Publishing, Inc. is an imprint of Kathryn Le Veque Novels, Inc.
P.O. Box 23
Moreno Valley, CA 92556
ceo@dragonbladepublishing.com

Produced in the United States of America

First Edition December 2023
Trade Paperback Edition

ARE YOU SIGNED UP FOR DRAGONBLADE'S BLOG?

You'll get the latest news and information on exclusive giveaways, exclusive excerpts, coming releases, sales, free books, cover reveals and more.

Check out our complete list of authors, too!

No spam, no junk. That's a promise!

Sign Up Here

www.dragonbladepublishing.com

Dearest Reader;

Thank you for your support of a small press. At Dragonblade Publishing, we strive to bring you the highest quality Historical Romance from some of the best authors in the business. Without your support, there is no 'us', so we sincerely hope you adore these stories and find some new favorite authors along the way.

Happy Reading!

CEO, Dragonblade Publishing

Additional Dragonblade books by Author C.H. Admirand

The Duke's Guard Series
The Duke's Sword (Book 1)
The Duke's Protector (Book 2)
The Duke's Shield (Book 3)
The Duke's Dragoon (Book 4)
The Duke's Hammer (Book 5)
The Duke's Defender (Book 6)
The Duke's Saber (Book 7)

The Lords of Vice Series
Mending the Duke's Pride (Book 1)
Avoiding the Earl's Lust (Book 2)
Tempering the Viscount's Envy (Book 3)
Redirecting the Baron's Greed (Book 4)
His Vow to Keep (Novella)
The Merry Wife of Wyndemere (Novella)

The Lyon's Den Series
Rescued by the Lyon
Captivated by the Lyon

Dedication

For DJ ~ my Heavenly Hubby

Acknowledgments

A special thank you to Arran McNicol, my wonderful editor! I greatly appreciate your attention to detail, ability to find dropped plot threads, and making sense out of some of my longer run-on sentences. You totally rock, Arran!

For my loyal readers, thank you for reading my books and letting me know how much you love my stories. A special shout out to Sandra, Jackie, Fredine, Millie, Wendy, Mariah, Anne, Sherry, Linda, and Suzonne!

CHAPTER ONE

"HELP! WE'RE OVER here!"

Ryan Garahan reacted instantly to the youthful voice and its cry for help. He leaned forward and whispered in his horse's ear as they raced toward the ancient oak on the edge of the village. "Hang on, lad!"

He leapt from his horse, glanced up, and noticed two things at once: a pair of scuffed half boots and stocking-clad legs dangling directly above his head. He quickly averted his gaze, but not before he got a healthy glimpse of a curvaceous length of leg attached to—

"I brought help, Miss Barstow! It's Garahan from Summerfield Chase!"

Garahan recognized the lad standing beneath the tree as one of the squire's twin sons. The lads were always getting underfoot whenever he patrolled the village. Garahan snapped back to attention. Truth be told, he was grateful for the interruption—it distracted him from thinking about the lovely vision above him.

You'd have to hold his feet over a roaring fire before he admitted that parts of him were still reacting to the lovely sight. Whoever she was, she had not called for help…and she was no lad! He assessed the situation, the height of the lass—given the length of her legs, she was tall—and the distance she'd have to drop into his arms. 'Twas not all that far—she could fall into his arms and not end up with a scratch. "If ye let go, miss, I'll catch ye."

"If I could let go, I would have already done so!"

Her sharp reply had him swallowing a snort of laughter. "Well then," he drawled, "why haven't ye?"

The sound coming from above him was a cross between a growl and a screech before her strained reply reached him. "Has it escaped your notice that my hair is wrapped around a branch?"

How in the bloody hell would he have noticed? He couldn't see beyond the heavenly sight of her long legs adorned with white silk stockings—tied with ribbon garters in a shocking shade of scarlet!

The damned breeze chose that moment to swirl beneath the chemise and gown above his head, flashing the curve of her delectable *derrière*! He nearly swallowed his tongue. He'd been far too long without a woman. With the never-ending onslaught of slander and threats against the duke and his family, he hadn't even thought of it until now. With a silent groan, he called on his steely control and girded his loins to ignore the goddess above him. He'd have to if he was going to extract her from her predicament.

Cursing his reaction to the lass, he wondered when in God's name he would find the time to woo a willing lass into bed when he was on duty twenty-four hours a day.

He climbed the tree, hesitating for a moment when a shadow moved above him. Narrowing his eyes, he got a better look. It was the squire's other son sitting securely above them. The lad grinned; Garahan would get to the why of that later. He noticed the branch and the irritated expression in the lass's wide blue-violet eyes at the same time.

He straddled the limb, leaned down, and wrapped an arm around her. Mindful of the long blue-black tangle in the branch above them, he lifted her into his arms. Instead of relaxing in his embrace, she started squirming. "Be still, lass, else ye'll be pulling a chunk of yer hair out."

She stilled, and he began the arduous task of extricating the silky-soft strands from the branch above them. The strands were long enough to wrap around his wrists, multiple times. He quickly squashed where that image was leading in order to extricate her.

"Can't you free me any faster?"

He felt her tremble. Was it temper or fear? Either way, he was grateful she wasn't in a panic. *Brave lass.* "Aye, I can. Reach in me boot and extract me knife."

Her gasp of shock had him chuckling, as a voice from beneath them called out, "Maybe you should cut her hair."

Her face paled as she replied, "Percival, you are not helping!"

The voice from above him said, "If Mrs. Ball discovers we've snuck out again, we'll be in the suds for sure! Cut her hair!"

"You're not helping either, Phineas! If I wasn't trying to help *you* down, I wouldn't be stuck up here."

"Percival, lad, why don't ye run on home and—"

"They'll sack me for certain!" the young woman interrupted.

The entreaty in her unusual-colored eyes had him wondering if this governess would join the others who hadn't lasted more than a fortnight. It had been rumored the squire's twin pranksters—and something slimy—had been behind the trail of governesses. Their antics were always good for a laugh whenever he passed through the village—reminding him of his twin cousins, Thomas and Eamon O'Malley, when they were young lads getting into scrapes together.

"If they let me go because I've failed to properly care for my cousins," she whispered, "I won't receive a letter of recommendation, then I have no idea what I'll do."

Surprised, he paused in his delicate task. "I thought ye were their governess."

"It's not an official position, but they are under my care. Since I'm family, my aunt and uncle do not have to pay me for watching the boys."

"Well now, doesn't seem fair to me," he said. "'Tis work, isn't it?"

Her eyes welled with tears, and he wiped them away. "Don't be crying, lass," he soothed her. "I've just a few more strands, and ye'll be free to return to yer charges. Though if I were yer relations, I'd be paying ye a fair wage. I've heard and witnessed for meself that those two are more than a handful."

She sniffed back her tears. Needing to distract her while he continued unwinding her hair, he asked, "How badly did ye hurt yer hands, lass?"

"What makes you think I injured them?"

"I've been climbing trees since I was younger than yer cousins. 'Twas a necessary skill growing up, and it added to the calluses to me hands." When she remained silent, he asked, "Now then, how badly did ye scrape them dangling from the limb—while trying to hold yerself up so as to not tear yer hair out?"

She let go of the limb, showed him one hand, grabbed hold of the branch, and showed him the other. He winced. "Ye'll be needing those scrapes and that cut tended to before infection sets in."

"How do you know so much about cuts and scrapes?" Phineas asked.

Percy answered before Garahan could. "Don't you remember the stories everyone tells at the inn about the duke's guard? All sixteen of them were injured when the Duke of Wyndmere's estate was attacked!"

Phineas snorted. "Not all of them. Besides, it wasn't scrapes or cuts—they were shot at!"

Garahan agreed, "Aye, and clubbed or stabbed, as well. Me older brother James survived being hanged, but that was before the duke hired us. Me cousin Finn O'Malley survived a hanging just a few months back."

Both boys whistled at that last statement. "Truth?" Phineas asked.

"I don't lie, lad. Took three men to save Finn. 'Twas me brother James, and two former soldiers, Tremayne and Hennessey, both friends to Captain Coventry."

The lads were properly impressed as they mulled over the information. Finally, Percy asked, "Did your cousin steal a horse?"

As they warmed to the topic, Garahan realized his error. "I shouldn't have said anything, lads. 'Tis not something me brother—nor me cousin—speaks of. Can I have yer word ye'll not mention it to anyone?"

"They'll promise," Miss Barstow answered for them. "Won't you, boys?"

"What's in it for us?" Percy demanded, hands on his hips.

"Yeah!" Phineas echoed from above. "How much will you pay for our silence?"

"I'll not hear such talk, boys," Miss Barstow proclaimed. "Bribery is as evil as placing a wager! The two of you will give Mr. Garahan your word—"

"Just Garahan, if ye please, Miss Barstow."

"Very well. Percival and Phineas, please give Garahan your solemn word that you will not speak of what happened to his brother."

"But we'd have one up on all the other boys in the village," Percy whined. "We actually know someone who had a noose around their neck!"

"Two someones," Phineas added. "And they survived!"

"Ye're a pair of bloodthirsty hooligans," Garahan told the pair, who didn't seem to mind the epithet at all. He loosened the last silken strand and said, "I'll have yer word now, lads, or I'll turn ye over to me cousin, Thomas O'Malley. He's head of the duke's guard at Summerfield Chase."

"Is he related to Finn?" Percy asked.

"Did he have a rope around his neck, too?"

"Thomas is one of the Wexford O'Malleys, cousin to Finn of the Cork O'Malleys."

"Anyone else have a noose—"

Garahan interrupted Percy, "Enough! I'm after yer solemn word, lads." He glared at one and then the other, before telling them, "A man of honor keeps his word."

Miss Barstow squeaked as she was suddenly freed from the branch and lost her grip. Garahan caught her in time, pulling her roughly to his pounding heart. Their eyes met, and he swore he saw his future unfolding in the blue-violet depths of her eyes— hands joined, standing before a man of the cloth, while the baron and baroness beamed at them. Miss Barstow in his arms as he stepped across the threshold of a pretty little thatched cottage. Pressing his lips to hers as he helped her remove her gown—

"Are you all right, Prudence?" The worry in Percy's voice was evident, and thankfully brought Garahan back to the present.

"We're not supposed to use her name, remember?" his brother said. "No one is supposed to know she's our cousin and not a real governess."

"Well now, lads," Garahan said, "it seems as if ye have a secret ye want to keep, too. I'll be keeping yers, if the two of ye promise to keep mine."

"Once a Clarkson gives his word," Miss Barstow reminded them, "they keep it."

"We're Honeycutts," Percy protested.

"True," she agreed, pulling the remaining pins from her hair to shake bits of twig and leaves from it. "But your mother—like mine—was a Clarkson before she married your father." When she shook her head, midnight silk rained over her shoulders to the middle of her back.

Garahan's tongue was tied, and for a moment, he lost the ability to speak. She lifted her gaze and smiled as she nimbly fashioned a braid. "Thank you for refraining from using your knife on my hair."

Angry with his momentary loss of concentration, he frowned at her. "If it were a matter of life and death, I'd have cut it all off."

"Surely you exaggerate," she said.

"Nay," he replied. Intrigued by the fire simmering in the depths of her gaze, he explained, "'Tis me job to save lives. Even if ye aren't under the duke's protection, I would never let ye or your cousins come to harm, lass."

She worried her bottom lip, as if troubled by his words. Need arrowed through him, as the temptation to haul her close, and discover the taste and feel of her lips, threatened his ironclad control. He dug deep and conquered the need to sample them.

No distractions, his head warned.

Just one kiss, his heart reasoned.

Angry with the crack in his control, he dug deep and pulled it around him like a shield. "Phineas, lad, will ye be all right until I set yer cousin—er, governess on her feet?"

"I'm not really stuck," Phineas confessed. "I just pretended to be so I wouldn't have to eat porridge this morning."

"We hate porridge!" his twin added.

"Do you mean to tell me—" Miss Barstow began.

Garahan interrupted, "Scold them later, lass. We need to climb down."

She glanced at the ground and shut her eyes. He wondered if her fear of heights would make the climb back down more difficult than it had to be. "I need ye to wrap yer arms around me neck and hold on tight—but mind that cut on yer one hand."

She opened her eyes, and the determination he glimpsed there warmed his heart. Fear of heights was not the problem.

"There's a lass."

She reached up and did as he asked. Her womanly curves pressed intimately against him had an immediate effect on him. He silently cursed his bloody control as the need to do far more than plunder her sweet lips scalded him on the inside.

He climbed down, set her on her feet, and immediately climbed back up to make sure Phineas wasn't boasting about his tree-climbing ability.

When his three new charges were beneath the tree, he asked, "Would ye like me to carry ye home on me horse?"

"I would!" Phineas shouted, while Percy shook his head.

"If you wouldn't mind taking the boys home," Miss Barstow said, "they could still arrive in time for porridge."

Garahan grinned, sensing she planned to walk. "Well now, Duncan—me fine gelding—is used to carrying me weight and would not bat an eye at carrying the three of ye."

Before she could protest, Garahan lifted the lass onto his horse and set one boy in front of her. She wrapped her arms around Phineas and turned a worried glance at Percy.

The lad backed away when Garahan reached for him, protesting, "Duncan is really big. His back is higher off the ground than I thought. What if I fall off?"

"Aye, he comes from a long, proud line of warhorses. His ancestors were destriers—warhorses that would carry their lords into battle wearing armor." He patted his mount. "Duncan's a fine horse. He wouldn't let ye fall off." As if on cue, the horse lifted his head.

Phineas laughed, but the solemn-faced lad standing off to the side didn't. "I...I can't," the boy insisted, and Garahan realized the real problem—the lad was afraid of the horse. He needed to remedy the situation quickly if he was going to deliver the twins and their governess to the squire's home.

"Well now, I may have a solution."

Percy stared up at him. "You do?"

"Aye." Garahan knelt in front of the lad. "Climb on me back." When the little boy did, he said, "Put yer arms around me neck." When the lad was clinging to him like a burr, Garahan slowly stood. "Let's be off, then, Miss Barstow. We wouldn't want yer cousins to miss out on a fine bowl of porridge."

His worry gone, Percy snorted. "Prudence doesn't eat with us. She eats in the kitchen with the rest of the staff."

Garahan filed that information away, wondering what other slights the lass endured working for her aunt and uncle...aside from no pay and being treated like a servant.

A SHORT WHILE later, the trio arrived at their home. Garahan set Percy on his feet before helping Phineas down, and then the lass.

They were greeted by the stable master. "If you don't want to get caught, you'd best hurry—Mrs. Cabot is keeping your breakfast warm, and I believe Mrs. Ball has been looking for you."

The boys raced around to the back of the house.

"I won't ask you not to say anything, Gifford," the lass said, "when I know it may get you into trouble with my uncle."

"I didn't see anything but a pair of scamps who'd been visiting the stables before breakfast, Miss Barstow," the stable master replied without expression.

Garahan observed the exchange and sensed the stable master was someone the lass could rely on. "I'll be taking me leave, then, Miss Barstow. I'd keep an eye on those two—they remind me of me cousins Thomas and Eamon."

"Twins?" she asked.

"Aye, though not identical like your cousins. Mine were always getting into trouble when we were young."

He turned to leave, but paused and looked over his shoulder when she called his name.

"Thank you for rescuing us this morning. I'm grateful—*we're* grateful."

He smiled. "Well now, 'twas a pleasure, as it's been some time since I've climbed a tree." Garahan grinned at his horse. "Duncan enjoyed carrying Phineas and yerself. He knew it was an important task."

Her smile bloomed, like a rosebud unfurling in the warmth of the sun. Beauty such as Miss Barstow's was rare. Midnight hair, blue-violet eyes, and curves to drive a man to thinking thoughts he'd best be reserving for his wedding night—

Bloody hell!

He'd taken enough time rescuing the lass and her cousins. It was time to resume his duties before he lost what little was left of his wits. O'Malley was bound to be waiting for his return—and an explanation of what had kept him.

Duty called.

CHAPTER TWO

PRUDENCE WATCHED GARAHAN mount his horse and ride away.

The stable master loudly cleared his throat, and she turned back. "I should have been more firm with Phineas when Percival dared him to climb that tree."

Gifford shook his head. "Those two are only happy when they manage to escape this house—and you."

"Am I too hard on them?" she asked. "Is that why they constantly try my patience?"

He smiled. "Those boys think the world of you. I can't tell you how often they've told me how much they're enjoying having their cousin mind them instead of—in their words—'one of those pinch-lipped, vinegary, old-maid governesses.'"

Prudence shook her head. "The women who take on the position of governess cannot help being pinch-lipped, Gifford. I've found myself making that same face whenever I turn my back and find they've run off again."

"Like this morning."

She sighed heavily. "They were such perfect angels, getting up and dressing themselves when I asked them to. I should have known something was up when they were so cooperative."

"Sharp, devious minds lurk behind the camouflage of their bright blue eyes and freckled faces."

She laughed, delighted with the accuracy of Gifford's deduction. "I never spent much time with young children growing up. I'm the youngest. The first time we attended a harvest dance in our village, my two older sisters received proposals from half a dozen young men! My parents often reminded me it was most unfortunate that I was nearly equal in height to my father…unlike my shorter, older sisters."

She smoothed her gown, wondering what had possessed her to tell Gifford even the tiniest bit of her past. She brushed bits of bark and leaves before noticing the dirt that stained one of the three serviceable gowns she owned. They complained about the extra cost for gowns to accommodate her height. But that wasn't the only thing that concerned her parents. They often lamented her overly generous curves, insisting that while young men flocked to her, not one had marriage on their minds. When she obeyed her parents, not showing any interest in them, the rumors started. Rumors that cut her to the quick, calling her character into question, as the *on dit* spread that she was easily convinced to part with her favors.

"Well, miss," the stable master began, "if they did not take note of you, they were blind as bats and will regret it when they realize they've saddled themselves with a wife who cares more for the latest fashions than her children."

Buoyed by Gifford's kind words, she confessed, "You and Mrs. Cabot are the only ones who have not constantly echoed Aunt and Uncle's claims that I am not a proper governess—and will never be. I think they expect me to fail, and enjoy reminding me that I'd best learn quickly, because they are tiring of pointing out my faults and failings in that regard."

She was perilously close to tears when he noticed and held up a hand. "None of that now, else the squire will be lecturing you about bemoaning your circumstances before you've had your morning tea."

He was right, and she knew it. Wiping her cheeks with the backs of her hands, she heard his sharp intake of breath and wondered if the squire was behind them. When she turned around, no one was there.

She turned back and saw concern on his weathered face. "What have you done to your hands?" he asked.

Putting them behind her back, she murmured, "Er…nothing."

The stable master's frown was fierce. "Why didn't you wait for them to climb down? They're agile as monkeys."

"Phineas sounded so scared," she told him. "No one was about, so I did what I had to do. Besides, I used to love climbing trees."

Gifford shook his head at her. "Best wash up and let Mrs. Cabot tend to your hands—especially that cut—or Squire and Mrs. Honeycutt will have even more to browbeat you for if they have to summon the physician."

She knew he was right. "I'm becoming accustomed to it."

The stable master frowned at her. "I do not want you to worry, but if someone saw Garahan rescue you and the boys this morning, tongues will start to wag."

"But the duke's guard are men of honor and integrity. They would never do anything to give the local gossips anything to talk about."

"I did not say tongues would be telling tales about Garahan or the others who protect Baron and Baroness Summerfield."

"Then what—Oh." She placed a hand to her ample chest and let it fall. "I understand, but you are wrong. I haven't done anything improper to give them fodder for gossip…other than trust my two darling little cousins."

"Mrs. Cabot and I will keep our ears to the ground and let you know if we hear anything untoward."

She stood on her toes and gave him a peck on his cheek. "Thank you for being my friend, Gifford."

"It's an honor, miss."

She waved, lifted her skirts, and dashed toward the back entrance, crossing her fingers that her aunt and uncle were still upstairs.

"There you are, miss." The cook smiled. "I sent the boys off to wash. It's your turn," she said, nodding toward the room off the pantry. "Best see to it before the mistress sees you." Tilting her head to one side and then the other, she sighed. "From the looks of your gown, those boys were telling the truth. You climbed the old tree on the edge of town! Whatever made you think Phineas was stuck?"

Prudence started to wring her hands together and ended up sucking in air between her clenched teeth. They hurt!

Mrs. Cabot put down the large spoon she'd been using to stir a pot on the stove, wiped her hands on her apron, and walked toward Prudence. "Let me see your hands."

"I'd rather wash them first."

Mrs. Cabot was twice her age, and had a formidable temper when crossed. Her intense frown decided for Prudence, who reluctantly held out one of her hands.

The cook's frown was every bit as fierce as Gifford's. "Dirt, bits of bark—and Heaven only knows what else—is ground into that hand." She motioned with her free hand. "Let's see the other one." Prudence slowly extended her other hand and winced when Mrs. Cabot accidentally brushed against the cut. "I have just enough time before Squire and Mrs. Honeycutt come down to breakfast to clean these out." The cook pulled Prudence along behind her.

Mrs. Cabot tutted over the state of the abraded skin on Prudence's hands while she cleansed them, then shook her head over the depth of one cut. "You may need threads to pull that closed."

That prediction had Prudence's stomach feeling queasy and her head going light.

"Easy now, miss. Lean on me."

Prudence had no other choice—she leaned against the cook and let herself be led to the stool next to the pitcher and bowl on the long sideboard. "I'm sorry. I don't know what came over me."

The knowing look on the cook's face had Prudence suspecting the older woman could see right through her. Her suspicions were confirmed when Mrs. Cabot said, "You don't like needles, do you?"

Prudence gulped. "I don't mind needlework, but I prefer being out-of-doors—thankfully, the twins do, too." When the cook pressed her lips into a thin line, a sure sign she was irritated, Prudence immediately apologized. "I'm sorry for being flippant, Mrs. Cabot. Please forgive me—I do not wish to be a bother and truly do have an aversion to needles…when they are to be used on my person."

Lifting her chin, she continued, "Do you see the jagged scar beneath my chin? I was the same age as Percival and Phineas when I fell out of the tree I was climbing." She shuddered. "I stopped counting after ten stitches."

"But that did not stop you from climbing that tree to save your cousin." The cook handed her a cup of water. "Do you think you can hold on to the cup with your fingertips, or do you need my help?"

"I can manage." Prudence took a few sips and then one long swallow. "Thank you. I do feel a little less shaky."

"A good breakfast will take care of that," the cook predicted.

"Oh, but you know I'm not allowed more than toast and tea for breakfast. Aunt is determined that I shall lose weight before they allow me to appear in public with the boys." Prudence hesitated before adding, "My parents tried to hide me away when it became obvious my appearance was attracting too much attention."

"Fiddle-faddle!" the cook admonished her. "You'll eat what I fix for you. A proper meal will give you the energy to keep up with those two. Leave the mistress to me."

Mrs. Cabot gently cleansed Prudence's hands and inspected the worrisome cut. "Now that it's clean, I can see it is not quite as deep as I feared."

Prudence sighed with relief.

The cook applied the healing salve with great care, then wound a thin linen strip around her hand. "Now then. You are not to get that bandage wet until I see how you are faring after teatime."

"My duties—"

"Will have to be modified…or curtailed. We cannot have those scamps who instigated your scaling that old tree taking advantage of you. Why not ask them to pitch in and help you with your tasks? They may enjoy it, as they have none of their own—and should."

Prudence struggled to keep her composure as her mind raced through a tangle of emotions: worry, fear, and helplessness. It did not matter if she was related to the Honeycutts. Her aunt and uncle would insist she leave without compunction if she were no longer of use to them.

Resigned to the inevitable, she said, "It was a pleasure getting to know you, Mrs. Cabot. You and Gifford have treated me like family. Better than my own," she whispered.

"Now, now, I'll not listen to any talk of you leaving. Do not borrow trouble. I shall speak to the mistress first. If she balks, I will speak to the squire. She hates when I go over her head."

"Please don't on my account," Prudence begged. "I wouldn't want to cause you to lose your position, too."

"Now, now," Mrs. Cabot said. "Have a little faith, and while you're searching for it, why don't you keep me company in the kitchen while I finish preparing breakfast?" She winked at Prudence, adding, "Tell me all about that handsome-as-sin Irishman with those dark and dangerous eyes."

Prudence felt her face flame before she leaned close and confessed. "His eyes got this mysterious look in them when he kept me from falling off the limb—it was dark and…desperate."

"Oh?" the cook asked as they returned to the kitchen. "How did he keep you from falling?"

Prudence sighed and closed her eyes for a moment, then slowly opened them. "He yanked me against his broad chest."

She looked around her to ensure they were alone before adding, "I think his muscles have muscles!"

Mrs. Cabot's delighted laughter filled the room and lightened Prudence's heavy load. The older woman brushed her hands on her apron, lifted the kettle from the stove, and poured hot water into the waiting teapot. Setting out two teacups, she sat down and smiled conspiratorially. "Tell me more."

CHAPTER THREE

"WHERE IN THE bloody hell have ye been?"

Garahan knew he returned later than he'd planned, but still within a reasonable time frame, allowing for unforeseen circumstances. His heart warmed at the thought of the curvaceous Miss Barstow of the blue-violet eyes…and her precarious position hanging from that limb. It certainly qualified as an unusual circumstance in his mind. O'Malley had never questioned him before. "What's got the bug up yer *arse*?"

O'Malley vibrated with anger. Something was wrong, but Garahan wouldn't know what happened while he was on patrol unless his cousin told him. Either that, or if he pushed his cousin to the edge of *his* control. It had been a sennight since they'd had time to hone their bare-knuckle skills. He'd welcome the opportunity to go a few rounds with O'Malley. He flexed his hands while he waited for his cousin to answer.

O'Malley shoved him out of the way. "We've no time for a bout of bare-knuckle right now! The baron's waiting to speak with us."

Garahan shoved back. "What happened?"

O'Malley strode toward the stables. Garahan kept pace with him and stuck his foot out to trip his cousin, but O'Malley anticipated the move and evaded it. "'Tis serious, Ryan. I've never seen the baron this angry."

"Our patrols do not run on a bloody timepiece. If his lordship intends to keep track of us that way, I'll be speaking to His Grace about a transfer."

O'Malley jolted to a stop and grabbed Garahan by his cravat. "Shut the *feck* up! 'Tisn't always about what ye want or think ye need."

Garahan slapped his cousin's hand away, chastised, and rightly so. He had been thinking about himself. "Bugger it, ye're right, Thomas." Shame mixed with worry. "'Tisn't the baroness, is it? Is she ill?"

O'Malley shook his head and followed the path toward the entrance to the kitchen.

"Why are we meeting inside?"

O'Malley mumbled a curse, then answered, "An urgent message arrived for the baron. Her ladyship heard the baron's reaction to the message and insists on being a part of the discussion with us and his lordship's reply. 'Tis why we aren't meeting in the stables."

Garahan sighed, well used to the volatile personality of the baroness. "Her ladyship is not one to stand quietly off to the side."

"I lost ten years off me life chasing after her when she received the ransom note for the baron. 'Twas before they were married," O'Malley admitted.

Garahan snorted with laughter. "Didn't ye say she held off more than one of the kidnappers with a bundle of ribbon-wrapped hatpins and a paperweight?"

"With the paperweight in her hand, her right cross was as effective as it was a thing of beauty." O'Malley opened the door and held it for his cousin. Walking past the small room next to the pantry, he nodded to the young man who'd delivered the message, who was currently eating a scone piled high with jam and clotted cream while he waited for a reply. "We'll be with ye shortly."

The lad nodded. His mouth was full.

Walking along the hallway toward the kitchen, Garahan wondered what the message involved this time. Whenever one arrived involving any of their ladyships, the baron stalked around Summerfield Chase, growling at everyone. Garahan understood the baron's reaction from years of watching his parents—and more recently his brother and his cousins, who had met and married the loves of their lives. Each in turn became fiercely protective of their women—even more so once they married.

Ever since the duke inherited his title, there had been constant rumors, threats of scandal, and physical attacks upon the duke, his brother, and their cousins. But worse, Garahan remembered, were the attempted kidnappings of the duke and duchess's twins—who were infants at the time—and their lordships' wives! Though the baron and his cousin, Viscount Chattsworth, were only distant cousins to the duke, His Grace treated them as if they were brothers. Given the striking resemblance to His Grace, and the earl, and the fact that they were eerily alike in mien and looks, it was assumed they were in fact *closely* related, if not brothers born on the wrong side of the blanket.

Garahan would keep that thought to himself, unless anyone made the mistake of uttering such a claim. The fourth Duke of Wyndmere never strayed from his beloved wife. Their son, the fifth duke, was another story that ended in tragedy. The sixth duke was cut from the same cloth as his sire. Garahan was proud to serve His Grace.

"Fresh scones, Mrs. Green?" O'Malley asked, interrupting Garahan's thoughts as they passed the doorway to the kitchen.

The baron's cook smiled and brushed a lock of gray off her forehead with the back of her hand. "I'll be sure to set aside a batch for the three of you."

O'Malley thanked her and kept walking, but Garahan paused to wink at her. "Ye're an absolute angel, Mrs. Green!"

Her laughter followed them to the door that led to the main side of the house. Timmons was giving instructions to one of the new footmen when they walked through the door. "O'Malley, Garahan, his lordship's waiting for you in the library," the butler informed them.

The door to the library opened as they approached. "I heard your footsteps," the baron remarked. Turning to Garahan, he glared at him, demanding, "What in the bloody hell kept you?"

"I had to rescue a lass and her charges from the old oak at the edge of the village, then escorted them home."

Summerfield's expression changed from irritated to interested as he accepted that his guard had not been lax in his duties. None of the guard currently stationed at Summerfield Chase had ever given him reason to think so. "Tell me later."

"Aye, yer lordship." Garahan nodded to Flaherty and followed the baron into the room.

O'Malley shut the door behind them. "Now then—"

The door swung open, and the baroness swept inside, walked up to her husband, and poked him in the chest. "You promised to wait for me," Baroness Summerfield reminded him.

His gaze softened. "Ah, my love, you know the messenger has another missive to deliver within the hour. You would not want to be responsible for him being derelict in his duties, would you?"

She narrowed her brilliant blue eyes—so like the baron's that one would think they were closely related. The Lippincott genes were strong, even though they were very distant cousins. She walked past him to settle into one of the leather armchairs Garahan knew she favored. Lady Phoebe waved a hand in the air. "You may begin, husband."

He raised an eyebrow in silent question before speaking. "Apparently the recent salacious gossip about my wife and myself has not died down completely, as we had hoped."

"Even with the servants and ourselves helping to spread the truth?" Flaherty asked.

"Yes. Apparently, the duke's sources have informed him that someone in our village is fanning the flames to keep the rumors alive."

"Who in the village would speak out against ye?" Garahan asked.

"We will find out," O'Malley promised.

The baroness shot to her feet. "I'll rout out whoever it is, Marcus!"

Summerfield rolled his eyes at his wife. "For the love of God, Phoebe, let the duke's guard handle the matter."

"While someone in our village spreads vicious lies about us? Do they not remember who supplied the coin—and the man-power—to repair the church's roof?"

"Now, love—"

She crossed her arms, demanding, "What of the repairs to the inn when that tree branch crashed in through the front window during the terrible storm last summer?"

Garahan enjoyed watching Lady Phoebe when she was on a crusade. Her passion for life was a delight to watch and reminded him of a young woman he'd met an hour before. He glanced at his lordship and knew, from the heat in the baron's gaze, that he felt the same about his wife.

The baron walked over to where she stood and reached for her hand. She uncrossed her arms to take it. He reached out to brush the tips of his fingers across her cheek. "Once we discover who the malcontent is, and take care of the matter, our lives will finally return to normal."

She sighed, and he tucked her against his side.

O'Malley and Flaherty moved to flank Garahan. "Leave it to us, yer ladyship," O'Malley said. "We have the connections."

"Aye," Flaherty agreed. "And ways of extracting infor-mation."

"The rumors are beyond detestable," Lady Phoebe rasped. "Never in my life could I even imagine anything so vile or disgusting. Who would gain such pleasure repeating something so heinous?"

Summerfield shifted his wife into his embrace. Tucking her

head beneath his chin, he said, "We will get to the bottom of the situation and reveal the source. Worry not, my love."

He lifted his head and locked gazes with O'Malley. Garahan watched the exchange. He recognized the baron's need to do bodily harm to whoever reignited the flame beneath the pot of vicious lies that slandered his wife and himself, and the silent agreement from his cousin.

The baron said, "See to it."

"Aye, yer lordship, we will," O'Malley answered for the three of them.

"And give the messenger my reply to the duke," the baron added.

"What would ye have me tell him?" O'Malley asked.

"Thank him for alerting us," Summerfield answered. "Tell him we will handle it."

"Aye, yer lordship." With a nod to the baron and baroness, the guard exited the library.

"Ye know as well as I do there's more than one person in the village who enjoys passing along rumors. We need to find the one who has the blackest heart," Flaherty said.

"And the biggest mouth, though I'm thinking it might be hard to decide, as there are a few candidates I can think of right off," Garahan remarked.

O'Malley glared at his cousins. "Keep yer voices down. We don't want to upset her ladyship any more than she already is."

Garahan sensed there was more to the situation than the passing along of gossip. "I'm thinking there's coin involved."

"Aye," O'Malley agreed.

Flaherty waited a beat then said, "Mayhap an old score to be settled."

"No matter—we'll do what we've done in the past," Garahan said. "It has turned the tide of those ready to believe the worst of the duke and his family before, and will work again."

The guard dispersed to their assigned shifts. It was Flaherty's turn to patrol between Summerfield Chase, the village, and beyond. Garahan would be on guard within the house, while O'Malley patrolled the grounds. In four hours, they would change shifts again.

By teatime, the duke's guard planned to have the information they required. If everything went according to their plans, by nightfall, the rumormonger would be standing before the baron and baroness begging their forgiveness!

CHAPTER FOUR

A FEW DAYS later, the situation remained unchanged. Garahan had his suspicions, but he needed proof. Mulling over who else to question to obtain the proof, he entered the hallway from the outside to man his post guarding the inside of the house. Raised voices coming from the library distracted him, and for a moment he felt relief that he hadn't been caught in the parson's noose. With a nod to the footmen stationed near the library, he wondered if his brothers were experiencing similar problems with their wives as the baron was with his.

Striding toward the entrance to the servants' side of the home, he opened the door and nearly knocked Lady Phoebe's maid off her feet. He reached out to steady her. "Forgive me, lass. I did not intend to knock ye to the ground."

She shook her head. "My fault, Garahan. I tend to rush about without paying attention when her ladyship is out of sorts."

He let go of her arm and nodded. "Anything I can do to help?" She blinked away tears, and he stifled a groan. "We're here to help. Ye need to tell meself, or either of me cousins, if something is wrong. We cannot protect her ladyship otherwise."

Her face reddened, but she did not look away. "You're right, of course, but this isn't a new problem. It's... I just..."

Sensing it had to do with the horrendous tale that had started circulating a month ago and was currently making the rounds again, Garahan sighed. "His Grace thought the gossip would end once the person responsible for starting the vile claims had been exposed."

"I know, but—"

"And ye know that the duke called upon his connections in London," Garahan interrupted, needing to fix the maid's problem so he could continue on his rounds. "Gavin King of the Bow Street Runners and Captain Coventry, the duke's London man-of-affairs."

"Yes, but—"

"The entirety of the duke's guard, along with the servants at each of his households, did their part," he continued, needing Beth to understand. "Spreading the truth should have stopped the false and vindictive tale from spreading."

The maid lifted her gaze to meet his. "I think Lady Phoebe suspects she knows who is responsible for countering all that you and the others have done, adding to the rumors…"

Garahan squared his shoulders. "Finish it, lass. Tell me what else is being spread about their lordships."

"It's about you," she whispered.

He frowned. "What about me?"

When her face flushed for the second time, he thought she might refuse. He was more than prepared to make her talk if she refused to tell him. Then the maid surprised him by blurting out, "There's talk in the village involving two young women. One was seen being accosted by you; the other is reported as having been seen being compromised by you."

He didn't know what to make of the sordid tales. The ramifications would harm not only the reputations of the baron and baroness, but the duke and his family, as well as the duke's guard. "'Tis a lie. Since transferring to Summerfield Chase, I haven't even had the time away from me duties to visit the inn and share a pint with me cousins!"

She turned away from him, and Garahan could have kicked himself for dismissing her words. "Pardon me, lass, for acting the part of an *eedjit*! Thank ye for bringing these claims to me attention. Do ye know who's made these claims?"

He waited for Beth to speak, while the need to gallop off to the village and prove his innocence nearly choked him.

"If not a name, then mayhap where ye heard these claims?"

"A scullery maid, and one of the footmen overheard the tale escorting Mrs. Green on her shopping earlier in the day. 'Tis said you accosted the blacksmith's daughter."

He'd spoken to the smithy on more than one occasion, but they never spoke of family. "The blacksmith has a daughter?"

The maid nodded. "The rumor spreading like wildfire is that you were seen holding the young woman against a gravestone in the churchyard."

He scrubbed a hand over his face as if he could wipe the evil words from his mind. "So not only have I tried to hold a young woman against her will, but I did so within sight of the church on hallowed ground?"

The maid nodded.

He raked a hand through his hair and asked, "What other charge have ye to tell me about?"

"'Tis said the vicar's daughter was seen running from behind the church with the sleeve of her gown torn, her hair tumbled down. She was weeping…and you were chasing after her."

Garahan's gut clenched with anger at the lies, and sorrow that two young women who were innocent in this were having their reputations torn to shreds. "Not a word of what ye've said is true."

The maid's hands trembled as she held them to her waist. "I believe you, Garahan, but what can we do about such talk? I have lived here all of my life, except for the short time I was a maid in London. I know that neither the vicar's daughter nor the blacksmith's daughter would allow themselves to be lured into such dire straits."

He wondered who had such a blackened soul that they would make up and spread such vicious gossip. "Lass, do ye know when

I'm supposed to have been seen with these young women?"

Beth shook her head. "It wasn't mentioned. Given the rumors resurfacing about her ladyship—and the fact that she and his lordship are under your protection…"

Garahan finished what she had not said. "The good people in the village are more apt to believe it of me than they are inclined to believe the other."

"The footman spoke up on your behalf, and both reported what they'd heard to the cook, who told his lordship. None of the staff would believe it of you—or your cousins, let alone what is being spread about her ladyship, and his lordship." The sorrow in her gaze matched his. "Why would anyone want to spread lies that could ruin the reputation of those who have never done anything but help them?"

"I'm afraid I don't have the answer, lass. Thank ye for confiding in me. I'll be needing to speak to the footman and the maid to thank them for sticking up for me, but I need to speak to me cousins and his lordship immediately."

"You're welcome. If I hear anything else, I will be sure to let you know."

"Thank ye, lass."

Garahan turned around and retraced his steps through the door into the main part of the house. He was relieved to find the butler in the entryway. "Timmons! Did ye see Flaherty ride past?"

"Not as yet." The butler hesitated, then asked, "Problem, Garahan?"

"Aye. I must speak to Flaherty before he goes on his rounds." Garahan yanked the door open and stepped outside in time to see the back end of a horse headed toward the village. Instead of shouting to get the attention of his cousin—who would no doubt ignore him—he used their signal for danger, a short, sharp whistle.

Flaherty immediately reacted, spinning his mount around. He pulled to a stop, demanding, "What's happened?"

Garahan was about to reply when O'Malley rounded the

corner of the house, sprinting toward them. Relieved they had arrived, Garahan told them, "I'll be needing the two of ye to vouch as to me whereabouts for the last few weeks."

"Would that be when yer *arse* has been glued to the saddle on patrol between the village and Summerfield Chase?" Flaherty asked.

O'Malley met Garahan's gaze. "Or during the household shift and guarding the perimeter?"

"All of it. I wanted ye to know before I speak to—"

"I understand that you need to speak with me, Garahan," the baron said, arriving.

"Yer lordship!"

"Phoebe just confided what she heard earlier when she and her maid were visiting with the vicar's wife. Though her daughter is vehemently denying the talk, the poor woman was in a state of shock."

Garahan clenched his jaw, then relaxed it. "On me honor, yer lordship, not a word of what's being said is true!"

The baron did not hesitate to agree.

"Her ladyship's maid spoke to me just now. I was just letting me cousins know they'll be asked to vouch for me presence while performing me duties, yer lordship. I haven't told them what I'm being accused of yet."

The baron patted Garahan on the back. "From your deeds, and those of your cousins, I have no doubt they will stand with you and help end these vile rumors. Have faith. We'll get to the bottom of the gossip and expose the culprit."

"I do, yer lordship. It's just that…"

What could he say? He wasn't immune to the powers of a winsome woman. He'd succumbed to the lure of a whispered offer and crook of a feminine finger many times—just not recently. Come to think of it, since he'd started working for the duke, he'd had far too little time to enjoy the charms of a willing woman.

A curvaceous, black-haired beauty—wearing scarlet garter

ties—slashed through his thoughts, discombobulating them.

The baron seemed to think that Garahan needed reassurance. "No one understands what you're feeling right now better than me, Garahan, having been in the middle of accusations and scandal myself. We know the truth. And you can count on every one of our staff to stand behind you as they've stood behind Phoebe and me. Trust in the truth." With a glance at the men surrounding him, Summerfield nodded. "I'll let you men return to your posts."

Flaherty mounted his horse, and O'Malley started to walk away, but Garahan stood glued to the spot, rubbing a hand over his heart. "This must be what me brothers felt when their reputations were cast in doubt, tangled up in heinous lies and innuendo."

The baron nodded.

"It hurts me heart," Garahan admitted. "I would never do anything to bring censure to His Grace or his family—of which ye're a part, having married His Grace's sister. I hold each and every one of ye in such high regard. 'Tis an honor the duke bestowed on meself, and me family, when he hired us as his personal guard. What kind of a man would I be if I was to forsake that vow?"

"Ye wouldn't be kin of mine," O'Malley answered, pausing.

"Or mine," Flaherty added before flicking the reins and riding off.

"We count on every last one of you," Summerfield rasped. "To honor your vow to protect our families with your lives, as we proudly stand beside you, ready to lay down our lives for them, too."

"Ye've fought alongside of us more than once, yer lordship," Garahan reminded him. "Along with the duke, the earl, and the viscount. It has been an honor."

The baron waved a hand in the air, as if dismissing Garahan's words. "You will continue to honor your vow, and you will not leave the duke's guard because someone has decided to attack your honor."

Garahan shook his head. "I'd be leaving in order to prove that I am guiltless. Then I'd be returning to resume me duties."

The baron clamped a hand to Garahan's shoulder. "You may do so while performing your duties."

"Then ye don't want me to step back?"

"I do not, and I know I speak for my cousins when I tell you that nor would they wish it either. You are an integral part of the sixteen-man team that has been with His Grace since he accepted the title." Summerfield smiled. "You're stuck with us."

The sharp arrow of betrayal eased out of Garahan's heart. "I'll not be letting ye down, yer lordship."

"I never thought you would. Now get back to your post."

Feeling as if a weight had been lifted from his shoulders, Garahan returned to his shift patrolling the interior of Summerfield Chase, though a dark thought took root in his brain: would the squire's niece become the next young woman he supposedly accosted or compromised? Faith, even he had to admit, if someone had seen them at a distance, it would have looked as if something funny was going on.

He'd best be prepared. Mayhap he'd need to speak to his cousins in more detail about his early morning rescue of the distractingly curvaceous, midnight-haired goddess and her twin hooligan cousins.

CHAPTER FIVE

PRUDENCE HAD MANAGED to hide the injuries to her hands from her aunt, until it no longer required a bandage, for the last few days by keeping the boys busy with their studies in the schoolroom upstairs. Her aunt surprised her by complimenting her on their excellent behavior when she was in the kitchen picking up their midday meal.

"They are such good little boys and will grow up to be fine, upstanding young men."

Instead of agreeing, her aunt blurted out, "Those three Irishmen stationed at Summerfield Chase will never be mistaken for upstanding men! I just knew they would be trouble!"

Prudence tried to ignore her aunt, who was building up a head of steam, but she needed to find out just what the woman was talking about. Deciding to appear as if she agreed with her aunt without question, she remarked, "What have the duke's guard done now?"

Warming to her topic, her aunt expounded, "That dark-haired, dark-eyed one with the devilish good looks has compromised the blacksmith's daughter—and the vicar's daughter! Both young women have impeccable reputations—now they're ruined!"

"But Aunt—"

As if just realizing her niece had been addressing her too

familiarly, she corrected her, "Mrs. Honeycutt."

"Forgive me, Mrs. Honeycutt, but isn't His Grace's reputation and that of Baron and Baroness Summerfield also being maligned if the men in his employ are suspected of such horrific deeds?"

Her aunt's expression changed from indignation to interest. "Why yes, Miss Barstow, I believe you are correct."

Prudence hid her dismay at being spoken to as if she were a complete stranger. She should be used to it by now. She fought to control the urge to snap at her aunt, reminding her of their familial connection. It would do no good. Once her aunt's mind was made up, she was immovable. "Are we not, as residents of Summerfield-on-Eden, dependent upon the baron and baroness's largesse, and owe it to them, and the duke, to do all in our power to squelch the awful rumors?"

The look of abject horror on her aunt's face had Prudence wishing she had held her tongue.

"Do not, for one infinitesimal moment, think that you are counted among the good people of Summerfield-on-Eden! You were sent here because of your gauche ways, embarrassing height, and your overblown figure. My sister could not mold you into a proper lady, as we were brought up to be, and nor could my brother-in-law find a man willing to wed such a blot, such a stain, on the Clarkson and Barstow names." Her lips thinned and her eyes narrowed. "So, they sent you to me, while they continue to seek an advantageous marriage for you, despite being deemed unmarriageable by your mother. You will either learn to accustom yourself to your duties as governess to Phineas and Percival and comport yourself as a proper lady should, or I will have no choice but to turn you out without a recommendation."

Prudence tried to swallow past the lump of anguish in her throat, wishing she were anywhere else but in the presence of another family member who could barely stand the sight of her. It was not her fault that she resembled her father's side of the family—especially Grandmother Barstow, who was the complete opposite in looks and personality from her mother and her aunt, who were of average height and figure, with pale blonde locks and paler blue eyes.

Society deemed their looks acceptable, while finding Prudence an anomaly. One to be shunned, bullied...and all because of the way she looked! Not one of the people who openly mocked her at the dances hosted by the local inn, nor those who treated her as if she were a leper when she accompanied her mother to the dressmaker's shop, saw her as more than an object to be ridiculed, despised...pitied.

"Yes, Aunt...er...Mrs. Honeycutt. I shall strive to improve my shortcomings and remember my place so that I may please you."

"And Squire Honeycutt! You have a fortnight to show a marked improvement, or mark my words, we will send you packing! I shall keep my promise to my dear sister and give you the opportunity to learn a skill—caring for our sons. You will need it, as I highly doubt any gentleman could be bribed...er...convinced to offer for your hand."

Tears pricked the backs of her eyes, but she refused to shed them. She would not give the woman the satisfaction of knowing how deeply her words had cut. She drew in a breath to steady herself. "Percival and Phineas asked if I could take them to the marsh to study the plants and creatures living there—as part of their biology and botany studies."

Her aunt considered the request. "They have been quite diligent attending to their bookwork, and they would do well to know the land surrounding their home. After all, it will be theirs one day. I will allow the trip, but make it a short one, and ensure they wear their old boots. Bring plenty of containers for whatever slimy things they deign to collect—Mrs. Ball was most displeased when advised they forgot to remove them from their pockets the last time they went to the marsh."

"Er...yes."

When Prudence didn't move at once, her aunt shouted,

"What are you waiting for? You are dismissed!"

Prudence hurried to escape the woman's formidable temper. She had her hand on the doorknob when her aunt added, "See that they are home in time for tea. I'm expecting the ladies, and wish to present my darling sons looking their best."

She bowed, murmured a proper goodbye, then fled. How in the world would she be able to coerce the twins away from their favorite haunt in time for tea? It was already half an hour past their midday meal! Rushing to do as she was bidden, she clamored up the servants' staircase and nearly collided with one of the boys at the top of the stairs.

"Mother raised her voice again," Phineas whispered. "It makes my stomach hurt when she does."

She had taken on the duty of shielding her cousins from their mother's censure and temper from the moment she arrived. Prudence vowed to continue to do so for as long as she was still acting as their governess. Smiling down at the boy, she said, "I'm sorry it bothers you, Phineas, but sometimes, we must be brave and face a confrontation to settle matters, rather than turn from it."

"But when she squints, her lips disappear… It's scary."

She hugged him to her. "We need to find Percival, because your mother has given me permission to take you to the marsh as part of our studies today."

Phineas shouted for his brother, "Percy!"

Prudence covered her ears and laughed. "Remember, gentlemen do not shout, though I am certain he heard you. He's probably in the schoolroom drawing."

The door at the end of the hallway room swung open. "I'm busy! What do you want?"

Before the brothers could get into an argument—as they were wont to do—she said, "You two need to change into the shirts and trousers I mended the other day. Oh, and put on your old boots and jackets, while I collect the specimen jars and a leather satchel to carry them in."

The brothers grinned at her, and her heart melted. Those darling, freckled faces were worth facing down their dragon of a mother!

"Hurry now. Your mother expects us home in time for tea—and dressed in your best!"

Phineas groaned. "She only does that when she invites her ladies over for tea."

"We don't like them," Percy added. "They talk about everybody and always say mean things about them."

Prudence sighed. "I cannot understand why some people need to act that way. But you don't have to listen to them—or believe what they say if they are disparaging others. My parents and those in our little village said terrible things about me…because of my height, and how I look. In spite of that, I always did my best to treat others as I would want to be treated." She sighed.

"Did it make them stop?" Phineas asked.

"Er…no, but in the end, it made no difference."

"Why is that?" Percy asked.

"My mother wrote to her sister—your mother—and, well…here I am."

The boys wrapped their arms around Prudence, melting away the hurt that their mother had caused over the years with her harsh words and threats. "Don't listen to Mother," Percy told her.

"Father never does," Phineas added.

"Thank you both for listening. I didn't mean to speak of my troubles to have you feel sorry for me, but to help you understand that you are the only ones who can make yourself feel inferior. Be true to yourself and don't listen to idle gossips. They thrive on spreading lies with the intention of hurting others."

"We will!" the boys promised.

"And remember, there are times in life when we have to do things distasteful to us, but if it be something our parents ask of us," she said, "we must obey."

"Is that why you let Mother speak to you the way she does?" Phineas asked.

"She didn't speak to the governesses we dispatched with those worms that way." Percy slapped a hand over his mouth, while his brother elbowed him in the side.

Prudence cleared her throat. "Yes, well, I do recall hearing a tale of slimy things; however, I know you boys would never slip them beneath *my* covers."

They looked at one another, then crossed their hearts. "We wouldn't do that to you," Percy said. "We love you—besides, you told us you wouldn't take us fishing again if we did."

Touched by his words, she kissed their foreheads and shooed them toward their room. "Hurry along now and change—it will take me a few moments to match the lids to the proper jars. You boys have amassed quite a collection of them."

"Don't leave without us," Percy warned.

"I wouldn't dream of depriving you of your favorite outing."

And she meant it. These two boys, though a trial to her patience, could not help their boisterous ways and excess energy any more than she could help that she was just shy of six feet tall, with curves that had embarrassed her until last week—when a certain handsome-as-sin Irishman's eyes had nearly popped out of his head upon his discovering her dangling from that tree limb. His smile was genuine. It had not made her feel as if she were a trollop. She had overheard her mother referring to her by that name more than once. The insult had hurt, because it was not true.

Turning her thoughts back to Garahan, she called up the image of him in her mind's eye and remembered his expression. It was as if he admired the way she looked—and was mayhap interested in speaking to her again. Perhaps not all men were put off by her height and figure. Garahan had stood a head taller than her.

Once again, she relived the moment when they stood face to face, and she watched his eyes darken as he studied her lips. Hand to her breast to calm her racing heart, she wondered again, what would have happened if he dipped his head down just a smidgeon? Would he have kissed her?

She'd never been kissed before...

Her cousins called to her as they raced out of their room, slipping their arms into their coat sleeves. "We're ready!"

The trio made their way along the paths from their home to the marsh. It was a lovely day, and she let the boys get a bit of the vinegar out of their systems as they pushed and shoved at one another, racing toward their goal—the pond.

They were faster and lower to the ground. *Where do they get that energy from?* she wondered, rushing to catch up to her charges. Thoughts of Garahan were set aside as she called out to her cousins to wait for her. Their laughter trailed behind them, leaving her to realize they had no intention of letting her catch up.

What mischief were they bent on getting into now?

She hurried along the path toward their favorite spot in the marsh—a wide pool of brackish water. They loved to explore the area surrounding the pool. On their other trips to the marsh, they'd found all manner of things—from six-legged creatures to ancient spearpoints—and their latest find was a piece from what she thought must have been an ancient shield.

Truth be told, she loved these forays into the wild marshland at the edge of Summerfield-on-Eden—nearly as much as she enjoyed when they were able to convince her uncle to allow them to spend an afternoon along the banks of River Eden.

Sorrow lanced through her at the realization of how much she would miss the twins and these outings if her aunt followed through with her threats to dismiss her. She set that worry aside and concentrated on ensuring her cousins enjoyed the few short hours they were allowed to spend in their favorite place.

Mindful of where she stepped—it wouldn't do if she ended up knee-deep in mud and ruined her only pair of half boots—she heard a desperate cry for help. She dropped her leather satchel and broke into a run. "I'm coming!"

"Over here! Hurry, Cousin Prudence!" Phineas called out.

She skidded to a halt at the edge of the pond and grabbed hold of the back of his trousers, pulling him to safety. "You nearly fell in."

Before she could ask where his brother was, Phineas turned his tear-stained face to her. "Percy already did!"

She shot to her feet. "Where is he? Show me!" she ordered him.

"There!" Phineas shouted. "Do you see him?"

"I do. Hang on, Percy, I'm coming!"

Phineas shouted to his twin, "Prudence will save you!"

She jumped into the water knowing full well her clothing may slow her down, but she couldn't worry about that now. Percy needed her! Ignoring the worry curdling in her stomach, she set out with strong strokes that had her reaching the boy as he was about to go under again. "I have you, Percy." She grabbed hold of him. "Wrap your arms around my neck and don't let go!"

Percy was crying too hard to answer her, but he did as she asked. In that moment, she recognized that their bravado made it seem as if they were far older than their years.

Striking out for the grassy edge of the pond, she prayed for the strength to lift him from the water. Her arms were growing heavy with fatigue. Her aunt had intercepted the hearty breakfast Mrs. Cabot had been about to serve Prudence that morning, reminding the cook that her niece was not to have a heavy meal at the start of the day, insisting she would never be able to handle her duties due to sluggishness from eating too much.

As she drew closer to shore, she said a prayer of thanks that Percy had eaten the porridge he hated. He would never have been able to tread water as long as he had without it. Why had she not gone to the squire to let him know her aunt had not allowed her to begin the swimming lessons he had approved of? Would it have helped their precarious situation now?

Ignoring the emptiness gnawing in her belly and weakness

stealing into her limbs, she kept one arm about Percy and began to tread water. "Phineas! I'm going to need your help pulling your brother out of the water."

"You're too far away! I can't reach you."

"What will we do, Prudence?" Percy asked.

"Don't worry, either of you. We're nearly there."

"Why are you stopping?" Phineas demanded.

She did not want either twin to worry. Digging deep, she strove to answer with a calm she did not feel. "I need to float on my back for a few minutes to conserve my energy."

"What about my brother?"

"He'll hold on to me, and we'll both be floating while we rest."

Seemingly satisfied with her answer, Phineas sat down to wait.

Before the boy in her arms started to struggle, she said, "I'm going to wrap my arm around your back, Percy, and you're going to trust me—and float with me."

"What if I sink?"

"You won't," she told him.

His lips trembled. "What if *you* sink?"

"I won't. Trust me." Relief speared through her when he nodded and followed her lead. Courageous little boy, trusting her to hold on to him while they floated toward the edge of the pond.

"I can't see Percy!" Phineas shouted. "Where's my brother? Did you lose him?"

Prudence couldn't ignore the boy's shouts. She had to reassure him, even it was going to sap more of her strength to answer. Every bit of it was crucial to make it back to the edge of the pond. "He's right here tucked against my side—we're on our backs, almost ready to swim again. Aren't we, Percy?"

"We're...c-c-coming!" Percy answered. *Brave, brave boy.*

"Hang on, lad!"

The deep shout had Phineas running toward the voice.

Fear slammed into Prudence with the force of a blow. Dear

Lord, she couldn't do this alone! "Phineas, wait! Don't leave us! We need your help!"

The sound of hooves and a loud splash had her tucking Percy close. While she used her tired arms to stay afloat, he struggled against her, draining more of her strength. She focused on the boy. "We need to swim again, Percy."

"But I'm so tired," he moaned.

"It's getting late, and we cannot miss tea with your mother and the ladies. Can we?" He started to let go, and her heart nearly stopped. "Percy!" She hugged him tighter to her. "Just a little bit further. We can make it."

"I've got ye, lad!" came that booming voice.

"Garahan?"

"Aye—loosen yer hold on him."

She did as he asked. Their eyes met over Percy's head. "Can ye make it back on yer own?" Garahan asked.

"Yes." But as soon as her charge was no longer clinging to her, every ounce of her strength seemed to drain away. She refused to call out for help until after Garahan had her cousin safely out of the water next to his sobbing brother.

A lassitude swept up from her toes, and all at once, she noticed how cool the water had become. It was a lovely feeling just floating atop the water. If only it was just a bit warmer, she might be tempted to stay where she was, but a violent shiver racked her tired body, forcing her under.

CHAPTER SIX

GARAHAN PICKED UP the coat he'd torn off before diving into the water, wrapped it around Percy, and watched for the lass out of the corner of his eye. Where in blue blazes was she? He scanned the pond and finally saw the top of her head as she slipped beneath the water. "You two, sit. Now!"

The boys hugged one another and sat.

Garahan dove into the water and swam like a man possessed. He had to reach her before she got tangled in the weeds at the bottom of the pond. He struck out and then dove under, reaching for the hand just below him. He hauled her up, and they broke through the surface. Worry filled him—she wasn't breathing. "Hang on, lass!"

He made it to shore and pulled her out. "Stay back, boys. I've got to get the water out of her lungs."

"We want to help," Percy cried.

The sight of the lass's inert body terrified Garahan. "Then pray, lads. Pray hard!" He flipped her onto her stomach and began to press on her back to expel the water.

"You're going to hurt her!" Phineas said.

"If I don't get all of the water out, she'll die," Garahan replied without looking away from the woman he straddled. "Lord, I could use yer help!"

"Faith, but ye're a lucky son of bitch, Garahan," a deep voice called out from behind him. "The Lord sent me!"

He nearly choked on his laughter, hearing the familiar sound of his cousin's voice, but did not look away from the lass. "O'Ghill, keep an eye on the lads for me, will ye?"

"Who are you?" the twins asked at the same time.

Before O'Ghill could answer, Garahan heard the sweetest sound—the lass coughed! He quickly shifted until he was holding on to her side when she started to gag. He rubbed her back while she got rid of the brackish water she'd swallowed. "There's a lass. Don't hold back—ye need to purge it out of ye."

When he sensed she was empty, he wrapped himself around her, trying to warm her while risking a glance at the others. He nodded to the man, then the lads. "O'Ghill is one of me cousins."

"Not to be confused with one of the sainted O'Malleys or Flahertys," O'Ghill told the boys. "Me ma is a Garahan, but an O'Ghill by marriage."

A shiver racked the woman in Garahan's arms. She'd closed her eyes but was breathing normally. "I need yer coat, O'Ghill. The lass is icy to the touch, and I've wrapped mine around Percy."

His cousin handed over his coat, then squatted next to the limp woman. Garahan ignored the appraising look in his cousin's eyes. "Now's not the time."

O'Ghill slanted him a look but inclined his head. "'Tis a bit chilly for a swim, isn't it, lads?"

Garahan cursed beneath his breath. He'd finally met a woman who interested him, and his rake of a cousin showed up. He loved the man, but he had never won a woman's affections if O'Ghill was involved.

Burying his feelings deep, he asked, "Want to tell us what ye were thinking, Percy?"

The twins shared a glance, reminding Garahan of himself and his brothers when they were young—and in trouble. The lads were thick as thieves.

Percy hung his head, while Phineas asked, "She'll be all right, won't she?"

Garahan glanced at Prudence, watching her lashes flutter. Her red-rimmed eyes and pale-as-flour skin were a testament to how close he'd come to losing her before he'd even had a chance to know her.

She stared at him. Was she trying to guess his thoughts?

He brushed the tip of his finger along the curve of her cheek. "Aye, lad," he answered, never taking his gaze from hers. "Once we've safely delivered the lass home, and yer ma tucks her into bed with a hot water bottle at her feet and a fire in the hearth. A day or two of rest, and she'll do just fine."

The twins started arguing in a loud whisper.

Garahan looked away from the lass and asked, "Something wrong, lads?"

"Mother will insist she return to her duties," Percy said.

"The both of ye nearly drowned!"

"Mother will put Percy to bed for a sennight and summon the physician," Phineas predicted.

"And ignore her," Percy added.

"What ails yer ma?" Garahan asked.

Before either lad could answer, his cousin nudged him in the shoulder. "Where's the lass's other boot?"

"Must have come off when she was in the water," Garahan replied.

"It got stuck in the mud on the bank," Phineas told them, handing him the boot.

Garahan studied it, noting how worn it was. "'Tis a good thing she wore her old boots today, lad."

The boy stared at him. "These are her *only* boots."

He could not help the protective feelings he had for the lass, nor the desire to help her—even it was to buy her a new pair of half boots! Uneasy with the feelings rioting within him, he asked, "How far out did ye swim, Percy?"

The lad lifted his head, and Garahan watched Percy's eyes well with tears. They magnified the fear he'd seen in the other boy's eyes when he'd dismounted and dived into the water. Phineas tried so hard to bury his fear, as Percy was trying to do now. Garahan sensed the lads were concerned about their cousin, too. "Well?" he asked, and repeated the previous question.

"He was halfway across," Phineas answered.

"So, the lass had to swim a good distance, out and back," O'Ghill said. "Is she a strong swimmer?"

"Aye," Percy and Prudence answered at the same time.

"She's teaching us how to swim," Phineas added.

"And I will be," Prudence said. "As soon as your mother agrees to allow it. Your father already has."

Listening to the weakness in the lass's voice, and noting the unshed tears on Percy's face, Garahan could not keep the frustration from his voice when he asked the boy, "Then why were ye in the water alone?"

The lass shifted in his arms. "I was going to ask Percival that very question," she rasped, struggling to sit up.

When he accommodated her, a deep, racking cough had him stroking the hair off her forehead and whispering, "Easy, *mo chroí.*"

"Is the lass yer heart?" his cousin asked.

"Leave off, O'Ghill."

"'Tis a simple question."

Garahan frowned at him. "Later." Another coughing spasm hit, and he tried to soothe her. "Easy, lass, ye're safe—*they're* safe."

When the fit passed, she asked, "When did you get here, Garahan?"

"In time to save ye from drowning, lass."

She blinked, then turned to stare at the dark-haired man beside him. He had a similar build to Garahan and resembled him. "Are you another of the duke's guard?"

He snorted. "Not bloody likely. Killian O'Ghill, at yer service, lass. If ye need the shirt off me back to go with me coat, ye've but to ask."

"I…uh… Thank you, Mr. O'Ghill."

"Killian will do, as ye're wearing me clothes."

Garahan tightened his hold on the lass and growled at his cousin. "She's borrowing yer coat, as Percy's wearing mine. And if she's in need of a shirt, she'll be wearing mine!"

His cousin's eyes lit with amusement. "Staking a claim, boy-o?"

Garahan knew his cousin was after getting a rise out of him. "Ye're a bloody pain in the *arse*, but faith, I've missed ye, O'Ghill."

His cousin grinned at him, then turned to the woman as Garahan helped her don her other boot. "Ye've yet to tell me yer name, lass."

"Prudence…Prudence Barstow."

"It's miss," Phineas added, helpfully.

"She's our cousin…well, governess," Percy added. He turned to his twin. "We'll be in the suds for sure this time."

Prudence squirmed as Garahan pulled her back onto his lap, stirring the lust he'd been striving to control. The sweet *derrière* he'd caught a glimpse of the other day pressed against him, hardening him to the point of pain. He leaned close and whispered, "Ye'd best be still, lass, if ye don't want to embarrass yer young cousins and meself."

She immediately stopped moving, and he wondered if she knew what he'd meant. But she interrupted the direction of his thoughts when she apologized, "Forgive me, but I need to take the twins home. If we're late, Aunt—er Mrs. Honeycutt—will punish the boys. They're much too young to go without more than toast and tea for meals. They're growing boys."

He looked at his cousin, and then the twins. "Yer ma would punish ye that way?"

"She hasn't since I've been here," the lass said.

He knew wondered if the lads' ma would hold back food from the lass, too. A woman of her height—and curvature— needed more than a meager meal to get her through the day.

"'Tis a credit to ye that ye intervened on behalf of the lads."

She shivered.

"Are ye still cold?" Garahan asked.

"Ye're adding to her chill, as ye're as wet as herself," O'Ghill said.

Garahan knew he'd have to turn her over to his drier cousin. "Do ye trust me, lass?"

"I do."

"Thank ye, lass. Ye've been introduced to me cousin. Know that I trust him with me life, and that of me brothers and cousins." Their gazes met and held. "I don't give me trust lightly, and do not expect ye to either, but I'm asking ye to let him carry ye home. He's dry."

"And warmer than the soaking-wet *eedjit* cousin of mine holding on to ye," O'Ghill said. "Besides, it's plain as the nose on yer face that Garahan cannot keep yer chills at bay."

She blinked and slowly smiled at the man who held her. "Thank you, Garahan. For saving my life and coming to our rescue a second time."

"Second time?" O'Ghill asked.

"'Tis nothing," Garahan answered.

"It was to me—and to the boys." She turned to his cousin and added, "I was losing my grip on the limb, and the twins would not have been able to unwind my hair from that branch without help."

Interest shone in O'Ghill's eyes as his gaze swept from the top of her head to her well-worn boots, igniting Garahan's fierce temper. "I'm sure ye'll charm the rest of the tale out of her," Garahan said as he loosened his hold on her.

His cousin got down on one knee, scooped the lass into his arms, and stood. Garahan felt the loss as soon as she was taken from him, but he'd think about that later. When she started to tremble, he said, "We'd best get ye in front of a fire with hot tea to warm yer insides before ye catch lung fever."

"Which is closer," his cousin asked him, "Summerfield Chase

or where the twins live?"

"Summerfield Chase." Garahan stalked over to his mount and scratched behind his horse's ears. "I'm after me spare shirt, Duncan, me lad. Once we're home, I'll see that ye have the rubdown ye enjoy, along with an extra cupful of oats."

His horse twitched his ears in reply.

"But our mother—" Phineas started.

Percy interrupted, "Would be even angrier if we arrive in the middle of her tea with the ladies—with Cousin Prudence and me soaked to the skin."

"Being carried in by a stranger," Phineas added.

"I'm not a stranger," Garahan reminded them.

Percy nodded, and Phineas pointed at O'Ghill. "He is!"

His cousin chuckled. "He's got ye there, Garahan. Toss me the shirt—ye'll only get it wet holding on to it."

Garahan complied, wishing he could wipe the satisfied grin off his cousin's face. He'd see to the chore before O'Ghill went on his way—to wherever that might be. O'Ghill was the rover—and the rake—in the family.

Shifting his thoughts to the lads, Garahan could not help but worry about the lass. She'd turned him upside down and inside out from the moment he rushed to her rescue when he spied her hanging on to that limb. It was just the physical, though, Lord help him, that caught his interest at first. But upon his observing the way she had with the twins on their way home—and now again today—he felt a need for her that went deep. Too deep. He had a duty to see to and a vow to keep.

Ordering his thoughts, he knew they had to deliver the lass and her cousins to Summerfield Chase. It would be an imposition upon the baroness and her staff, though he'd never seen Lady Phoebe turn away anyone in need—from stray kittens and hungry dogs to strangers looking for work. The baron was always on hand to observe when a stranger arrived, but after careful questioning, he too was always willing to lend a hand. Heaven knew Percy and Prudence had no doubt swallowed far too much of the brackish water to be good for either of them.

Prudence—the name did not suit the woman at all! She deserved something bolder—a strong Celtic name. *Aisling*: because her beauty was almost unreal. She was a dream…a vision. *Ciara*: for the midnight locks he imagined wrapped around his wrists as he pulled her to him. *Maeve*: for her queenly stature and goddess-like beauty—she intoxicated him!

"Are ye daft?"

O'Ghill's question brought his mind back to where it should be, in the here and now.

"Well now, that depends on who ye ask." Garahan stared at the lass, wondering if he was bringing trouble to the baron's door. But there was no hope for it—Summerfield Chase was closer. They would have to impose upon the kindness of the baron and baroness while Percy and the lass were tended to. He'd need to impose further and ask the baron to send a missive off to the squire and his wife, explaining where they were and why they were late.

A thought rocked him to the core: what if the lass fell ill with a fever? How in the bloody hell would he be able to keep his distance from her when she was right there underfoot?

"Bollocks!"

"What did you say?" the lass asked.

"He said *bollocks*," O'Ghill happily repeated, setting the lass on her feet next to his horse, steadying her when she swayed.

"Isn't that a bad word?" Percy asked.

"'Twould depend on how ye use the word, lad," O'Ghill told him. Before Garahan could stop him, he'd eased the lass's arms out of the coat and slipped Garahan's dry shirt over her head, then quickly bundled her back into the coat. "It'll have to do until we reach Summerfield Chase. I'm after setting ye on me horse. Are ye afraid of heights?"

The twins looked at their cousin and promptly burst into laughter.

O'Ghill glanced at the boys and back. "I'll take that as a no, then."

"Aye," Garahan said, lifting his gaze to meet hers. "Ye'll have to ask Miss Barstow how we met."

O'Ghill nodded, as if he sensed it was an interesting tale. "I'm a good listener," he told her, placing her on his horse. He climbed up behind her, then shifted her onto his lap. "Rest yer head against me, lass. Ye'll soon warm up."

Garahan's teeth hurt from clenching them at the sight of his cousin holding the woman who had been stuck on his mind for days. When Percy shivered, Garahan realized Phineas was bound to get wet leaning against his brother while riding on Duncan. He grumbled, "Lend me one of yer shirts, Killian. Percy's starting to shiver. I need ye to think about all the water ye swallowed—and yer cousin as well, Percy—and ask ye to be braver than ye already have been."

Percy's face paled, but the lad nodded, understanding without being asked what Garahan needed him to do.

"How far is it to our destination?" O'Ghill asked.

"Riding double—triple, in me case—less than ten minutes. If ye spend yer time blathering, instead of keeping yer mind on the road ahead of ye, it'll take ye longer."

"Me cousin has a fair temper," O'Ghill warned the lass. "'Tis best that ye know it ahead of time."

"Shut the *feck* up!" Garahan barked.

Percy leaned close to Phineas and whispered, "I've heard that word…it's a bad word, too."

"Aye," O'Ghill called out cheerfully. "'Tis. It means—"

The lass cut off his explanation with her hand over his mouth. From the sly look in his cousin's eyes, Garahan knew what O'Ghill had in mind to do. "Keep yer tongue inside yer trap, and yer lips to yerself, boy-o, or we'll be going three rounds right here…right now!"

O'Ghill sighed. "I warned ye, did I not? Me cousin has a fearful temper when riled."

"What do you suppose has him so upset?" the lass asked.

His cousin glanced at him and snorted with laughter. "Ask me again when ye're feeling better. Let's be off, lads, before either of ye catches a chill."

Garahan helped Percy on with the dry shirt and then turned his coat inside out, so the dry side would be against the lad. Thinking of his cousin holding heaven in his arms, while he held the hooligans, he muttered, "Bloody bastard."

Before Percy could ask, Phineas whispered, "That was two bad words together."

CHAPTER SEVEN

PRUDENCE SIGHED AS the heat of the man started to ease the chill racking her bones. "Th…thank you for the u…use of your c…coat, Mr. O'Ghill."

He tightened his hold on her. "'Tis Killian, remember? Save yer breath till ye stop shivering, lass. Rest now, or me cousin'll have me head when we arrive at the baron's home for talking yer ear off and wearing ye out."

She wondered at the sneer in Killian's voice when he said the word *baron*. Did he know Baron Summerfield, or was it for some other reason?

As they rode, she marveled at the difference a dry shirt, and nearly dry coat, made as her limbs stopped shaking and the tension in her jaw—from trying to keep her teeth from chattering—eased.

"Do you know Baron Summerfield?"

"I see ye've got yer shivers under control enough to start asking questions."

"Is that a problem for you?"

His rumbling chuckle reminded her of Garahan's. The man's cousin insisted that she call him Killian…and not O'Ghill. Garahan was more formal. "Not at all." Apparently, he was not going to tell her why he laughed.

Rather than pester the man with endless questions, to quench her thirst to know anything and everything, she fell silent, grateful to be above the water—not under it. She'd have to thank Garahan again—and would make sure Percy did too, right after she finagled from him the reason why her cousin was in the water in the first place! The twins had proven more difficult to pry answers from than she expected.

The low whistle near her ear had her turning her head in time to see the windows of Summerfield Chase glistening in the late afternoon sunlight. She knew from listening to her aunt expound on the merits of the estate—albeit with a jealous tinge to her voice—that it was a few hundred years old. Was it two, or mayhap three?

The sharp whistle off to their right had her jolting in Killian's arms.

"Easy, lass—'tis just one of me boneheaded O'Malley cousins on patrol."

"O'Ghill, what are ye doing here, and who have you brought to us?"

"Well now, 'tis Miss Prudence—" He paused. "Begging yer pardon, lass, but I don't recall yer last name."

"Barstow," she said loud enough for O'Malley to hear. "I work for—"

"The squire and his wife. Ye're the latest governess, riding herd on their twin hooligans," O'Malley finished for her, reaching up to help her off the horse. "Where's—"

Another sharp whistle sounded from behind them, and she spun around and wobbled. O'Malley was quick to steady her as he nodded to Garahan. "Care to fill us in on what's happened?"

"Later," Garahan promised. "The lass and Percy went swimming in the marsh and need to dry off and warm up."

Prudence watched the cousins share a glance, as if they shared a silent conversation with a look. "'Twas closer to come here than Squire Honeycutt's," Garahan added.

"Aye," O'Malley agreed.

Prudence had started to reach up for Percy when Garahan

cautioned, "Let O'Malley help the lads down." She wanted to remind him that they were her responsibility, but from the set of his jaw, she decided to save that conversation for another time.

Her knees started to shake from the cold and exhaustion. She hoped Garahan wouldn't notice that she had to fight to control her limbs.

With a nod to a stable lad who rushed over to take the horses, Garahan swept her into his arms without a by-your-leave. He followed O'Malley and Killian, who carried the boys, to the rear entrance of the house. "Please, put me down. I don't want my aunt to hear I was being carried into the baron's home." He quirked an eyebrow at her, but her explanation was too convoluted and would take too long. "Please?" she asked.

He set her carefully on her feet but kept his arm around her waist. "If I see ye having trouble, I'll be scooping ye up again."

"You cannot keep doing that." She hesitated, then added, "I'm too heavy."

Garahan chuckled. "I'll admit ye're a delightful armful, lass. What ye're not is heavy."

"But I… That is… My parents…"

She fell silent. Had she truly been about to confess what her parents had drummed into her head over and over for the last decade? Their disappointed tone hurt almost as much as their list of why she was a constant embarrassment to the family: she was too outspoken, too tall, too curvy, and too heavy to attract any good man's notice.

A tear escaped, past her guard, and she brushed it away.

Garahan leaned close and whispered, "Let go of whatever troubles ye, lass. Ye've been given a second chance at life." He cleared his throat to add, "Ye were halfway to the bottom of the pond when I grabbed hold of yer hand."

His eyes met hers, and she wondered if Garahan would be different from the gentlemen her mother praised so highly while reminding her that not one of them would ever offer Prudence marriage. She looked into his dark brown eyes and felt herself being pulled toward the man who'd saved Percy—who'd saved *her*!

She swallowed against the tightness in her throat to speak. "I hadn't realized that I was. I will never forget that you came back for me, Garahan. I—" Could she tell him that she'd already accepted that she would die? As soon as the question popped into her head, the words came out of her mouth. "All I could think of was that you'd saved my cousin's life just as my strength drained and my arms and legs felt leaden. When I started to sink, I knew I was meant to die today."

Garahan stopped and grabbed hold of her upper arms, shaking her. "Never accept death willingly when there's a chance to live yer life, lass! Ye weren't meant to die today, and neither was Percy. God granted me excellent hearing. I heard when Phineas called for help, and arrived in time to save ye both."

Gratitude swept up from her toes as a prayer left her lips. "Thank you, Lord, for sending Ryan Garahan in our hour of need." Their eyes met, and the turmoil in his went straight to her heart. "Thank you, Ryan, for saving our lives. I will find a way to pay you—"

His mouth possessed hers in a kiss that shook her to her soul. The hand splayed against the middle of her back slid to her waist, pulling her flush against him. His kiss demanded a response…and she gave it, as every thought in her head evaporated.

"We'll hear no more about payment. That kiss makes us even."

Hand to her breast, she could only stare at his beautifully sculpted lips. The urge to trace her finger along the curvature of his mouth had her aching. He may have thought one kiss was worth her life, but she knew he deserved far more. What could she do for him? What could she give him?

The intensity in his gaze deepened as his eyes locked on hers, then dipped lower to her mouth, her breasts, her belly, her bare feet. Heat seared through her body, igniting a flame she hadn't known existed inside of her. Was this passion…desire?

Her hand trembled as she reached out to cup the side of his face in her hand and rasped his name before slipping her hand to the back of his neck. Lifting to her toes, she pressed her lips to his in a soft, tentative kiss—the antithesis of the sensuous melding of mouths from moments before. "I will never forget the gift of life that you returned to Percy and me."

He looked deep into her eyes and slowly lowered his lips—

"Garahan!"

He sighed at the sound of his name being bellowed and eased back slowly. His arm was still around her waist as he opened the door. O'Malley stood watching them. The silent question in his cousin's eyes had her wondering if she had taken too much of Garahan's time away from his duties.

When Garahan stared at the man, she immediately apologized, "Forgive me, Mr. O'Malley. I wasn't steady on my feet, and Garahan picked me up."

O'Malley nodded. "But ye're walking now."

She tipped her chin up and said, "I didn't want to be carried."

O'Malley's eyes lit with humor. "Didn't ye, now?"

She found herself reacting to the blond giant's easy charm. "I just needed a moment to collect myself."

Garahan snorted with derision. "If I hadn't pumped the water out of ye, ye would not have been worried about whether or not ye walked inside or I carried yet." He frowned, reminding her, "Nor would ye be smiling at me *eedjit* of a cousin."

O'Malley chuckled. "Me cousin has the right of it—ye should be thanking the man for saving yer life, not arguing about whether he helps ye regain yer strength by carrying ye."

Shame made her stomach ache. "You're right, Mr. O'Malley—"

He rolled his eyes. "O'Malley will do, if ye don't mind." He looked at his cousin. "Does she call ye mister, too?"

Garahan's frown eased. "Not anymore. Lass, the lot of us prefer to answer to our last names."

"Except for Killian," she said. "He asked me to call him by his first name."

"Aye," Killian said from behind her. "That I did, lass."

Surprised that she hadn't noticed the man, she spun around, and had to put a hand to her head as the room swirled, nauseating her.

"Easy, lass. I've got ye." Garahan's familiar, deep voice was her lifeline for the second time that day.

She buried her face in the crook of his arm and told him, "The room's moving."

"Close yer eyes and be still. Give yer head a chance to right itself, lass."

She decided to do as he suggested.

"O'Malley, have ye told Mrs. Green we've two patients who require something hot to drink?"

The deep rumbling of his voice was soothing when he spoke to his cousin. She compared it to Killian's voice and realized they were quite similar, but only Garahan's had a tingle of awareness skittering along her spine.

"Where are the lads?" Garahan asked.

"We sold them to gypsies," Killian replied.

Prudence's eyes shot open. "Gypsies? Garahan, do something!"

O'Malley groaned. "Ye haven't changed, have ye, O'Ghill?"

"Why would I, when I've already achieved perfection?" Killian replied.

"Our cousin was after having a laugh at yer expense, lass," Garahan said.

She squirmed in his arms until he set her on her feet, then rounded on him and poked a finger in his chest. "I do not find selling my cousins to gypsies even remotely amusing!"

"I'm not the one ye should be angry with," Garahan said.

"Aye, 'tis meself," Killian said. "Begging yer pardon, lass."

"What in God's name is going on here?" a deep voice boomed from outside.

Prudence reached for Garahan's arm and held tight.

GARAHAN EASED HER closer when she wavered on her feet again—stubborn lass. He'd never understand women. "Yer lordship, I fished Miss Barstow and her cousin out of the marsh."

Baron Summerfield paused to study the woman standing beside Garahan. "Welcome to Summerfield Chase, Miss Barstow. I heard that the squire and his wife hired a governess. Why was the governess not tending to the boys?"

"I took the boys to the marsh to study the creatures that live in there and take samples."

"For their studies?" the baron asked. "Shouldn't their governess be doing that?"

Garahan felt her tremble and knew she feared retribution from her aunt and uncle if word got out that she was related to them. The lads had been adamant that no one know the lass was their cousin. Though why was beyond him. "'Tis a bit of explanation as to that, yer lordship. Would ye mind if we speak of it after Miss Barstow and the lads have dried off and warmed up?"

"I'd be grateful if you let Percy take a hot bath, your lordship," she hurriedly added. "I rescued him from the pond, but I tired more quickly than I thought I would. We were halfway to the bank when Phineas started to panic on the bank."

"Because…?" the baron asked.

"My arms were growing tired, and I needed to rest them. I decided to stop and tread water. While I was showing Percy how to float on his back, Phineas got worried."

Summerfield took in her appearance and started giving orders for the baths and a hot meal to be prepared immediately. Garahan admired the baron's ability to bark commands and be instantly obeyed. Percy and the lass would be taken care of.

When they were whisked away in the baron's wake, he asked O'Malley, "Would ye mind if I speak to Phineas before I change me clothes?"

"I think that would be wise. I'll join ye." O'Malley paused and looked around him. "Where in the bloody hell did O'Ghill go?"

Garahan chuckled. "The lure of a hot meal was too much for him to resist. No doubt ye'll find him in the kitchen cozying up to Mrs. Green and the lad."

When they entered the kitchen, O'Ghill was indeed entertaining them with tales of his travels, while the lad emptied a bowl of stew. He paused to smile at them. "Ah, if it isn't me illustrious O'Malley and Garahan cousins."

"Leave off, O'Ghill," O'Malley grumbled. "I have a few questions for ye after we speak to the lad."

Phineas stared at his empty bowl while Mrs. Green tutted. "Poor mite was frightened out of his wits when his brother fell into the pond. Let him digest his meal before you upset him with questions."

O'Malley met her direct gaze and asked, "And if I choose to question him now?"

The determined look on the cook's face had O'Ghill chuckling. "I'm thinking Mrs. Green may not be apt to bake any more scones for ye."

O'Malley started to speak, but O'Ghill interrupted him. "Leave off, O'Malley. The lad and his brother were terrified when Miss Barstow went under that last time."

Phineas looked up, and Garahan knew it was the truth. Tears streamed from the lad's eyes as he silently continued to weep. "She's fine, lad," Garahan assured him. "I fished her out, too."

The lad nodded. "But she was so pale...and not moving."

"That was before I coaxed the water out of her," Garahan reminded him. "Remember?"

Guilt-ridden eyes stared at him. "Thank you for rescuing Prudence. She's the only one who lets us be ourselves. We've never had a governess climb trees and rock walls...or collect bugs and frogs..." He paused. "She *listens* to us."

Garahan knelt beside the boy's chair. "'Tis what we do—the rest of the duke's guard and meself—guard those under our care, and every now and again, we rescue a lad or lass when the need arises."

Phineas wiped his eyes with his sleeve. "When I grow up, I want to do that, too."

Garahan stood. "Ye're a fine lad, Phineas Honeycutt, and ye'll grow up to be fine man. Ye'd be a welcome addition to the duke's guard—wouldn't he, O'Malley?"

His cousin took the boy's measure and agreed, "That he would."

The cook asked, "Are you ready for that slice of currant cake I promised you, Phineas?"

"Yes, thank you, Mrs. Green."

"You have lovely manners, Phineas. Your parents must be so proud."

He shrugged. "Percy and me didn't think they were all that important until Prudence came to stay with us. She said they matter and that it shows others that we care about them."

"Miss Barstow is right," the cook told him. "You are wise to listen to her."

He looked up and smiled at Garahan. "She likes you."

Garahan nearly swallowed his tongue. He knew who the lad meant, but pretended not to, winking at the cook instead. "Mrs. Green?"

Phineas laughed. "No. Cousin Prudence."

"How would a lad like you be knowing that?" Garahan asked.

The boy smiled. "'Cause she told us after you rescued her the first time."

O'Malley cleared his throat. O'Ghill snickered and said, "Faith, lad, we like Garahan, too. Even if he is a pain in the ever-loving *arse*."

"Language, Mr. O'Ghill!" Mrs. Green said.

"Begging yer pardon, Mrs. Green."

"Little pitchers…big ears," she said with a nod in Phineas's direction.

"I've never quite understood what that meant," O'Ghill said.

O'Malley moved to stand beside O'Ghill's chair. "A word."

O'Ghill sighed. "The mighty O'Malley has spoken, lad. I must away and see what the sainted man requires of me."

O'Malley mumbled something, and Garahan knew his cousin's patience was fraying. He warned O'Ghill, "Ye might show a bit of respect for the head of the duke's guard here at Summerfield Chase. Else ye may find yerself out on yer self-important *arse*."

O'Malley and O'Ghill walked out of the kitchen. Garahan sincerely hoped O'Malley would take the stick out of his *arse* long enough to realize they could use O'Ghill's help countering the rumors and lies.

The sharp intake of breath had Garahan wincing.

"Language!" the cook reminded him.

"I beg yer pardon, Mrs. Green."

Phineas's eyes brimmed with laughter, but a sharp look from Garahan had him swallowing it. No need to upset the woman who was about to serve the lad a slice of her famous currant cake.

"Finish yer cake, lad. Then ye can tell me what happened earlier."

In between bites, the boy told of the adventures they'd had with their cousin. Garahan's appreciation of what Prudence had done for the twins in the short time she'd been with them trebled. In the time he'd been assigned to the Duke of Wyndmere's guard attached to Summerfield Chase, he could not remember seeing the lads out-of-doors.

He remembered the fun he, his brothers, and cousins had had when their chores were finished. All lads should be allowed to run a bit wild in their youth. If not for her hair snagging on that branch, he had no doubt she would have had the twins home in time for breakfast.

And that thought led him to today's adventure. He needed to find out what Percy was doing when he fell in the pond.

The lad had picked up his plate and licked it before the cook could remind him not to. Garahan smiled, remembering wanting to do that earlier when he'd eaten a slice of the moist cake. If it had been just Mrs. Green and himself, he might have, but O'Malley was enjoying a piece, too. It was always wise to be on his best behavior whenever O'Malley was nearby.

"Now then, lad, about the pond…"

⟡

CHAPTER EIGHT

"Mrs. Chauncey, my housekeeper, and my maid Beth will remain to help you bathe."

"Thank you for the offer, your ladyship," Prudence said. "But I think I can manage on my own." It was simply not possible that a woman of rank would offer her housekeeper and personal maid to help a stranger. Wasn't it?

Lady Phoebe smiled. "You are positively soaked through to the skin. It doesn't matter if it is spring, summer, or fall—riding any distance in wet clothing will chill you to the bone. Now do be quiet and cooperate."

Prudence felt her mouth open in reaction to the command, and quickly forced it shut again. She dared not contradict the baroness, so she quickly nodded as she took in her surroundings. The room was quite large, with a lovely mahogany bed that looked to be as comfortable as a dream. It whispered her name, but she ignored it.

She glanced down at her hands and hid them behind her. If her hands were that dirty, she knew she had to be carrying some of the marsh—grass and leaves, as well as whatever was in the water from the pond—on her person. She would not dare soil the pristine white of the fluffy quilt by touching it.

"Beth will help you change behind the screen, while Mrs. Chauncey directs the footmen filling the tub in the adjoining dressing room."

"You have a separate room to dress in?" Prudence wished she could sink into the floor. What a complete antidote, asking such a question! Even the squire and her aunt had adjoining dressing rooms. "I do not mean to sound gauche, but I am not accustomed to such." Lady Phoebe extended her hand, and Prudence shook her head. "I'm more in need of a bath than I realized. Between diving into the pond after my cousin and then ending up lying on the bank while I..." Dear Lord, had she almost told of the humiliating way she'd cast up her accounts in front of her charges, Garahan, and his cousin?

"I understand, and thank you for your consideration," the baroness said as she linked arms with Prudence. "Do you know, I believe you are taller than my sister-in-law, the Duchess of Wyndmere. She's five feet, seven inches tall—not as statuesque as you." Smiling, the baroness added, "You are shorter than both of my brothers, who stand at six feet, two inches tall. Gives me a positive crick in my neck to speak with them—unless they are a reasonable distance away."

Charmed by the friendly baroness, Prudence felt her worries sliding off her shoulders. "Thank you for your kindness, opening your home to my cousins and myself, and letting us impose upon you in our hour of need, your ladyship."

"Nonsense, Prudence. It is my duty to care for those who live in the village, as well as our tenant farmers. We all depend upon one another. It would be foolish of me not to offer aid when it is within my power to do so."

Prudence sighed. "Not everyone feels as you do. I am so grateful to you and the baron, your ladyship."

"Your bath is ready," Mrs. Chauncey announced, shooing the footmen out of the room. She came to stop near the ornate screen in the corner of the room and folded her hands at her waist. "I thought you'd be undressed and wearing the dressing gown we left for you."

"We were chatting about this and that," Lady Phoebe replied.

"Beth will take good care of you," she told Prudence. "She was trained by Lady Farnsworth—the Duchess of Wyndmere's mother—and has been a wonder since the day she explained all of the reasons why I needed a personal maid." The baroness smiled at her maid before adding, "I didn't want one, you know."

Prudence had no idea if she was expected to respond or not, so she nodded enthusiastically, as if she agreed. When the baroness smiled at her, she relaxed. She would not want to irritate her benefactress.

"Mrs. Chauncey and I will be right down the hall in the upstairs sitting room—just a few doors away—if you have need of me. Beth knows to ring for whatever you need."

"Thank you, Lady Phoebe. Would it be too much trouble to find out how Percy is doing? He does have a tendency to, er…avoid bathing—whenever possible."

The baroness's laughter filled the room with light and happiness. "I believe I shall see how your cousin is doing. He could surprise you, you know. I believe my darling husband was planning to have Timmons oversee Percy and Phineas's baths."

"Oh, but only Percy fell in the pond."

Lady Phoebe shrugged. "I suggested to Marcus that it would be unneighborly of us to return one brother in his current state—and the other sparkling clean."

Prudence snorted and covered her mouth with both hands. Getting a good whiff of them, she made a face. "I believe I am in the same state and in desperate need of soap and hot water!"

The baroness and her housekeeper were smiling when they closed the door behind them.

Beth turned to Prudence and asked, "You do not have an aversion to baths, do you?"

Prudence opened her mouth to say something and ended up laughing instead. "Most definitely not. It will be a pleasure to have hot water for a change."

"A change, Miss Barstow?"

"Please call me Prudence."

"Do you not normally have hot water for bathing, Prudence?"

She sighed. It wasn't a secret, but she did not want others to think poorly of her aunt and uncle. "I…er…usually bathe after my cousins—" She did not mention the fact that she had to bathe immediately after them in the same tub…with tepid, already-used bathwater. "I have to be quick about it," she added.

Beth stared at her for a few minutes but did not question her further. She helped Prudence undress—no easy task with her damp clothing clinging to her. When Prudence had removed her garters and stockings and stood wearing just her chemise, Beth reached for the dressing gown.

"I wouldn't mind borrowing such a lovely garment," Prudence admitted. It was a pale shade of rose, with ecru lace around the collar and sleeves. "But I'm filthy. A few more minutes wearing my chemise wearing it won't make any difference. The water will be warm."

Beth smiled. "The water will be piping hot—that's how Lady Phoebe prefers it." She led the way into the adjoining room and walked toward the copper slipper tub, stopping at the washstand beside it. "Her ladyship enjoys changing her scent now and again and thought you might enjoy choosing which dried flowers to add to your bath. Lilac, rose, or heather?"

Prudence blinked back tears. She was not a weak woman, though she'd nearly died of fright when she discovered Percy had fallen in the pond. She reasoned that her tears were due to the fact that diving in after him, and swimming halfway across then back with the little boy, had used all of her energy. "Forgive me. I usually am not so emotional."

"If anyone was not after what you've been through today, they aren't human." Beth held up the first of three bowls with crushed blossoms in them.

Prudence sniffed them one at a time and decided on the lilac. Watching the maid add the dried flowers to the water, she admitted, "I'm not used to such luxury. Is this how it feels to be a lady?"

Beth frowned as she helped Prudence remove the chemise and step into the tub. "We may not be titled," the maid said, "but you and I are still ladies."

Prudence could not have answered if she wanted to—the heat of the scented water felt like heaven. She moaned in pleasure, then laughed. "Sorry, but it has been too long since I've felt so indulged."

"Prepare to suffer through more," Beth told her. "I have orders to help you wash your hair, as well."

Prudence did not offer any resistance.

An hour later, she felt like a queen. Pampered and cosseted, wearing a borrowed chemise and the lace-edged dressing gown, she found herself sipping tea while the baroness relayed the twins' antics as they both tried to evade the inevitable—a bath!

The royal treatment continued, as she was served tea with a dollop of cream and a spoonful of sugar—a treat for her. Though she had not asked for a second treacle tart, the baroness had served two to her. "These are quite delicious. Thank you for allowing me the luxury of the lilac-scented water, and now a wonderful tea with all the trimmings. I will always remember your kindness, Lady Phoebe."

"It is my pleasure." Phoebe eyed the remaining scones and tarts. "Do you know, Mrs. Green loves to bake, and once she found out our favorite sweets, she insisted on baking them daily."

Prudence dabbed her mouth with the linen napkin and smiled. "I'm afraid I cannot imagine, but it does sound lovely."

"Do you have a favorite sweet?"

Prudence set her cup and saucer on the table and stared at her hands.

"Is something wrong?" the baroness asked.

What could Prudence say? What *should* she say? *Nothing!* She owed it to her aunt and uncle not to mention their shabby treatment of her—after all, it had been on the express instructions from her parents. She decided to share part of the truth with the baroness. "Surely you will have noticed my height."

Lady Phoebe nodded.

"And my, er…curves. Not that you do not have them as well," Prudence said, "but yours are in perfect proportion to your height, your ladyship."

The baroness's direct look had Prudence squirming on her chair. Finally, Lady Phoebe exclaimed, "Botheration! Your curves are in proportion to your height, too. Whoever told you they were not should be horsewhipped! It is so wrong that anyone—no matter who they are—should feel they have the right to tell a woman that she is too tall or too short. Too thin or too curvy. And do not get me started on the color of our hair if our locks do not rival the sun… Bloody hell! Forgive me. The subject is one that constantly irritates me whenever I am confronted with it."

"Why? You are so beautiful, and carry a title as well," Prudence said.

"It is merely a circumstance of birth that I was born Lady Phoebe, the daughter of a duke. I bear the Lippincott genes proudly with my temper, my chestnut hair, and my brilliant blue eyes. I use them to my advantage when I pin someone who deserves my censure with the Lippincott stare of death!"

They were laughing when someone knocked on the bedchamber door. "May I have a word with you, darling?"

Phoebe jumped up from her seat. "Be right with you, Marcus. Please excuse me. Beth will help you into bed."

"Oh, but I cannot stay," Prudence said. "Mrs. Honeycutt will—"

"Do not even attempt to gainsay me," the baroness interrupted. "You and the boys will be staying until we feel you have sufficiently recovered from your ordeal. They, too, have been tucked in for a rest—they did not appreciate thinking they would be expected to nap."

"But I—"

"Will be accommodating—as Percy and Phineas have been—and hop into bed and close your eyes for at least an hour." When the baroness put her hands on her hips and tapped her foot, Prudence did as she was bidden.

After Lady Phoebe swept from the room, Beth said, "Her ladyship is used to giving orders. She means well, and it's not because she feels people should listen because of her title."

"I see." Prudence didn't really, but she felt she had to say something.

Beth smiled conspiratorially. "It's because she's always right! I'll check in on you in an hour."

"Make that half an hour," Prudence bargained, "and I will not argue about taking a nap."

Beth nodded. "Ring the bellpull in the corner if you need anything."

"I will." Prudence climbed into the bed, and the maid pulled the coverlet up to her chin. "Thank you, Beth." She heard the door close, and finally relaxed. Sinking into the cloud-soft bedding, she sighed and closed her eyes.

CHAPTER NINE

GARAHAN HEARD THE commotion as soon he stepped out of the kitchen. Knowing O'Malley, his cousin waited until he thought they were out of earshot before interrogating O'Ghill. His irritation with his cousins added to what he was already cursing—his cold, damp clothes. He hadn't had a moment to peel them off, and the bloody things were starting to chafe.

He shouldn't be complaining. At least the coat had warmed Percy after he'd been fished out of the pond. Garahan was proud to be a part of the duke's guard, proud to wear the uniform, and didn't mind the color at all. Black made the embroidered golden Celtic harp and brilliant green *Eire* over their hearts stand out. What bothered him was the duke insisting that his guard wear the blasted fitted frockcoat and waistcoat, when loose-fitting clothing would do. Then there was the damned cravat. Who in the bloody hell needed to wear one?

He paused outside the closed pantry door to listen to the rumble of voices, waiting for an opening in the conversation to shove the door open.

Then he heard O'Malley's perfect opening: "Not that I'm not happy to see family—"

Garahan grinned and shoved open the door. "Faith, but we both know our cousin would like nothing better than to see the back of ye, O'Ghill."

O'Ghill snorted with laughter while O'Malley grumbled, "Ye're both a pair of irritating buggers!"

Garahan grinned. "'Tis just part of the Garahan charm."

His cousin corrected him, "Nay, 'tis the O'Ghill."

"Shut yer gobs!" O'Malley ordered them. When they did, he continued, "I've an offer to make to ye," glancing at Garahan. "With the baron's approval."

Garahan guessed what the baron and O'Malley had discussed. He nodded.

O'Ghill held up his hands. "I'm not after working for the duke—or the baron. I'm just on one of me rambles."

Used to his cousin's itchy feet, Garahan asked, "Are ye headed to Scotland, then?"

"I don't report to either of ye," O'Ghill reminded them, "and I don't appreciate yer interference in me life."

"Sore nerve, is it?" Garahan asked, then turned to O'Malley. "Must involve a lass."

When O'Ghill didn't respond, O'Malley shrugged. "Well then, I'd be happy to show ye to the door. O'Ghill." He walked over and held the door open. "Be sure to thank the baron and baroness for their kindness in feeding yer ungrateful *arse* before ye leave."

Garahan watched their cousin's jaw tense and hoped they were getting to the bottom of why O'Ghill was in England— more specifically at Summerfield Chase. Was he in trouble, or was it a happy coincidence that his rambling had led him to the baron's door? Garahan did not believe in coincidences.

"Bloody hell, O'Malley!" O'Ghill sputtered. "Ye never give a man an inch, do ye?"

O'Malley didn't bother to answer. Garahan hadn't expected him to. One of O'Malley's tactics was to remain silent when everyone else would be shouting insults and challenges to one another. The Wexford O'Malleys had been butting heads with the eldest of the O'Ghill brothers since Killian had sweet-talked the lass Sean O'Malley had lost his teenaged heart to years ago.

'Twas in support of their older brother that the three younger O'Malleys had taken up the cause when Sean seemed to have set it behind him. Garahan thought they'd battered the anger out of themselves with that final bare-knuckle bout before the O'Malleys left for England to seek work.

Looking at the two raging bulls standing before him, he realized he was mistaken. He did not have time to act the peacemaker! He was overdue to man his post, needed to change into dry clothes, and all before he checked on the lass to see how she fared. His ear-piercing whistle had his cousins turning to glare at him. "Well then, now that I have yer attention, ye need to cut the *shite*. O'Ghill, listen to what our cousin has to say. Never have I known an O'Ghill to turn his back on family when he was needed."

His cousin blew out a breath and rubbed the back of his neck. "I've *shite* for brains, letting the past get in the way of the present. I apologize. How can I help, O'Malley?"

Satisfied that his cousins had gotten past their need to pummel one another, Garahan clapped a hand to O'Ghill's shoulder. "I'm off to change before I start to mold—going for a swim in the marsh pond was not what I'd planned to be doing today." He noticed the hesitation in O'Ghill's eyes and paused. "I'm thankful God sent ye here to aid me in getting the lads and the lass to where they could be taken care of. Though I'm thinking he's not done with ye yet, as we need someone who isn't known to the villagers in Summerfield-on-Eden."

O'Malley agreed, adding, "We need ye to gather a bit of information regarding a delicate topic."

Their cousin frowned. "I'll not be coerced into being the *eedjit* go-between for either of yerselves—or Flaherty, for that matter— if it involves a woman!"

Needing to defuse what could quickly become an argument, Garahan shoved O'Ghill into O'Malley, who shoved him back. O'Ghill's face was red, and his fists were raised. Garahan said, "Shut yer *eedjit* gob and listen, because it does involve a woman, but not the way ye think. I'll leave O'Malley to explain matters while I change." He paused in the doorway. "Don't be starting a round of bare-knuckle when the baron is already consumed with worry for the baroness."

O'Ghill lowered his fists and crossed his heart. "Ye have me word."

Garahan nodded to his cousins and closed the door behind him.

A QUARTER OF an hour later, he was waylaid by the stable master—he'd forgotten to speak to the man about O'Ghill's horse. Once the matter was handled, he stepped outside to find his cousins waiting for him in a semicircle outside the door. From the expressions on their faces, something had occurred in the short time he'd been away.

"Best tell me quickly," Garahan told them. "I've still to check on the lass and inquire after the lads."

"Ye don't have to rush," O'Malley said. "She was apparently rested enough to suit the squire's wife when she demanded to collect the lass."

Garahan cursed beneath his breath. He had not expected that to happen. "Did she at least have something more than tea and a scone before the harpy dragged her off? And what of the lads?"

Flaherty shrugged. "I was patrolling the grounds when the squire's wife arrived. She sounded like a shrew when she insisted the lads not be moved until her physician pronounced them well enough to leave."

"They looked well enough to me when they were stuffing their faces with currant cake," O'Ghill mumbled.

Garahan shook his head. "I'm guessing Phineas had a second slice."

"Aye," O'Ghill said.

"Did Mrs. Honeycutt see ye?" Garahan asked.

O'Ghill shook his head. "O'Malley insisted that I keep me distance, so I can make a bleeding entrance into the village later."

"'Twould be better if she didn't see ye," Garahan agreed, "until she sees ye." He looked at O'Malley. "How did the lass look when she left?"

O'Malley frowned. "Exhausted—and wearing her damp gown. Poor lass, needed a bit more rest, but the woman was impatient and insisted on dragging the poor lass back home with her."

Garahan felt his temper ignite. "Ye should have come to get me. I would have—"

"What?" O'Malley asked. "Insisted the lass stay, causing even more rumors about the two of ye than there already are?"

"What load of *shite* have ye been listening to? There's no gossip about the lass and meself. I would have heard it."

"'Tis all over the village that ye arranged for the lass to meet ye in the marsh," O'Malley told him.

"To have another *rendezvous*," Flaherty added.

Blood boiling, fists curled, Garahan demanded, "Who's spouting that load of *fecking* lies?"

"According to the squire's witch of a wife, she could not say or risk the young woman's reputation," O'Malley replied.

"Tell the baron I had to see the lass—"

O'Malley stepped in front of Garahan and shook his head. "Ye aren't leaving the property until after O'Ghill makes his appearance and secures a room at the inn."

"I'd rather stay in the stables with me knot-headed cousins," O'Ghill said.

"Sure and we'd love to have ye stay with us," O'Malley replied, "but ye've a job to do and a rumormonger to unmask."

Garahan stepped to the side, and this time Flaherty blocked his way. "Think of the lass's reputation. She'll only suffer more."

Garahan narrowed his eyes and grabbed Flaherty by his cravat. "Suffer more than nearly drowning earlier?"

Flaherty shrugged out of his hold and stepped back. "Tell him."

O'Malley placed a hand on Garahan's shoulder, but Garahan

was not certain if it was mean to calm him or prevent him from chasing after the lass. "We noticed she had a bruise on her cheek when she stumbled behind Mrs. Honeycutt."

He gathered from what they didn't say that the squire's wife was the one who struck the lass. He'd exact retribution later. "The lass needs rest—and a solid meal! Didn't the woman want the physician to see the lass as well as her cousins?"

"Nay," O'Malley told him. Seemingly satisfied that Garahan was going to stay put, he added, "Let O'Ghill do this favor for us. He has the devil's own luck, and the *fecking* O'Ghill gift of persuasion. He'll have the answers the baron needs...the ones we need."

Garahan didn't like the sound of that. "We? What else did the blasted woman have to say?"

"She accused the three of us of having our way with the lass," Flaherty answered.

White-hot rage had Garahan by the throat as he shoved against the trio of men blocking his way. They pushed back. "By the baron's orders, ye're not to leave Summerfield Chase until this has been resolved. 'Tisn't just the baron's and the baroness's reputations," O'Malley reminded him. "But the duke's and that of his entire guard. Our brothers have wives now—ye'll agree they must be protected at all costs."

Garahan relaxed his stance and let his hands drop to his sides. "Faith if ye don't have the right of it, Thomas." He met his cousin's gaze. "James and Aiden would have me head on a platter if their wives' reputations were slandered."

O'Malley sighed. "Sean and Michael would toss mine right next to yers and add an apple to me mouth."

"The two of ye are exaggerating," Flaherty said.

O'Ghill agreed, "They'd just beat us bloody."

"Well then, O'Ghill, ye'd best be fetching yer horse and heading to the inn for a room," O'Malley said.

"And see if ye can find work, while ye're at it," Garahan added.

O'Ghill threw his hands up in the air. "This is what I get for interrupting me ramble to stop and see me favorite cousins. Tangled up in their troubles, coerced into spying for them, and now…now…I have to find a *fecking* job!"

"Ah, ye were a sight for sore eyes, O'Ghill," Garahan said, giving his cousin a shove toward the stables. "Best be on yer way."

The duke's guard watched their cousin stalk toward the stables. As soon as he was inside and closed the door, Garahan rounded on O'Malley. "If the lass falls ill because of this, neither ye, Flaherty, nor the baron will stop me from checking on her."

O'Malley and Flaherty shared a pointed look, but neither disagreed. Satisfied that he had gotten his point across, Garahan asked, "How soon do ye think before the physician arrives?"

"Timmons sent one of the footmen as soon as Mrs. Honeycutt made her demand. Any time now."

"I'll stop in and speak to the lads, then I'll resume me rounds of the perimeter."

"Flaherty will take yer shift," O'Malley told him. "Ye're doing double shifts inside until we hear from O'Ghill."

Garahan wanted to punch something—O'Malley's pretty face was close enough. As if he sensed what Garahan was thinking, O'Malley stepped out of striking range. "Think of the lass's reputation."

"I want to do something… I *need* to do something!" Garahan said.

"And ye will, by doing yer duty to the duke, and performing yer duties here to the baron and baroness," O'Malley reminded him.

His cousin was right. "Aye. Ye're right. I'll not ask to leave again. I made a vow, and I intend to keep it."

CHAPTER TEN

PRUDENCE WAS QUIET on the ride back to her aunt and uncle's home. She had much to think about, mayhap much to change about herself. Garahan had saved her from a watery death, and she was not about to waste the gift he'd given her. She had been granted more time to live her life, and she intended to live it to the fullest!

Digging deep past the exhaustion weighing her down, she lifted her chin and watched the world as it flew past the carriage window. She may have made a mistake in allowing her aunt and uncle to believe she was submissive. Now that she thought about it, the expression of amusement on her uncle's face, when her aunt berated her for acting the hoyden for climbing a tree, led her to believe he didn't mind that she was teaching his sons the fine art of tree climbing. It was almost as if he sensed it was a side of herself she normally hid from others—her true self.

Just because her parents—to be honest, mostly her mother—treated her as if she were an embarrassment and complete antidote to Society, that did not mean that she had to continue to allow them to do so. She should have shown them the true steel in her backbone, but she had kept it from them in order to honor her parents. That was what she had been raised to do. How else would she have survived the slurs and insults once she reached the unfashionable height of five feet, ten inches tall? The comments were far worse, when her slender figure began to blossom into what her mother considered slatternly, something to be hidden as she ordered Prudence's breasts to be tightly bound to her chest to flatten them.

How would her father have reacted, she wondered, if she had spoken up when the bindings around her breasts became too painful to bear? Father appeared to agree with all her mother said…if Mother was present. If not, he had a decidedly different point of view. She should have been courageous enough to find out. But the time to do so was past. Even if her aunt had spoken the truth when she said her parents would continue to search for a suitable husband for her, Prudence doubted they would succeed. She had to make the best of the role she had been thrust into, but wondered, had she enabled those around her to press her into a mold she clearly would never fit into?

Leaning closer to the window, she inhaled the welcome scent of fresh-turned earth. She'd always enjoyed spending time out-of-doors when she was younger…before her figure had betrayed her by filling out here and curving there. "What is that God-awful smell?" her aunt demanded. "Draw the curtain! I cannot abide that odor!"

Prudence placed a hand to the curtain, holding it open. "I'm feeling nauseated, Aunt." She glanced at the window to add, "I simply must have the window open."

Her aunt's mouth opened and closed, but not a sound emerged.

Prudence added, "I must have swallowed too much marsh water."

"Why in heaven's name would you think to jump into that pond?" her aunt demanded.

"Percy was sinking. I could not let that happen."

Her aunt's expression returned to normal…one of complete and utter disdain. "It is completely your fault that my precious son was in that pond to begin with. I hold you responsible! Should he contract a lung infection, or fever, it will be your fault!"

"But I—"

"Do not try to extricate yourself from the situation or accepting the blame. This is entirely your fault. You know that I do not normally approve of my sons gallivanting about the countryside! They are to be raised as gentlemen, not farmers!"

Incensed that her aunt would cast blame without knowing the facts, Prudence retorted, "Isn't that Uncle's legacy and what a squire is? A farmer, albeit a wealthy one?"

The slap was vicious and stung more than her pride. Her aunt's penchant for wearing heavy rings added to the blow. But she did not show any reaction, knowing her aunt—like her mother—would feed off it. It was past time to stand her ground.

"You cannot change what is, Aunt, any more than I can. You are on the bottom fringes of Society, just as my mother is. No amount of social climbing would even put you in the same class as Baroness Summerfield. She is a gracious lady."

Her aunt's face flushed a bright crimson as her eyes narrowed and she shrieked, "She is a common trollop! Hosting orgies with the baron's contemporaries—and the duke's guard!"

All of the insults and degrading comments she'd received over the years swirled around inside of her until she saw red. Prudence grabbed hold of her aunt's hand and tugged on it until she turned. "How dare you disparage Lady Phoebe's reputation like that! Have you repeated such vile comments to anyone else?"

Her aunt glared at her, but refused to answer, and looked away.

The truth slithered inside of Prudence until her stomach felt raw. "You are contemptable, Aunt. I am going to send word to Garahan."

Her aunt yanked on Prudence's hair, loosening it from its pins. Twisting it in her hand, she pulled Prudence toward her. "You are not going to tell anyone anything, or I shall write to your mother and tell her everything that has happened and insist that she cease trying to find a husband for you. Without our recommendation, you will never find another position as a governess. You will be ostracized and forced to find the only work a woman who looks like you can get—on your back!"

The words were emotional blows, but Prudence did not crumble under them. She lifted her chin higher and glared at her aunt, saying nothing. Now was not the time. She knew once the twins were pronounced fit by the physician, they would immediately seek her out. She would hold her tongue until she had a chance to ask them to relay the message to Garahan for her. They would not let her down.

A horrible thought screamed through her mind—what if her aunt had been the one to recirculate the rumor involving the baroness?

Lord, I should have kept my mouth shut and continued to act submissive. Did I err the first time I tried to show my strength?

Her mind was blank; no words of encouragement were whispered in her ear. The jingling of the harness and rumbling of the carriage wheels were all she heard. Her aunt was silent as she seethed beside Prudence, as if that could possibly be any worse than the heinous accusation she had hurled at the kind baroness and her niece moments before. How could anyone possibly judge another based solely on their appearance, thereby forcing their opinions and ideals on an unsuspecting individual?

Before she drove herself positively mad trying to inject logic into her aunt's reaction and hurtful words, she set them aside. She would bide her time and find a way to escape from what was rapidly becoming an intolerable situation. Today was proof that she could not exist on the meager meals her aunt insisted Prudence's mother had instructed would change her daughter's embarrassing figure. If she had eaten more than tea and toast, she would have had the strength to make it back to shore with her cousin. But she hadn't. The cold, hard reality, that she and Percy would have been in imminent danger if not for the timely arrival of Garahan and his cousin Killian, was not lost on her.

If her aunt decided to lock her in her bedchamber—as she had recently threatened—she had to somehow let the stable master and cook know ahead of time. They had befriended her after seeing how happy and healthy the twins looked after a few weeks in Prudence's care. Percy and Phineas were staunch allies. She could count on them to sneak food to her room in the attic. They had angel's faces and engaging smiles when they chose to use them. Their mother always gave in to whatever the boys wanted. She prayed that would hold true now.

If they were prevented from helping her, she would survive a few days on meager rations and was not overly worried about it. What scared her down to her soul was the possibility that her aunt had already started rumors about the baroness. The words had spilled out of her aunt's mouth easily—too easily. Had she started rumors about Garahan of the duke's guard, too? Prudence had to act quickly, lest the baroness—and possibly the duke's guard—were on the receiving end of vile and vicious rumors and salacious gossip. Lady Phoebe had been kindness itself, and even remarked that Prudence reminded her of her dear friends Lady Calliope and Lady Aurelia, whom she missed terribly. Garahan had saved Percy's life and her own. She had to do something to stop the madness!

The carriage rolled to a stop and the door opened. The footman handed her aunt out of the coach and was about to assist Prudence when her aunt stopped him. "She doesn't need assistance. See to it that you follow Miss Barstow to her chamber and lock her in!"

"But Mrs. Honeycutt—"

"If you wish to retain your position within this household, you will follow orders without question. Is that clear?"

A quick glance let Prudence know he had no choice. She knew the young man was the sole supporter of his ailing mother and four younger siblings.

"Yes, Mrs. Honeycutt."

He turned to do her bidding, but stopped immediately when the woman demanded he escort her inside first. Prudence waited until they were out of sight before approaching the stable master.

"I need a favor."

He sighed. "Is it true?"

"About Percy needing to be rescued from the pond?"

"Aye. The rest of what I've heard is false. You would never throw yourself at Garahan or any of the duke's guard. I have heard each member of the guard has pledged their vow to protect the duke and his family—and extended family—with their lives!"

Her suspicions had been correct—her aunt had defamed the duke's guard as well. "Thank you, Gifford. It means the world to me that you don't believe those lies. But what my aunt said to me before..." She couldn't ever confide the rest to the kindly stable master. The words were too damning to hear, let alone repeat.

"If the squire's wife is anything, she's predictable. Mrs. Cabot and I will see to it that you have more to eat than bread and water. You're wasting away as it is."

She nearly laughed, knowing that she still had more curves than Society approved of. "Thank you. We would not have needed assistance if I'd been allowed more than tea and toast for the morning meal."

"You'd best present yourself in the entryway. I'm certain Mrs. Honeycutt is waiting for you."

Prudence sighed. "To exact her latest punishment in front of the staff."

"We are on your side... We just cannot let her know it."

She smiled and ignored the heavy weight of her limbs as she hurried to the front door and stopped. Her aunt would reprimand her for using the front door. With a heavy sigh, she retraced her steps and headed to the kitchen door.

Mrs. Cabot looked up from the tray of tarts she held as Prudence entered. She set it on top of the stove and asked, "What are you doing here? One of Baron Summerfield's footmen brought the message about what happened. The baron expected the three of you would be staying the night. Given what nearly happened, I'm very surprised to see you."

Prudence would not let the tears gathering in her eyes fall.

She bit the inside of her cheek and blinked them away. "Apparently, my aunt believes I am responsible for Percy's jumping into the pond."

The cook shook her head. "Those two scamps have been having the time of their lives since you arrived. Percy got himself into that pond—and don't try to tell me any differently. I know those boys. They're just like their father, and are constantly testing their limits. They are bound to get hurt every once in a while. Thankfully, you can swim—those are the squire's words, not mine."

"Thank you for believing that I would never let Percy or Phineas swim alone."

"You'd best go and report to Mrs. Honeycutt. Don't you worry—between Gifford and myself, you will have plenty to eat. You never would have been in such dire straits if you had been eating properly."

Prudence hugged the cook before rushing to the door to the main part of the house. She opened it and wished she hadn't.

"I want that creature banished!" her aunt screeched. "Do you hear me?"

The squire shook his head. "The twins love Prudence and have told me more than once that she is the best thing that has ever happened to them. High praise coming from boys that persecuted the last few governesses until they fled our home screaming."

"I do not care what the boys told you. She is a temptress! How else would that Irishman have ended up arriving in time to pull Percy, and then her, out of that pond in the marsh? She'd obviously arranged an assignation!"

Incensed that she was being accused without cause, Prudence asked, "How long have you been spreading lies about the baroness, the duke's guard, and myself?"

Her aunt closed the distance between them, her hand raised to strike. Prudence stared at her aunt, bracing for the blow, but it never came. Her uncle's hand was manacled around her aunt's wrist. "I believe you need to go have a rest and take one of your headache powders. I shall speak to our niece."

"Our *governess!*" her aunt insisted, but her uncle ignored her, waving to the lady's maid standing at the foot of the staircase. "Mary, see that my wife lies down after she takes something for the headache that is obviously plaguing her."

Her aunt had a mutinous expression on her face but did as he bade her to do. When they were alone, Prudence's uncle asked, "Now, tell me what really happened."

Prudence met her uncle's curious glance. There was no condemnation in his expression. It was open and waiting. "The boys were so excited to go on another of our scientific explorations to the marsh. They ran ahead of me after they promised to wait for me before they started exploring." She paused, and it hit her. They never promised *not* to go into the pond without her. Tears welled up and spilled over.

"I see there is something of import that you remembered, Prudence."

"I knew they were excited to learn to swim, but we weren't prepared to go swimming today, as Aunt hasn't agreed that we may begin our lessons. We were only to collect samples of creatures and insects. I was carrying the jars with the lids. I never thought to ask for their promise not to go into the water."

Her uncle's expression darkened. "My sons always keep their promises."

"I... Yes, of course they do," she agreed. "They are honorable young boys."

He inclined his head and put his hands behind his back—his thinking posture. "I am afraid I must side with my wife in this matter. By neglecting to gain their promise not to enter the pond today, you put their lives in danger. When they are in your care, you are responsible for anything and everything that occurs. Accidents, mistakes, what have you. Do you understand?"

"I understand. I am deeply sorry and promise that it will never happen again."

"My wife and I have been discussing the difficulties of your situation from the first day. Although your parents are hoping to make a suitable match for you, I doubt that will be possible now. After today's events, I must also agree with my wife's decision to hire another governess. By the time you have served your punishment for Percival's brush with death, the new governess will have arrived."

"But—"

"There will be no discussion of the matter. It is closed." He waved her toward the servants' staircase.

"Uncle, please—"

"Samuels will see you to your room—and lock you in."

She bit her bottom lip to keep from begging him to allow her to stay. She'd come to love her cousins and would hate to see them closed in a schoolroom for hours on end, instead of enjoying their romps outside in the fresh air.

"One more thing," her uncle said.

Hopeful that he would soften the punishment, she asked, "Yes?"

"I had discouraged my wife in her bid to turn you out without recommendation, but the peril you placed our sons in—and what nearly happened to Percy—has changed my mind. You will not be receiving a letter of recommendation from us."

His words hung around her neck like a millstone. She slowly made her way to the door to the servants' side of the house and slipped inside, failure dogging her heels. What would she do now? She would never be hired by any of the agencies her parents had mentioned. The reply from her aunt and uncle had arrived just as her parents were discussing which agency to write to. She thought she'd been granted a second chance, living with relatives and caring for her cousins. Prudence realized she should have paid more attention to the caveat in her uncle's letter, advising that they would allow a trial period to see if the boys would take to her, and see if she could handle the duties.

She heard heavy footsteps and knew who followed her. Their

faithful butler would accompany her to her bedchamber and lock the door. Without turning around, she asked, "Samuels? How many days this time?"

"A sennight, miss." He sounded resigned.

Her stomach clenched. Worry tangled with fear of the unknown and what might lie ahead of her once she left her temporary refuge. "Thank you for telling me, Samuels."

"I shall be delivering your meals to you—not one of the serving girls or footmen," he told her. "And the twins are not allowed to speak to you."

There was no way Mrs. Cabot or Gifford would be able to sneak food into her. "I understand."

She crossed the threshold and spun around to see if the butler's expression would give her a clue as to how he felt about keeping her prisoner. The closed, blank look on his face spoke volumes.

He shut the door, and she listened for the sound of the key turning in the lock. That final click broke her resolve not to feel sorry for herself. She sank to the floor and buried her face in her hands, not caring if anyone heard her sobs. No one would come to her rescue. She'd been neglectful. She'd put Percy and Phineas's lives in danger, and now she would pay the price.

✦

CHAPTER ELEVEN

GARAHAN RODE INTO the village on his daily rounds. It was part of the daily patrols performed by the duke's guard. To keep from becoming too used to their surroundings and miss something of import, the members of the guard rotated their route to and from the village of Summerfield-on-Eden. It had been a few days since he'd seen the lass and her charges. He smiled thinking of how quickly Percy bounced back from his ill-thought-out, impromptu dunking.

As he passed by the church, he scanned the graveyard. He remembered the ugly rumors Beth had spoken of. Bloody hell… He would never accost or compromise a woman—especially near a church in a graveyard! Women sought him out, not the other way around.

He forced those thoughts deep, to peruse his surroundings. *Nothing out of place.* Given the hour, he did not anticipate finding anything, but it was part of his duty to ensure the safety of the duke's family. The baron and baroness, and their staff, were part of those they protected.

Passing the blacksmith's shop, he raised his hand to the smithy, who was firing up his forge for the day. The man's expression had Garahan approaching. He dismounted as the smithy stormed toward him.

"How could you? I thought you were a protector of innocents!"

Garahan held up his hands. "You cannot believe the rumors. I did not even know you had a daughter."

The blacksmith was equal in size to Garahan, and a bit broader, like his O'Malley cousins. He braced for the first blow and did not bother to block it.

The blacksmith's shock was evident as Garahan dropped his arms to his sides. "So, you admit your guilt by letting me land the first blow?"

"Nay. I never touched any lass in the village. I've granted ye the first blow so you'd listen to what I have to say." The blacksmith launched a right cross, but Garahan deflected the punch. "I said the first blow—ye don't deserve a second until ye agree to listen."

The smithy's chest heaved with the effort to rein in his anger. "My wife would turn over in her grave if she knew what you did to our precious daughter."

"I didn't know ye lost yer wife—or that ye had a daughter. And before ye open yer gob and start spewing falsehoods, listen, for *feck's* sake!"

The blacksmith took a step back. "I'm listening."

"I vowed an oath when the Duke of Wyndmere hired me as one of the sixteen men in his private guard. I'd protect the duke, his family, and his extended family…with me life! I've been shot at, stabbed, and clubbed over the head while doing me duty. This is the first time me good name has been slandered. But that's not what has me and me cousins speaking to everyone in the village to uncover who started these ugly rumors—and to find out if the lasses rumored to have suffered at me hands have been given a chance to speak. Have ye told yer daughter that ye believe that she is a victim of an evil person's foul mind and mouth? Did ye ask if she was accosted?"

The smithy shook his head. "I'm ashamed to admit, I concentrated on exacting retribution when next I saw you, as my daughter begged me not to go after you."

"Ye thought she'd been a willing participant? Ye bloody bastard!" Garahan had the bigger man by the throat, and his feet dangling inches from the ground.

"Leave off, Garahan!"

He sighed but loosened his grip on the man's throat. "I didn't see ye there, Constable Standish."

"You were too busy trying to strangle Coleman. Let him go." When he complied, the constable said, "I take it this has to do with the latest rumors."

"'Tis all they are," Garahan replied. Turning to the smithy, he said, "All ye have to do is ask yer daughter, and she'll tell ye 'tis a vicious, slanderous lie."

"She won't stop crying long enough to talk to me."

"How did ye react when first ye heard that bold-faced lie?"

The blacksmith's hands curled into fists then slowly opened. "I told her I would beat you to death for sullying her reputation."

The constable shook his head. "Did you even think how your comment must have affected a shy young thing like Olivia? Your daughter is one of the sweetest girls. It must have devasted her."

Garahan put a hand on Coleman's shoulder. "Let me speak with her, and if she is open to listening to me, mayhap she'll accompany me to speak with the vicar's daughter next. I never laid a hand on either of the lasses, and I'll swear on a stack of Bibles that there is no way on this green earth that I'd ever accost a woman—let alone within spitting distance of the Lord's house, trampling on the graves of departed loved ones!"

When the other man agreed, he followed him into the forge, and out the side door to the house that stood a few yards away. "Wait here. I'll see if she wants to speak to you."

"Have you wondered why you haven't seen me at Summerfield Chase asking questions?" the constable asked as they waited.

"I haven't had the time," Garahan answered honestly.

"Ah, I heard about that business in the marsh. Miss Barstow and the twins were lucky you were nearby...and could swim. Since you haven't asked, I'll tell you. I took your measure—and that of your cousins—when you arrived at Summerfield Chase, guarding the baron and his bride." When Garahan remained silent, Standish continued, "I sent a missive to the duke, asking about you and the others in his guard. Everything he said confirmed my impression of you, O'Malley, and Flaherty. You are men who have earned His Grace's trust—and his eternal gratitude—for the number of times you and the others have stood between the duke, and his family, and certain death."

Garahan nodded.

Standish continued, "His Grace's reply contained a list of the number of times each one of his guard was shot, stabbed, clubbed, or had a rope around their neck." He stared at Garahan. "Care to read it?"

Garahan snorted out a laugh. "Thank ye, no. Having lived it, I'd rather not."

A few moments later, Coleman stood in the doorway and motioned for Garahan to come inside. Garahan looked over his shoulder. "Are ye coming, constable?"

"I believe I'll wait for you at the vicarage."

As soon as Garahan stepped into the small parlor, Coleman's daughter rushed over to him with one hand to her throat and the other reaching for Garahan. "She was right! You came! She knew you would want to see for yourself that I was unharmed."

Garahan glanced at the blacksmith and then back at his daughter, who quickly let go of him. "Who is the 'she' ye speak of?"

"Lady Phoebe. She was here early this morning—you were taking care of our horses, Father."

"How is it you are not crying, Olivia?"

His daughter smiled. "Lady Phoebe explained that even though you acted as if you believed the rumors and wanted to kill Garahan, you knew I would not have gone out of my way to entice him or lead him to the graveyard, of all places."

"She said that, did she?" Garahan asked. "Her ladyship is a rare woman, unafraid to flaunt convention if it means saving the life of the man she wed. Ye should ask her about her ribbon-wrapped hatpins sometime."

Olivia smiled. "I will. Thank you for coming, Garahan. It's a pleasure to meet you. Can I go with you to speak to the vicar and his wife? Melanie is as distraught as I was."

"'Tis an honor to meet ye, Miss Coleman. If yer da doesn't mind, then I'd be pleased to have ye accompany me to speak to the Chessy family. No doubt I'll have to let him land a blow to me battered face before he'll feel obliged to listen to me, too."

She narrowed her eyes at the bruise on Garahan's jaw. "Did my father hit you?"

"'Twas nothing more than a conversation opener, if ye will," he replied. "Now then, do ye have a wrap? There's a bit of a breeze, and ye wouldn't want to catch a chill."

She rushed over to the chair by the window, retrieved her shawl, and wrapped it around her. "I'm ready. Let's go."

CHAPTER TWELVE

HOURS LATER, GARAHAN headed back into the village after putting in a full day. He'd been quick to volunteer to meet with O'Ghill at the ungodly hour of midnight—a time when no one else would be about to ask questions about the latest gossip, or the dark-haired lass he'd pulled from the marsh pond. He'd righted a few wrongs since his first trip to Summerfield-on-Eden earlier that day.

Thankfully, he had not had a repeat of the blow he'd accepted from the blacksmith, or the awkward conversation he endured. The vicar questioned him not only about his background, but what church he'd attended since leaving Ireland. After that conversation was exhausted, the vicar, being a man of God, had not immediately thought to exact retribution from Garahan. He'd taken the time to calm his daughter's fears at hearing such horrible gossip about herself—and her very good friend Olivia Coleman. After he had assured his daughter Melanie that he believed she and Olivia were never accosted by Garahan, he sent word to the baroness requesting her assistance in sorting out this disastrous debacle involving two of the shyest of young women in their village.

Garahan smiled, remembering the way Lady Phoebe tossed her head as if her part in smoothing things out at the blacksmith's home and the vicarage were akin to her arriving at teatime, prepared to discuss the latest projects the vicar's wife was working on with those on the church committee. He felt blessed to have been assigned to protect such a caring person. He would miss his time guarding the baron and baroness when his rotation in the Borderlands was over and he was assigned to another of the duke's properties.

A whisper of warning brushed against the back of his neck. The fine hair there stood on end as unease slithered into his gut. Scanning his surroundings with an eye out for anything out of the ordinary—or trouble—he found nothing. As he approached the inn, he realized it wasn't what he saw that had acid searing his gut; it was the absence of something—or make that some*one*! O'Ghill wasn't waiting where he promised he'd be.

Another thought struck Garahan: he'd not seen hide nor hair of the twins, or their lovely governess, during his rounds earlier that day—or at all since they left Summerfield Chase. His hands tightened on the reins, and his horse immediately responded, his flesh quivering as he anticipated Garahan's next command.

"Sorry, lad. 'Tis a bad feeling, is all—no need to gallop off to rescue anyone tonight."

Slowing his mount to a walk, he looked deeper, not just at but *into* the barrels stacked at the end of the alley alongside the blacksmith's, searching for something—anything—that was out of place, wishing O'Malley had relented in his decision to keep Garahan away from the lass and her cousins. "If wishes were all it took, Duncan, me lad, I'd have captured the king of the leprechauns and his crock of gold years ago."

The thought helped dispel a bit of the unease he felt. He'd kept his word to O'Malley, as he'd kept his word to the duke and the baron. He had not sought out Miss Barstow, nor had he stopped by the squire's home to see how the lads fared after Percy's ill-advised attempt to swim. A Garahan never went back on his word, and nor did he forsake any vow freely given. For that matter, neither would his cousins, the O'Malleys and Flahertys who served with him in the duke's private guard. Nor would any one of his other cousins, the O'Ghills, Fitzpatricks, or McGreevys. Loyalty to family and honoring a vow were pledges that could not be forsaken—even in death. Those that came after the one who'd given his life would continue to honor any vow given.

He felt a pinch of guilt at persuading Phineas into confessing what had happened the other day. A life could be at stake if he had not used his considerable charm to uncover the facts: Percy had been bound and determined to swim. It had not been the plan, and nor had Miss Barstow mentioned the possibility of a swimming lesson the day he'd ridden to their rescue.

It was no coincidence that he had not seen the trio in the village earlier. He did not believe in coincidences. Something was wrong.

Garahan noticed a familiar horse and rider in front of the inn. *He's late.* He rode toward them, hoping to have a word with O'Ghill. They'd spoken a few times before—after hours—during the midnight shift. Because of his vow to O'Malley, Garahan had not specifically asked O'Ghill about Miss Barstow or the lads.

O'Ghill lifted a hand in greeting, and Garahan wondered, had his cousin uncovered any information that would indicate Miss Barstow was ill, or worse—had been dismissed? As soon as the thought occurred, he banished it, thinking, *We would have heard the rumors by now if she had been.*

His cousin was tying his horse's reins to the post outside of the inn when Garahan slowed to a stop and asked, "Have ye been for a ride? 'Tis a fine night for it."

O'Ghill's expression was bleak, but his tone cheerful enough as he replied, "Excellent weather for a ride. It has lightened me mood. Care to join me for swig of whiskey?" He reached into his waistcoat pocket and pulled out a flask. "I'm buying."

Garahan had to keep the surprise from his expression. O'Ghill never offered to share his whiskey. "Thank ye, no. Not when I'm on duty."

O'Ghill nodded. "If ye're after a spot of tea, ye'd be out of luck."

Garahan snorted with laughter. "Another time. Ye're late. Is there trouble?"

In answer, his cousin patted his horse affectionately and waited for Garahan to dismount and secure his own mount. Side by side, they walked toward the smithy and on past it. When they reached the church, they headed for the gate to the graveyard. When they had walked to their meeting spot—the huge Celtic cross—they agreed they were far enough away from prying eyes and ears.

Garahan asked, "Have ye been to the squire's place?"

"Aye. And before ye hound me about it, no, he's not looking to hire me on. But he did mention being plagued by a family matter."

"Did he now?" Garahan noticed his cousin's hesitation. "Best just to tell me whatever is weighing ye down."

"'Tis the lass—not that I heard it from the squire, but from the stable master, who's taken a shine to me."

"Aye, we all know how ye preen yer blasted feathers when someone notices ye. What did the man say?" Garahan asked.

"The lads are inconsolable over losing their favorite cousin as their governess."

He dug deep to control his shock. Had the lass been dismissed? Was she gone? "When did this happen? Where did she go?"

O'Ghill grabbed a hold of Garahan's sleeve to stop him from turning around. "'Tis the middle of the night! Hear me out before ye go off half-cocked!"

Garahan was seething inside, but knew he had to listen to what his cousin had to say. "Ye have the right of it. Just tell me where the lass is."

"As far as I know, she's still living with the squire and his family."

"But she hasn't had the lads out on any adventures," Garahan said. "Is she ill?"

"Nay, or at least no one has told me that she is ill," O'Ghill answered. "From what I've gathered, from bits and pieces of conversations I've overheard, Squire and Mrs. Honeycutt blame the lass for Percy nearly drowning."

"But he didn't. The lass was more than halfway to the bank when I heard Phineas shouting, and jumped in to bring him to shore. Ye know the rest, as ye were instrumental in aiding in their rescue."

"That I do. Percy and Phineas are beside themselves with worry for the lass. They tell me there's a new governess arriving at week's end."

Garahan struggled to hold on to his temper. "Do they plan to boot the lass out?"

"From what the lads have told me when they were helping to groom their horses, that's exactly what their parents have planned."

"The very least they can do is give her a recommendation..." Garahan trailed off when he saw his cousin shaking his head. "No recommendation?"

"Nay."

"Isn't it expected for an employer to give credit where credit is due with a letter of recommendation? Securing her next position depends upon it. Their treatment of the lass is criminal!"

O'Ghill agreed. "The lads have admitted to their parents that it was their fault. They knew they were not supposed to jump in the pond because every other time they'd been there with Prudence, she reminded them. After it became part of their excursions, she did not have to repeat what was a hard and fast rule."

"Then why the ill treatment? What has she done to deserve this?"

His cousin met his gaze and told him, "I overheard Mrs. Cabot speaking with the stable master."

"Gifford," Garahan said. "Good man."

"The cook heard Mrs. Honeycutt raving about improprieties

and inexcusable, lewd acts being performed at Summerfield Chase involving the baron and baroness, their guests…and the duke's guard."

Garahan blew out a breath. "'Tisn't a new rumor. Flaherty mentioned it, but we thought it would die down, as it had been circulating more than a month ago. The matter has already been handled by the baron's cousin, Viscount Chattsworth, the duke's contact within the Bow Street Runners—Gavin King—and those of the guard assigned to serve at Chattsworth Manor."

O'Ghill asked, "Were charges made against whoever defamed the duke and his family?"

"Aye," Garahan replied. "Me brother James was there when they were publicly proclaimed during a bare-knuckle bout."

O'Ghill grinned. "A fine way to spend a day, beating the bloody snot out of a worthy opponent."

Garahan nodded. "When the culprit was unmasked, witnesses came forward concerning the deaths of the man's cousin and his cousin's wife. Bloody bastard paid to have them murdered so he could take over the barony."

"*Fecking* bastard," O'Ghill swore. "I'll never understand why a man cannot be happy with the gifts he's been given in life. As to that, apparently 'tis the squire's wife who is intent on keeping the vicious rumors alive."

Garahan felt knots forming at the base of his neck. He rubbed them. "I received a message two days ago from the lads that did not make a lick of sense, but with what you've just told me, I think I understand it now. The lads were trying to tell me about the rumors their mother has been circulating, without actually telling me she was responsible. Poor lads. The next question has to be, is she the one guilty of starting them up again in the first place?"

O'Ghill shrugged. "'Tisn't easy trying to get the squire or his wife to talk about their niece, or the baron and baroness. I've tried a few times."

Garahan noticed his cousin's rounded shoulders. O'Ghill

always assumed that position when he felt he'd failed. "Take heart, O'Ghill. Mayhap 'tis time for me to pay a call on Squire and Mrs. Honeycutt—I'll speak to O'Malley first to gain his permission to release me from me vow not to."

"Ye'll not do or say anything to jeopardize the lass or the lads' safety."

"Ye have me word," Garahan promised.

O'Ghill nodded. "I've grown fond of the rascals. They remind me of our cousins when we were all the same age."

Garahan chuckled, knowing which cousins. "Thomas and Eamon O'Malley."

O'Ghill grinned. "'Tis something about twins their brains are linked. If one's addlepated, the other one is worse!" He lifted his arm and sniffed his sleeve. "I've got clean the scent of horse off me. I'm expected at the vicarage for supper tomorrow, and I'm not sure I can convince the innkeeper's wife to wash me coat after she did her best with the other one—marsh water stinks to high heaven when it dries. I'll be riding with the squire first thing in the morning, and there again at suppertime. That should give ye the time ye need, if O'Malley cuts ye loose."

"Bring back whatever news ye hear."

His cousin nodded. "Whether it be good or ill."

"Aye," Garahan agreed. "Though, truth be told, I'm hoping for some good news."

"I second that," O'Ghill replied. "Until tomorrow night."

"Meet me here—"

"Behind the tall Celtic cross in the cemetery at the stroke of midnight," O'Ghill interrupted. "I'm standing here now, aren't I? Even though ye know how I feel about graveyards and spirits. Though why ye have this penchant for meeting at all hours of the night in strange places is beyond me."

"No one else is usually about at midnight, and no one frequents graveyards," Garahan reminded him.

Satisfied his cousin would be there, Garahan gave a quick nod and strode back to where he'd tied his horse. He mounted, leaned down, and whispered in his horse's ear, "Time to be off, lad."

As if he sensed what Garahan hadn't said, Duncan retraced his steps, keeping his gait smooth, as he picked up the pace at the edge of the village. The moon lit their way. Once they were on the open road, Garahan let Duncan have his head, encouraging him when his horse quivered with the need for speed.

He needed to return to Summerfield Chase to flesh out his plan to speak to the lass—or at least the lads—with O'Malley's approval. He'd go without it if he had to, but he wasn't after breaking his vow to the duke, and therefore the baron. He took comfort in the knowledge that he, and the others serving the duke, had been given license to use discretion in urgent matters, and would not be accused of breaking any vows to do so.

The unease in his gut confirmed what he'd been worrying about—this was an urgent matter! He sensed the lass was in trouble. She needed him, and time was of the essence!

CHAPTER THIRTEEN

PRUDENCE HAD PLENTY of time to think while incarcerated—a horrible word, but she *was* being held against her will inside of a locked room. There were no bars, and at least she did not have to bed down on a pile of straw. But being forced to remain indoors, instead of showing Percy and Phineas the wonders of what lay beyond their front door, was a form of pure torture. She missed the boys and their enthusiasm for their jaunts through the countryside surrounding their home.

The whisper of a breeze caressed her face, carrying the scent of the wildflowers blooming in the lovely meadow the boys loved to run, tumble, and play in. Her uncle always encouraged her to take the boys on excursions out-of-doors, though her aunt wasn't as keen on the idea of her sons playing outside.

Aunt was equally as cross as her own mother had been about the stains the meadow grass left behind. Heaven forbid if she dared to open the subject of making mud pies with her cousins. Truly, who ever heard of a child growing up in the countryside and not having perfected the fine art of creating a pie out of mud, twigs, and leaves?

She loved listening to the birds singing, especially when dawn broke over the horizon. The sound never failed to lighten her heart. The soothing sound was lovely, but when one was outside, the experience was vastly different. One felt as if they were a part of nature, watching the rays of the sun peek through the trees, while the birds each added their own note to the chorus that seemed to coax the sun higher in the sky.

Enough! she thought, annoyed with herself—and her situation. "Stop bemoaning the situation you are responsible for!" she said aloud. "If you had remembered to remind the boys not to go in the water, you would not be locked in your room."

But they had spoken of it daily, and her cousins knew it was her strictest rule. She hadn't even had a chance to ask Percy what he'd been thinking to jump into the pond. The least he could have done would be to wait until she was just a few feet away from him. Then she could have fished him out before his struggles to stay afloat pushed him away from the bank, instead of toward it.

The fault had been laid squarely at her door. And how could she blame her uncle and aunt, when she blamed herself? She *was* the adult—the person responsible for their safety. Thank goodness Percy had not succumbed to a fever or lung infection. Though she was afraid that *she* had. The room was growing warmer by the hour. While she had been coughing, it seemed to alleviate whatever was in the water that irritated her lungs, because she was able to draw in a breath without issue.

She opened the window in spite of the chilly day, knowing that a fever could be worrisome, but not as much as her aunt's response to her request for more water. Her aunt told her that she could bang on her door to call attention to herself, but it would do her no good. *"God has chosen to punish you."* Prudence knew she was in dire straits when her aunt suggested she pray for forgiveness for leading her much younger, impressionable cousins into danger. One thing was for certain—God had not locked in her in her room in the attic!

The newly hired footman, who delivered the one meal a day that she had been allotted, had promised to bring more water, but that had been hours ago. She was desperately thirsty, and her skin felt hot to the touch. The fever had begun the morning after they'd been rescued and become more noticeable by the day, more intense by the hour. She could no longer speak. Her throat was raw from her having swallowed—then regurgitated—the foul marsh water.

Every inch of her body ached, protesting when she rolled off the bed and landed on her backside on the floor. Her only chance of receiving help, or water, was to somehow get word to the stable master, or mayhap the cook. Mrs. Cabot had a special herbal for reducing a fever. Prudence dearly wished she had had a chance to speak to the baroness or baron before she was summarily ousted from their home, but her aunt had all but dragged out of the house and into her uncle's carriage before either appeared.

Mayhap she could shout or throw something out of the attic window. She opened her mouth to call for help, but the pain in her throat brought tears to her eyes. It felt as if she'd swallowed shards of glass. Pushing to her knees, she scanned the room to think of what she could toss out the window that would catch someone's attention.

"Lord, please hear my prayer," she rasped. "I need to send a message—"

Before she finished the prayer, the answer filled her mind. She laughed, holding a hand against her aching throat. She knew how to get word to Gifford, Mrs. Cabot, or one of the boys. She'd forgotten about the leather satchel she'd dropped in her rush to get to the boys. Had it been wishful thinking that she'd heard one of the boys telling Garahan they needed it? She distinctly remembered adding paper, pencils, and drawing charcoal, along with the glass jars and lids. Please let it not be just her fever-ravaged mind projecting what she hoped to find. Let the satchel be here!

She tried to stand, and ended up on her bottom when her legs gave out. Determined, she got on her hands and knees and crawled over to the chair. Thank goodness—someone had tossed the satchel and O'Ghill's coat on it! Why hadn't Killian come by to ask for his coat? Why hadn't Garahan? The hazy memory of the strength in Garahan's arms, as he pulled her from beneath the water, surfaced, and she remembered the strong strokes necessary to reach the bank and pull her to safety. Well, she didn't recall that part exactly, but her cousins had told her what happened.

She'd been semi-conscious at the time and could only recall the large hand gripping hers and tugging hard... The next thing she remembered was strong hands on her back, urging the brackish water out of her. She understood why Garahan had not since inquired after her welfare, but it did not make sense that he hadn't stopped by to see how Percy and Phineas fared.

Or mayhap he had, and no one told her.

She pulled one of the charcoals out of the leather bag and reached for the worn linen on the washstand nearby. After setting them on the floor, she began to tug on the corner of her bed linens. The sheet resisted at first, then slowly loosened. It required more strength than she had, but she kept pulling, tugging, as she braced her back against the chair. She let out a huff when the bed covering finally slid free. Her head throbbed from her efforts, and her eyes burned with fever. For a few minutes all she could do was sit there... She could not think what to write! Finally, she decided on one word: *help*. Then she decided on another: *fever*. After inscribing her message, she set the charcoal aside and tied the cloth to the corner of her bedsheet. Her strength was waning, so she fashioned one knot instead of two, desperately hoping it would hold. It took longer to crawl to the window, but she finally managed it, hanging the bed linen out of the window.

Relief speared through her as the breeze lifted her message, as if beckoning someone—anyone—to see it. Then the sheet slipped over the frame and disappeared.

Had it worked? Would anyone come to investigate? For a moment, she wondered what her aunt or uncle would do if they discovered she was trying to send for help. She struggled to clear her fever-soaked mind to concentrate on the sounds below. Were those voices she heard outside the window? Had someone noticed her plea for help?

Her fever spiked, and she slumped to the floor as darkness pulled her under.

⁂

GARAHAN ARRIVED AMIDST chaos. The twins were standing on the side of the house crying, holding on to what looked to be someone's bed linen, while the squire and his wife were arguing—loudly. His whistle cut through the din. The boys immediately stopped crying and ran toward him, with the linen flapping behind them.

"Mind ye don't startle Duncan, lads." They stopped a few feet away. The tears on their upturned faces reminded him of his nieces and nephews back home in Ireland, and affected him the same way. He would move mountains if they needed him to.

"Will you help us, Garahan?" Percy pleaded. "She's so sick!"

"She needs water. Can you please rescue her again?" Phineas asked.

Garahan glanced at the arguing couple and knew his gut had been right—the lass was in trouble. "Ye have me word, lads. I'll rescue the lass."

"We aren't allowed to see her—" Percy began, only to be interrupted by his twin, who confided, "We snuck upstairs to see her and promised to get help…but they stopped us. We failed."

He'd find out later what had prevented the lads from visiting with their cousin. Right now, it was imperative to find out what had happened to her and where she was—then he would be able to lend her his aid.

Keeping his expression neutral, he asked if they could smooth out the linen so he could read the writing. It was indeed a bedsheet with a small, drying cloth tied to it. Two words were scrawled in what appeared to be charcoal: *Help. Fever.* The message left no doubt in his mind what had reduced the lads to tears. Their cousin must have been desperate to resort to this. "I'll be needing to hang on to this, lads." *As evidence.*

They handed it to him. Working together, they folded it until the size was manageable. He draped it over Duncan, patted his horse's neck, and told him to guard it before dismounting.

The older couple ceased arguing and noticed him. The squire asked, "What brings you here, Garahan?"

"I always check on those I rescue." Garahan winked at the lads, grateful they'd stopped crying. Hoping to ease their fears, he added, "I haven't seen the lads or Miss Barstow in the village in the last few days. I was on patrol to the village. Thought I'd stop by to see how they were." The lads rushed over to him, and he ruffled their hair as they flanked him. When their mother glared at them, they scooted closer to Garahan. In that instant, he knew who was behind what happened to the lass. By all that was holy, he'd protect the lads—from their own parents, if need be.

"You should not have gone to the trouble," Mrs. Honeycutt told him. "As you can see, the boys are fully recovered."

"And obviously upset about Miss Barstow." Garahan placed one hand on Percy's shoulder, and the other on Phineas's. The boys squeezed up against his sides, as if the proximity to him eased their fears. This would not be the first time he protected a child from their mother or father. Faith, it wouldn't be the last.

Instinctively, he knew all was not always as it appeared on the surface. He remembered the first time they met, and the way they quickly corrected themselves after referring to Miss Barstow as their cousin. The lads had told him their mother instructed them not to acknowledge the lass as their cousin in public. There was something strange going on at the squire's home. 'Twas just beneath the façade they showed the rest of the village. He would not leave until he got to the bottom of it!

"'Tis no trouble. How may I be of help?"

The squire's wife stared at him, narrowed her eyes, and said,

"By leaving."

"Well now, thank ye for yer gracious invitation, but I won't be doing that. Ye see, there is another matter entirely that I've come to discuss with yerself and the squire—privately." He squatted down so he was eye level with the lads. "Tell Miss Barstow I'm here to speak with her, if she is well enough to receive visitors."

The squire's wife shrieked, "Impossible! Leave here at once!"

The squire remained silent, seemingly immune to his wife's hysterics—a sure sign it must happen with some frequency. If Garahan gave in to what he wanted to do and put the harpy in her place with a harsh reply, would the squire speak up?

As soon as the thought crossed his mind, he knew he would have to keep his comments to himself. Garahan's temper was as volatile as O'Malley's. But without a doubt, O'Malley would have his hide if he spoke his mind.

Resolved to be patient, he replied, "I've been given leave by Baron Summerfield—and O'Malley, head of the duke's guard at Summerfield Chase—to call upon Master Phineas and Master Percy to see how the lads are feeling. As they have taken a liking to the twins, they are naturally concerned. As is the baroness, who is also concerned about Miss Barstow, who was completely worn out from jumping in the water after Percy. The baron and baroness were surprised that you'd come and gone without waiting to speak to them—and that you forced Miss Barstow to leave."

The squire cleared his throat. "I agree with my wife. You have seen for yourself that our sons are hale and hearty." He glanced at his wife, adding, "No thanks to Miss Barstow."

Garahan moved like lightning. One moment he was standing by the boys, the next, he was crowding the squire, standing so close that the shorter, rounder man had to tilt his chin up to meet Garahan's intimidating gaze. "Ye owe the lass yer thanks for leaping in after yer son. Had she not already swum halfway across the pond, and back—before I arrived to lend a hand—Percy would not be standing here asking for me help."

He turned to face the squire's wife. "If Miss Barstow isn't with the lads, she must be ill. 'Tis no surprise she wasn't feeling well after swallowing that brackish water. She was exhausted when she was whisked away from Summerfield Chase. Take me to her. After I see for meself how she fares, I'll report to his lordship that she has contracted a fever but is recovering."

The woman glared at him, refusing to speak. Her reaction pushed him closer to the edge.

"Is there a reason why she wouldn't tell ye if she fell ill? Is it not yer duty to take care of yer governess, and the rest of yer staff? If one of them was ill, would ye ignore them, too?"

This time the squire's wife glanced at her husband. His slight shake of his head kept her silent.

Garahan wanted to wrap his hands around their throats. Instead, he resolved again to remain calm, knowing he'd never get in to see the lass otherwise. "Did ye send for the physician?" He paused for a moment, appalled that they refused to answer his questions. "If she's truly kin, as the lads have said, isn't that even more of a reason to take care of her?" Studying the short woman and rotund man, he couldn't find a familial resemblance, but the lass could resemble a grandmother or grandfather instead of her aunt and uncle.

"That is none of your affair." Mrs. Honeycutt turned to her husband, demanding, "Send someone to fetch the constable!"

The lid on Garahan's anger lifted, but he forced it back down. The only way to defuse what bubbled inside of him was to go a few rounds with O'Malley or Flaherty—or better still, he'd trade a few blows with O'Ghill. It had been too long since they'd squared off in a bare-knuckle bout. Imagining trading blows with three of his cousins at once kept his anger from erupting.

He heard a rider and looked over his shoulder. Relief flowed through him. He trusted the rider approaching to keep his word and not to be put off by any excuses the squire or his wife offered. "No need to trouble yerself, Mrs. Honeycutt." He raised a hand in greeting. "Constable Standish! I see ye received Baron Summerfield's message. Thank ye for coming so quickly."

"Happy to oblige the baron and his wife. Without their constant support—and lending men, such as yourself, who are ready at a moment's notice to lend a hand when trouble arises—our village would not be as safe as it is. Not to mention the fact that we'd never have been able to complete the needed repairs to the church or the inn without the added men."

The squire shot a concerned glance at Garahan before he and his wife pasted false smiles on their faces to greet the constable. The squire stepped forward, hand outstretched, shaking the constable's hand when he offered it. "What brings you here?"

The official looked from the squire to Garahan and back. "As Garahan mentioned, I received a message from Baron Summerfield. I'd like to speak to you and your wife—privately, after I see to the task the baron asked of me."

"Task?" The squire's wife appeared confused. Garahan wondered if it was all an act, and decided it was when she added, "I don't recall asking the baron for assistance."

"He has asked me to ascertain the well-being of your sons, and their governess, Miss Barstow."

Mrs. Honeycutt immediately held up her hand to prevent him from entering their home. "You can see for yourself that the boys are well, but I'm afraid it is impossible for you to see Miss Barstow. She is indisposed."

"You haven't been to see her since you brought her home from the baron's house," Phineas said.

"She needs help," Percy added.

The constable stared at the squire's wife until she dropped her hand and let him pass. "I cannot refuse a request from the baron," he told her. "We owe our livelihood to Baron and Baroness Summerfield. It is a small thing for me to check on your sons and their governess."

Percy yanked on the constable's sleeve. The man bent down, and the boy said, "She's our cousin, too."

Phineas moved to squeeze in between the constable and his brother. "But we aren't supposed to tell anyone."

The constable straightened to his considerable height, nearly eye to eye with Garahan, and leveled a hard look at the squire. "I am going to need to speak with you and your wife about that, and another troubling matter the baron has apprised me of."

"What matter?" the squire asked.

The official ignored him and motioned for the boys to precede him. "Take me to your cousin." He looked over his shoulder at the squire and his wife. "Do not leave before I speak with you."

Garahan watched the squire's face turn red, and coughed to cover his snort of laughter.

"You have no right to issue orders to me while you are standing on my land!" the man boomed.

"When it is official business," the constable replied, "I do. Stay here!"

The couple looked as if they wanted to follow, but another gruff command from the constable changed their minds.

The stable master approached to take care of the horses. "I'll water the horses and see that they each receive a handful or two of oats."

"Thank you, Gifford," Garahan called out as he accompanied Standish and the boys inside.

The group walked in through the rear entrance of the house in time to see Mrs. Cabot rushing toward them from the kitchen. "Oh, thank goodness you're here. Miss Barstow is not answering her door. She must be in a bad way."

Garahan was incredulous. "Why didn't ye open it?"

Tears filled the cook's eyes as she clutched her apron. "There is only one key to that attic room, and I don't have it."

"Bloody hell!" Garahan shoved the back door open and shouted, "Bring me the bloody key!"

The squire looked at his wife, who paled and backed away from him. "Where is the key?" When she did not answer him, he added, "I gave it to you with instructions to see that Prudence was taken care of." She nearly tripped as she continued to step backward. He grabbed hold of her elbow, stopping her. "What have you done?"

"I could not take the chance Mrs. Cabot would feel sorry for our governess and unlock the door." She wrung her hands together. "You said yourself the incident in the marsh was entirely Miss Barstow's fault. Our sons are in her care, and it was her duty to watch out for them. She failed to do so. Percival nearly paid with his life because of it!"

The squire let go of his wife and held out his hand. "The key, Hortencia."

"I put it in a safe place."

"Bugger it!" Garahan slammed the door and met the constable's concerned gaze. "We don't have time if the lass is as ill as the lads think. I'll break the door down."

"What if she's leaning against it?" Phineas asked.

"We heard her banging on it earlier," Percy added.

Fear curdled the meat pie Garahan had eaten earlier, as worry sluiced through his gut. "Show me where she is, lads."

The boys rushed over to the door to the servants' staircase, opened it, and raced up the stairs, with Garahan and Standish hot on their heels.

They opened the door at the top of the stairs, to the second level, and Garahan's worry increased. When they took the stairs to the third floor and opened the door at the top, Mrs. Honeycutt's maid was waiting for them. "Mrs. Cabot told me you needed the key. I found it in her ladyship's top drawer, beneath a stack of handkerchiefs." She handed it to Garahan.

He unlocked the door, grabbed the doorknob, and said, "Stand back, lass, I'm opening the door."

He clenched his jaw to keep from swearing in front of the lads when she didn't answer. He opened the door slowly, until he could see around the edge. She wasn't lying on the floor behind the door—she had collapsed next to the open window!

"Lass!" He rushed to her side and scooped her into his arms.

She stirred but didn't open her eyes. "She's burning with fever!" He looked up and noticed the lads standing just inside the door, holding on to one another. "I need the two of ye to help me. Go downstairs, lads, and ask Mrs. Cabot if she has herbs to bring down a fever. Can ye do that for me—for yer cousin?"

Percy looked at Garahan and whispered, "You promise you can save her?"

He immediately replied, "Aye, lad."

"Promise you won't let anything else happen to her?" Phineas asked.

"Ye have me word."

The twins looked so much older than their years as they inclined their heads and scurried out of the room. He could hear their footsteps clattering on the stairs. Pride filled him—the lads had shown nothing but courage and compassion since he arrived. Garahan knew without question that—despite their parents—they'd grow to be fine men.

"Before ye speak to the squire and his wife, Standish, would ye send someone for the physician?"

The constable nodded, spun on his heel, and followed the twins downstairs.

Garahan gently laid the lass on the bed and brushed a lock of midnight hair off her forehead. "We'll need to bathe her face with cool water."

The maid appeared shocked when she held up a dented metal pitcher. "It's empty."

"What about the bowl on the washstand?"

The bleak expression on the maid's face was his answer. *Unconscionable!* They'd locked the lass in a room without water. Before he could shout for someone to bring some *fecking* water, a footman appeared with two pitchers. Another footman entered behind him, carrying a tray with a small, steaming mug, an assortment of bowls, and a stack of linens.

Relief filled him when Mrs. Cabot marched in behind the footmen. "Faith, ye're a sight for sore eyes, Mrs. Cabot. Thank ye."

He watched the cook take in the sight of the fevered lass. The woman blinked back tears and started giving orders. One footman set the pitchers down on the washstand, while the other man set the tray on the small table on the back wall, before bowing and retreating. Within moments, the maid had washed her hands and was bathing the lass with cool water.

Mrs. Cabot approached the bed with the mug from the tray. "I keep a supply of healing herbs on hand. This will help bring her fever down."

"Before ye try to shove me out the door, I gave me word to the lads. I'm not leaving till she's swallowed every drop, and her fever is under control. Then I'll be asking ye why the lass has been treated so poorly."

She frowned at him. "It wouldn't be proper for you to remain in Miss Barstow's bedchamber. You can wait in the hallway."

He crossed his arms. "Nay."

Mrs. Cabot protested, "She's in her nightrail."

"'Tis an emergency, and I'm the man you can count on at such a time. The duke and duchess commended me for being quick on me feet, catching Viscountess Chattsworth when she collapsed at Wyndmere Hall after she married the viscount. Besides, ye may need me help moving the lass."

The cook sighed. "Well, she is half a foot taller than me, so suppose I will. But propriety—"

"Be damned!" Garahan interrupted. "I'm not leaving till the physician arrives. After what I've witnessed today, I wouldn't trust the squire or his wife if me very life depended upon it. And ye know the lass's life depends on it!"

"They weren't always like this," Mrs. Cabot told him. "They seemed to change after the governesses they hired left. I overheard them speaking about their niece when Miss Barstow arrived, but it's not my place to repeat what I heard."

Watching the maid brush the cool linen cloth across the lass's forehead, Garahan tucked that information away. He'd speak with Mrs. Cabot, the butler, housekeeper, and the others—after he questioned the squire and his wife. "Let me ease the lass up, so she can drink the concoction ye've brewed for her." He didn't bother to wait for the cook to agree. Crouching next to the bed, he slid his arm around the lass and carefully lifted her. Fear tightened around his heart as heat poured off her, searing though his frockcoat and waistcoat.

"Miss Barstow," the cook called, "can you open your eyes to have a drink?"

Shock had Garahan swearing beneath his breath when the lass's eyelashes fluttered, and she slowly opened her eyes. "I thought ye unconscious, lass."

"Heard your voice," she rasped, settling in the crook of his arm. "Thought I was dreaming until I felt your arm around me."

He noticed she winced when she spoke. "Well, ye're awake now. Mrs. Cabot has something for yer fever. Drink it up now."

She slowly lifted her arm to take the cup but could not control the trembling enough to do so.

"Let us help ye." Between them, the cook and Garahan helped steady her and hold the cup.

She tried to gulp it down, but Mrs. Cabot cautioned her, "Slowly." When she sipped from the cup, the cook nodded. "Much better."

"Drink all of it, lass."

This time Prudence put a hand to her throat before she spoke. "Why are you here, Garahan?"

"I haven't seen the three of ye climbing the tree at the edge of the village, nor have I seen the lads skipping ahead of ye as they raced one another to the churchyard and back while ye stopped to speak with the vicar's wife."

Tears welled up and spilled over, but she ignored them, asking, "How are Percy and Phineas?" She hesitated before adding, "They wouldn't let me see the boys."

"Both boys are fit and fine," Mrs. Cabot answered, taking the empty cup from her.

"The baron and baroness were concerned when I mentioned I had not seen ye with the twins in the village," Garahan told her. "They sent me to check on the well-being of the lads and yerself."

"Why would they worry about me?"

"If I answer this last question, will ye rest yer voice? I can see it pains ye to speak."

"Yes."

"The baroness is like her brothers—the duke and the earl—and takes her responsibility to others to heart. Baron Summerfield is cut from the same cloth as his brothers-in-law. They care about their tenant farmers, their staff, and the people in the village… That includes the lads and yerself."

"She was so kind, offering me tea and conversation when I arrived on their doorstep looking like a drowned rat!"

Garahan studied her face. That she was in pain was evident, but was it just her throat? "Does anything else pain ye, lass?" She opened her mouth to speak, but stopped when he warned, "Have a care, lest ye do yer voice damage, lass."

The woman in his arms was still feverish, but she was awake, aware, and, dare he think it…adorable when she grunted in reply. She probably would not care to be thought of that way, but to him, she was adorable—nay, precious. "Ye remind me of a certain soaking-wet kitten I pulled from a stream back home. Only ye weren't spitting mad at me when I pulled ye from the pond. Ye waited until I tried to bring ye inside the baron's home, instead of letting ye stay outside, while the lads and yerself were seen to."

"I was filthy, covered with dirt and weeds from the brackish water."

She struggled as she spoke. The way that pain dulled the spark in her blue-violet eyes slashed clear down to the bone. But instead of reminding her to rest her voice, he listened. Mayhap speaking of what happened would help her cope with being locked away, not knowing if her cousins were ill. "Are ye ready to lie back down?"

"May I have a little water first, Mrs. Cabot?"

"Of course."

Garahan noticed a tear slip past the lass's guard as she waited for the cook to refill her cup. To distract her, he said, "I didn't know ye'd left Summerfield Chase, lass." He stared into the depths of her eyes, sensing she did not know what to think of his confession. "I would have stopped the squire's wife, had I known. Anyone could see ye had not recovered enough of yer strength to get out of bed."

"I had no choice."

He ached for the lass and her situation. "I'm sorry for whatever happened since ye left the protection of the baron's home. Sorrier still that I never got to say goodbye to ye."

The lass's reply was interrupted by the kindly cook, who handed her the cup. "Drink slowly now." Prudence nodded and struggled to thank Mrs. Cabot, who placed a hand on the lass's shoulder. "Garahan is right—you should rest your voice. I know you do not want to prolong your recovery. We cannot help but see how much it pains your throat to speak. I have a recipe my mother used to make for sore throats. It has honey in it."

"And what else?" Garahan asked.

"As my mother used to tell me whenever I asked," Mrs. Cabot answered, "all good things."

When the lass handed the cup back, Garahan was pleased to see her trembling was not as pronounced. "Ye can have more water as ye need it. Can she not, Mrs. Cabot?"

"Certainly," the cook answered. "But right now, we need you to try to rest."

Garahan took the hint and eased Prudence back onto the bed, smoothing the wrinkles from the covers. "Close yer eyes, lass." She surprised him by doing just that. Unable to resist, he brushed the tip of his finger along the curve of her cheek. It took every ounce of his control to step away from the bed and walk over to the window to observe what was happening below.

"Mary, would you mind staying while I check on the boys?" Mrs. Cabot asked. "You will be doing double duty, taking care of

Prudence, while acting as chaperone."

The maid was quick to agree, "I would be happy to, though I have a feeling we can trust Garahan with our lives."

No use wasting words, but he wanted the women to know he heard and agreed. He grunted in response.

"Would you please tell Mrs. Honeycutt where I am?"

The cook nodded. "Of course, Mary. I'll remind her that there are other maids who can do her bidding while you sit with Prudence and Garahan, waiting for the physician."

The maid thanked Mrs. Cabot, then dipped the cloth in the cool water once again. "I'm going to place a cool cloth over your eyes, Prudence. It will help bring the fever down and ease the dryness in them."

Garahan glanced over his shoulder to see the lass reach for Mary's hand and squeeze it. He heard her faint rasp of thanks. *Poor lasses*, he thought, turning back to his post at the window. Both of them were under the thumb of the squire's wife.

A glance out the window had him struggling with impatience. There was no sign of the physician yet. No matter—he would keep watch until the doctor arrived.

He wondered how long the women had been subjected to the whims of the squire's ill-tempered wife. Was it something new, or part and parcel of the woman's personality? He would plant a flea in the ear of O'Malley, who'd say it in passing to the baron. The staff would hear, and, with everyone knowing how well the baron and baroness treated their staff, word would reach others in the village.

Garahan felt a bit of satisfaction with the plan. Rumors weren't always a bad thing—if they improved a working person's situation. Mayhap he could do something about the lass's situation… After all, she'd become his responsibility the moment he climbed that bloody tree and untangled her hair.

He remembered the sight of her long legs above his head, and had to bite the inside of his cheek to distract himself from the rest of the view that had kept him awake nights, dreaming of her. The pain reminded him that thoughts of her delectable form were best left till late at night, when he was alone, supposedly sleeping, while in truth he would be tossing and turning, dreaming that the raven-haired lass was curled up next to him—or around him.

The rumble of carriage wheels announced the latest arrival. "The physician's here!"

CHAPTER FOURTEEN

GARAHAN WAS OUTSIDE waiting when the carriage stopped and the physician emerged. He'd never met the man, but he had seen him once or twice when he was summoned to Summerfield Chase. When the doctor's foot touched the ground, he nodded to Garahan and glanced around. "Is Constable Standish about?"

"Aye. He's inside speaking with the squire and his wife." Garahan offered his hand. "Name's Garahan. I'm part of the Duke of Wyndmere's guard stationed at Summerfield Chase. I'll escort ye to Miss Barstow."

"I'm not accustomed to being escorted by a guard—working for a duke, or the baron," the doctor replied. "I have been here on more than one occasion over the years. In fact, I was here a few months ago when young Percival had a fever, and Phineas a putrid throat."

Garahan filed that information away and opened the back door for the physician. To his surprise, the butler was waiting for them.

"I'm to escort Dr. Higgins to Miss Barstow's room on the second floor."

Garahan stepped in front of Samuels and the doctor. "I've only just left Miss Barstow with Mrs. Honeycutt's lady's maid, Mary...in the attic room Miss Barstow has been occupying since the squire told his wife to lock her in it."

Samuels's eyes widened, and the physician raised an eyebrow. "If Miss Barstow is the current governess, why then was she locked in the attic room at all?" the doctor asked.

Garahan's blood began to boil. "Ye'll have to be asking the squire. This is the first time I've been inside his home. I must tell ye, the accommodations in the attic are not quite as luxurious as the stables where he keeps his horses. There wasn't any water available in the pitcher or the bowl on the washstand!"

The doctor's eyes narrowed as he squared his shoulders. "I do not normally get involved in my patients' affairs, other than to treat them medically, Garahan. You would do well to obtain all of the facts before you slander the squire's name."

Garahan itched to reach out and grab hold of the physician by his over-starched cravat. Instead, he agreed with the doctor as he stepped into the man's way for the second time. "I'll have to assume ye must not be acquainted with His Grace, the Duke of Wyndmere, or his brother Edward, Earl Lippincott. Allow me to assure ye, Dr. Higgins, that part of me duties as one of the sixteen men who guard the duke and his family—which includes his sister, Lady Phoebe, Baroness Summerfield—is to use me gift for unearthing facts from those who are not always willing to share them. Sometimes, it is due to fear…then there are those who prevaricate to cover up their evil deeds."

The physician visibly blanched. "I believe it would be worth my time to verify your claims by speaking to Baron Summerfield."

Garahan leaned toward the doctor and said, "If I were ye, I'd go right to the top and send an urgent missive to His Grace. You can send it in care of Patrick O'Malley, head of the duke's guard at Wyndmere Hall in the Lake District. He's one of me eight O'Malley cousins working for the duke. Then there are me four Flaherty cousins, and me three brothers."

Samuels chose that moment to speak up. "I would trust Garahan, O'Malley, and Flaherty with my life, Dr. Higgins. The duke's guard have proven time and again that they are always willing to step in when there is trouble, or to lend their backs when needed—surely you remember how they worked alongside of us when part of the roof collapsed on the church in the village…and the time that large branch broke one of the inn's windows?"

Garahan met Dr. Higgin's direct gaze. "Thank ye, Samuels, for yer vote of confidence, but I'm thinking the doctor here would do well to send his request for verification of me character to the source." Taking the physician's measure, he added, "I believe the good doctor is wise not to take a man solely on his word. Faith, if me brothers or cousins were fool enough to do so, not one of us would have been offered positions within the duke's personal guard." He nodded to the doctor. "Send word to His Grace. I've nothing to hide, and ye'll have a clearer picture of the travesty of what has occurred here to Miss Barstow, who is not only the governess, but the squire and Mrs. Honeycutt's niece."

"Their niece?" The physician surprised Garahan by shoving past him to sprint up the steps as if he were twenty years younger than a man who sported a head full of gray hair. Garahan was right behind him when the man paused at the top to ask, "Which door, Samuels?"

"Third on the left."

Dr. Higgins proceeded to the room, knocked on the door, and, with Garahan's unspoken approval, waited until he was bidden to enter before doing so.

Mary opened the door and sent Garahan a worried glance. "I'm so glad you're here, Dr. Higgins. Miss Barstow is quite ill."

"Will ye be telling the physician how the lass came to be in such a sorry state," Garahan asked, "or shall I?"

"I can speak for myself," the lass rasped.

The doctor walked over to stand beside the bed and held out his hand to her. "I'm sorry to be meeting you under such circumstances, Miss Barstow." He released her hand and set down his bag.

Garahan watched the physician study the lass's flushed face and red-rimmed eyes while listening to her description of events. His estimation of the man improved when the doctor winced along with the lass every time she held a hand to her throat when it pained her.

When Prudence got to the part where she dove in after her cousin, the doctor held up a hand to stop her. "Do you mean to tell me that Percy—who does not know how to swim—decided to go for a swim without supervision?"

"I should have anticipated that they would run ahead of me." She paused, and it was clear her throat pained her considerably. "They ignored the rules I taught them," she rasped, "but they are children, and they love being outdoors. What happened is my fault. I take full responsibility."

Garahan's heart ached for the lass. Clearly, she was not entirely at fault. The headstrong lad knew full well what the ramifications would be if he jumped into that pond. What bugged the *shite* out of Garahan was the squire placing the blame squarely on his niece's head. The lads had already shouldered the guilt for their part in it. The brave boys were looking out for their cousin, and had told everyone that they knew they weren't allowed in the pond.

What sort of lesson did the squire think he'd be teaching the twins after this near disaster by placing all of the blame on the lass, instead of just a part of it? Did the squire and his wife realize that although they ignored the lads, everyone else knew the truth? Prudence was not solely to blame!

"I have three sons myself, Miss Barstow. Their mother and I are proud of the men they have become. Growing up, they were full of life, always getting into scrapes and mischief. Even though we forbade them to do so without supervision, I know they spent time in the pond. I suspect the blame lies somewhere in the middle of what I've heard."

"But I—" the lass protested.

The physician cut her off. "Please, let me finish."

That the man waited for the lass to nod raised Dr. Higgins another few notches higher in Garahan's estimation.

"Although there are those in my profession who would disagree with me, over the years I have found when a patient is harboring feelings of guilt or responsibility for whatever their ailment or injury happened to be, their recovery time slows considerably."

One of the tight knots in Garahan's gut loosened. Ma had said the same so many times over the years—it had become deeply ingrained in his mind and that of his brothers. He felt the need to add his weight to the physician's words. "Ye should listen to Dr. Higgins, lass. A very wise woman told me the same years ago."

Her eyes met his. "Was she the healer in your village?"

He grinned. "Aye, if the need arose."

The physician's interest was captured. "What did she do when she wasn't helping others?"

Garahan chuckled. "Raised four lads, all of whom now serve the Duke of Wyndmere in his personal guard."

Dr. Higgins slowly smiled. "Well then, Miss Barstow, I believe Garahan has just added proof to what I've said. If he and his brothers were anything like my sons growing up, and have managed to secure positions as the illustrious duke's guard, you should seriously consider my advice. Let go of the burden of guilt, so you can heal properly."

Tears welled up in the lass's eyes, but before they could fall, she blinked, and they disappeared.

In that moment, the pieces of Garahan's life shifted to form a new pattern, one that would include Miss Prudence Barstow. His life would not be complete unless she was a part of it. He only had to figure out how in the bloody hell he would accomplish that without forsaking his vow to the duke—and his eldest brother, James.

Ma's voice echoed in his head. *"Where there's a will, lad...there'll be a way."*

CHAPTER FIFTEEN

"I'M LEAVING YE in the good doctor's care, lass. Be sure to tell him everything."

"I will, Garahan."

He narrowed his eyes as if trying to decide if she were keeping something from him. She wished she had the gumption to ask him to stay with her. For the first time in her life, she'd met someone who did not want to change anything about her. He liked her just the way she was—height, curves, and all!

"I'm waiting to hear yer promise."

She blew out a breath, and wished she hadn't. Her throat felt as if it were on fire. "I promise."

"Well then, I'll take me leave of ye, lass. Listen to the doctor and send word if ye have need of me."

Her throat grew taut with emotion at his words, and the realization that she did need him, more than she realized. She nodded in response, aware that it wasn't one specific moment that precipitated needing Garahan nearby. It was a compilation of moments. Holding on to her and untangling her hair when she was hanging from that limb. Boosting a frightened Percy onto his back, so her cousin wouldn't have to ride on the horse he was so afraid of. Treating her cousins—and herself—as if they mattered. Watching over them whenever he saw them in the village. Diving into the pond to deliver Percy to the bank, then returning for her—even though he had to dive under the murky water to retrieve her. Forcing the water out of her lungs and bringing her to the safety of Summerfield Chase.

She not only trusted her rescuer, but she had come to depend upon him as a friend. She felt stronger in his presence…and heavens, the way he kissed her! Her body went weak as she remembered the passionate embrace. As if he knew what she was thinking, his dark eyes held her captive, until he inclined his head to her and left the room.

"Now then, Miss Barstow, I have a feeling the fever is only part of what I will be treating," Dr. Higgins said. "Let's have a look at your throat."

⇥⟫⟪⇤

GARAHAN SWIFTLY DESCENDED the main staircase and strode toward the sound of raised voices. The squire sounded angry. *The barrel-bellied blowhard.*

He knocked and waited until the door to the squire's study swung open. Standish's gaze met Garahan's. "I assume Dr. Higgins will be told the complete story?"

"Aye." Garahan immediately noticed the agitated state the squire and his wife were in. "Have ye asked them?"

"Aye, and they've denied any knowledge," the constable replied. "Why don't you add what you've heard, and we'll see if they remember any facts—no matter how insignificant."

The squire puffed up his beefy chest and barked, "How dare you imply that my wife and I are withholding information from you!"

Standish sighed. "Don't get your dander up, Honeycutt. There are serious accusations that have recently come to light. I would not be faithful to the office of constable if I ignored information that I have recently been apprised of."

Garahan watched the squire for a sign that the man intended to lie—again. Honeycutt shifted from one foot to the other, then

123

threw his hands in the air—a sign of someone trying to appear as if he were being forced to acquiesce when he did not feel the need to. Garahan cleared his throat to get the constable's attention, their gazes met, and he knew the official noticed and would not be swayed by what Honeycutt was about to tell them.

"I swear to you that my wife is as much a victim of the salacious gossip spreading through Summerfield-on-Eden and beyond as the baron and baroness are."

"Do ye now?" Garahan asked. "I'm not sure ye understand that the parties involved in starting the rumors have already confessed. A few of them have made amends—as their part in this verbal attack against the duke and his family could have cast a shadow over the title, the dukedom, and destroyed their family's reputation. The others are behind bars for not only igniting the gossip, but for their part in the murders of a member of the *ton* and his wife."

Garahan paused, pleased when the squire's face grayed. A glance at the smirk on his witch of a wife's face had Garahan wondering if the squire did not know as much about the situation in the village as his spouse did.

He asked the constable, "Do ye mind if I ask Mrs. Honeycutt a few questions?"

"Ask what you will."

Garahan hid the distaste he had for the woman. After speaking with the blacksmith's daughter and the vicar's daughter, he was certain she played more of a part in the local gossip than simply passing it on—he sensed she had rekindled it. Something the vicar's daughter had said yesterday had him wondering if the squire's wife was behind the resurgence of the vicious accusations spewed at Baron and Baroness Summerfield.

"How long have ye lived here, Mrs. Honeycutt?"

She held his gaze for long moments before deigning to answer, "All my life. Why?"

"Garahan and I are here to ask questions on behalf of Baron Summerfield," the constable reminded her. "I will consider answering any questions the two of you have—after you and the squire have supplied us with the information we require. We are expected to report our findings to the baron and Lady Phoebe immediately after we have spoken to you."

The woman's superior expression slipped for a moment. Garahan hoped she'd finally tell them what they wanted to know.

"How long have ye been married to the squire?"

"I do not see what—"

"*Hortencia.*" Her name sounded like a warning coming from her husband.

"But Harold—"

"Just answer the questions, wife. If we do as Constable Standish asks, he will answer our questions. Is that not right, Standish?"

"Aye, though we are pressed for time, as Garahan and I are expected within the hour."

The squire glared at his wife. "We beg your pardon, constable. Garahan, please continue."

Mayhap the squire sensed the direction of the questioning. Garahan met his gaze before repeating, "How long have you and the squire been married?"

"Fifteen years."

"And how long has it been since Summerfield Chase has been occupied?"

"A few years." When the squire opened his mouth to speak, his wife quickly added, "I honestly don't remember the date."

Garahan sensed that, at least, was the truth. "As the squire's wife, would you say that your position in the village was one of importance?"

She drew in a breath and lifted her chin. "Of the utmost importance. It is the duty of my husband, and myself, to see that those in the village show deference to his position in Society."

Garahan watched Standish for a reaction. When he did not see one, he said, "As I have learned in me time working for the duke, a squire is a local landowner of some wealth."

"And, as such, is due the respect of the people in *his* village," Mrs. Honeycutt said.

"Last I heard, the squire has no responsibility to those who live here," Garahan remarked. "Baron Summerfield, on the other hand, does, by seeing that his tenant farmers are well taken care of. As his father before him, the baron sees those in the village as his responsibility as well. 'Tis a circle, ye see—like an extended family. Everyone watches out for one another. When one prospers, they all do."

The squire's expression was one of agreement—his wife's was one of defiance.

"Ye see," Garahan continued before she could speak, "as part of the duke's guard, I had to learn the hierarchy of the *ton* beneath His Grace. Ye have the titles of marquess, earl, viscount, and baron, all of whom are members of nobility."

Mrs. Honeycutt narrowed her eyes. "You have forgotten baronet and knight."

Garahan wanted to end this verbal battle, but knew he had to respond to the woman, else she'd only add fuel the fire. "I haven't. They aren't nobility. One last question—how did it feel when Baron Summerfield married and brought his wife to live at Summerfield Chase, supplanting yerself from the position as the most important woman in the village?"

Her face flamed. It was obvious she had not taken it well.

To prod her further, he asked, "Did ye welcome Lady Phoebe—who is the daughter of a duke and His Grace's sister—to the village with open arms, bowing to her higher position in Society?"

The squire's wife spewed spittle, screaming, "I will never bow to that creature!"

Garahan turned to the squire. "Do ye have anything to add to yer wife's vehement statement?"

Squire Honeycutt raked a hand through his sparse gray hair. "I apologize for my wife's behavior. You have my word that no harm will come to Miss Barstow...er...Prudence while she is recovering."

"And ye'll not lock her in the attic after we leave?"

He sighed. "I will not." The squire frowned at his wife. "I will give you my wife's word that she will not do so either."

"I'll be by tomorrow to check on Miss Barstow. I'd best be seeing an improvement." Garahan didn't bother to threaten either of them, but he made a promise: "If she is still gravely ill, I have instructions to remove her from yer household."

"You have no right—"

Garahan turned his back on the squire's wife. "Heed me words, squire. Make certain yer wife heeds them as well." He strode from the room and nearly ran into Dr. Higgins in the hallway.

"I believe Miss Barstow will recover fully, if she follows my instructions to the letter. That includes rest, medicines I have prescribed, and a proper diet." The physician frowned. "I did not ask Miss Barstow, as I felt her strength was flagging, but would you happen to know if the young woman has been ill?"

"Not that I know of," he answered. "She did mention becoming used to a meager breakfast, no lunch, and a pitifully small supper."

"That would explain why she seems so weak."

"Aye, Dr. Higgins. I overheard the lads saying they would sneak food in to her."

The doctor shook his head. "I never would have thought the squire would treat a relative, let alone a member of his staff, so abominably as to deny them food."

Garahan scanned the hallway to ensure they were alone before responding, "She's related to him by marriage, to his wife by blood."

"I intend to speak to Samuels, as he is who I have been told to leave my instructions with. Miss Barstow is to have an invalid's diet for the first two days after her fever breaks, but after that, her body needs bolstering with savory stews and bread—maybe a bit of something sweet." The physician moved closer and pitched his voice low so as not to be overheard. "I suspect that you will be moving Miss Barstow to Summerfield Chase."

"Aye. Me gut tells me that as well. Mayhap as early as tomorrow."

The two men approached the butler. Garahan listened while the physician went over his list of instructions. When he'd finished, Garahan told him, "I've left word with Samuels, but I've also spoken to Mrs. Cabot and Gifford—if the lass needs me, they are to send for me at once."

The doctor nodded. "As you know, Samuels, I do not normally get involved in family matters, but I intend to make an exception in Miss Barstow's case. If Garahan is summoned on her behalf, I expect to be notified."

The grave expression on the butler's face left no doubt that he would obey the directive. "You have my word."

CHAPTER SIXTEEN

A FEW DAYS later, O'Ghill was cursing O'Malley. He should have been dining at the vicarage—or even the kitchen at Summerfield Chase. He didn't mind manual labor, but he hated being told to find work. Especially when one of the sainted O'Malleys gave the order. He quickly learned that he'd not be seeking a job as apprentice to a blacksmith again anytime soon. "Faith, how do ye stand the heat from the forge, Coleman?"

The blacksmith grinned. "You become accustomed to it. It's the only job I've ever known. I took over for my father when he injured his back."

Moving past the discomfort of the heat, O'Ghill set his mind on the current task, using the gigantic bellows to fan the burning coals.

"That'll do it, O'Ghill." Coleman glanced over his shoulder and said, "See that bucket on the wall?"

"Aye."

"Take it over to the rain barrel, fill it, and dunk your head in it."

The Irishman laughed. "Me ma often told me to do the same whenever I was feeling full of meself, antagonizing me brothers. I learned not long after, soaking yer head cools it. Though to be honest, I'd rather use me fists."

Coleman nodded. "I've been known to go a few rounds with

the duke's guard. Have you met any of the men yet? They're on assignment to protect Baron and Baroness Summerfield. I can put in a good word for you, if you think you'd like to try bare-knuckle fighting."

O'Ghill nearly snorted with laughter, but if he did, he might give away the fact that he more than knew the men—he was related to the lot of them! "Ye don't say? Work for a duke, do they? How many men are we talking about? I'm feeling stronger, having been working beside ye for a few days."

Coleman chuckled as plunged the last of the horseshoes into a bucket of water beside his anvil. "Three Irishmen. Likeable, though I recently was led to believe otherwise about one of the men."

"Oh?" O'Ghill wondered if he'd finally hear something he could report back to his cousins. He paused before pouring the bucket of water over his head, having gauged the size of the receptacle against his head and judging it too tight a fit.

Coleman wiped the sweat from his eyes with the back of his forearm. From the expression on the man's face, O'Ghill sensed he'd be hearing about the rumors that had yet to die down by now. Garahan had already spoken to the parents of the two young women he was rumored to have accosted. The lasses maintained the events never happened, and they had never even met Garahan before. Their parents believed them, yet the bloody rumors persisted.

"Ye cannot always trust what ye hear. 'Tis a lesson I learned as a lad." O'Ghill did not want to talk about his O'Malley uncles who'd been falsely accused and arrested. They had been cleared of any wrongdoing, but one uncle died in his brother's arms the night before they were released from prison.

"I can see from your expression that you understand," Coleman said. "If you've been in the village more than a day or two, you will have heard the ugly rumors. They're false and have been proven to be—yet somehow, someone is bound and determined to keep them alive."

The blacksmith curled his hands into fists, spun on the ball of his foot, and delivered two lightning-fast jabs to the wall behind him. O'Ghill was impressed and wary. "At the risk of having ye toss one of those jabs at me, I'll say yer speed and dexterity are impressive, Coleman."

The man drew in a breath and slowly exhaled. "When I find out who's been continuing to spread the false, vicious gossip about my daughter and her best friend…" His voice trailed off as he punched the wall a third time, cracking the already battered board.

O'Ghill had the feeling while the man had been taking his anger out on that particular board, he was imagining punching the faceless, nameless person bad-mouthing his daughter and her friend. "How can I help?"

Rather than accept the offer, the blacksmith asked, "Why would you?"

"I hate bullies who spread vitriol behind the backs of their target, rather than face them. Spreading those lies, while not the same as creating the gossip, is just as bad. Besides, ye took a chance, hiring a stranger. I was rubbing me last two coins together, wondering how I'd earn enough to fill me horse's belly…and then me own. I'm indebted to ye. Let me help."

"I could use a strong man like yourself around here. Are you interested in staying?"

O'Ghill shook his head. "As me ma likes to say, I'm on one of me rambles. I'll be moving on soon. I've kin in the Lake District who are next on me list to visit. Though I thank ye for the offer."

Coleman nodded, picked up the length of iron waiting to be fashioned into a hinge, and stuck it in the coals. Without being asked, O'Ghill operated the bellows until the blacksmith motioned for him to stop.

They continued working together for the next hour, until the blacksmith finally put his tools away and motioned for O'Ghill to follow him. As was their habit, they washed up at the pump between the smithy's shop and his home before they parted ways, with Coleman going home to his daughter, and O'Ghill taking the roundabout way to the baron's home. The need to keep prying eyes from discovering he'd been meeting with the guard these past few nights was essential to their plans to uncover the source of the rampant, continuous gossip. After working so hard to keep his connection to the men in the duke's guard a secret, he did not relish word getting out. His cousins had yet to force a confession from the squire's wife, though all evidence they'd uncovered—especially her damning response to one of Garahan's questions regarding the baroness—indicated she was behind the resurgence of the rumors…and the new ones.

O'Ghill liked the baron and baroness. He would do anything for his cousins—though at times he preferred to let them stew while he pretended to make up his mind to help. He'd been doing as they asked, passing along bits and pieces of gossip and rumor as he heard them. It was time to share what the blacksmith had told him tonight—someone was determined to keep the vicious gossip about the blacksmith's daughter and the vicar's daughter, and the salacious rumors about the baron and baroness, alive.

He intended to be there when the rumormonger was unmasked.

Pleased to find his gelding saddled and ready for him, he waved to Coleman and mounted. As he followed the road that wound in the opposite direction of Summerfield Chase, he let his mind wander. He ached from his labors, but it was a good ache—as Da liked to remind him, 'twas the ache of an honest day's work. He missed his family, but whenever he was home for more than a few weeks, his feet itched, and he knew it was time to set off again.

He had not planned on leaving Ireland, but found he'd missed the cousins who'd left years before to find better work, sending home a good portion of their wages. He patted his waistcoat pocket, and the coins jingled satisfactorily. Mayhap he would stay on a bit longer, especially if he could convince his cousins to pay him for his time and talents gathering information on behalf of the baron and his wife.

He was grinning as he turned onto the overgrown path in the forest that would take him around the back of the church. From here, he could make his way to the baron's home without anyone in the village being the wiser.

⬥⬥⬥

CHAPTER SEVENTEEN

PRUDENCE FOUGHT TO open her eyes, but could not. They felt weighted down. She swiped a hand across her eyes and discovered the reason. Relieved, she grabbed the cloth, dragged it from her eyes, and turned her head, expecting to see Mary. "I must be dreaming."

The deep chuckle had her blinking.

"Garahan? What are you doing here?"

He leaned close and studied her face. "I live here."

She closed her eyes. "I doubt the baron would release you, and know my aunt and uncle would never permit you to stay, so why are you here?"

He brushed the damp hair off her forehead. "'Tis the break his lordship has granted me since we brought ye to Summerfield Chase. I've been allowed to sit with ye for half an hour in between me shifts." His gaze seemed troubled, as if something preyed on his mind.

Words tumbled through her brain, and she struggled to make sense of them. *Break...shifts...* "Summerfield Chase?"

"Aye, lass." He laid his hand against her forehead. "Still warmer than Dr. Higgins would like, but faith, ye're not burning up." He tucked a loose strand of hair behind her ear. "I'm man enough to confide that ye scared the bejeezus out of me, lass."

She struggled to process what he was saying. Garahan would

never lie; somehow, she had ended up at the baron's home, without her knowledge. "How long have I been here?"

He ran the tip of his finger along the curve of her cheek. His touch soothed her, comforted her. "A few days, lass. Do ye not remember?"

She tried to call up the memory but could not. "I'm afraid I don't." She licked her dry lips, but it didn't moisten them. "May I have some water?"

Garahan clenched his jaw, as if he held something back—but what? He relaxed his jaw and rose from where he sat beside the bed, taking the now-warm cloth with him. She watched his motions—they seemed jerky, unnatural. His movements were normally fluid.

"Am I not supposed to have any water? I remember asking, and never getting any."

He mumbled beneath his breath, but she still heard what he said: "'Tis criminal."

"I remember you were there in the attic, and again after they moved me downstairs, where Dr. Higgins examined me. I may have been fevered, but I'm not daft and remember he said I was to be allowed to have water."

He returned to her side, cup in one hand, damp cloth in the other. "I'm not allowed to speak about what happened—'twas what I agreed to when I carried you out of that house." He set the cloth in the small bowl on the table beside the bed then slid one of his strong arms behind her, cradling her to his broad chest. "Drink yer fill, lass—but slowly."

Tears welled up, and she let them fall, sipping from the cup he offered. His whispered words that she didn't recognize—they sounded poetic, lyrical. Though she did not understand the language, the sound touched her heart. He cared about her. He was taking time when he should be eating—or sleeping—to take care of her. Unused to the attention, she was about to thank him and tell him he did not have to stay, but Lord, she wanted him to stay—needed him to.

The feelings she'd been trying so hard to deny filled her until she had no choice but to accept them. He'd captured her heart when he climbed the tree to rescue her. Garahan was a rare man… He seemed to appreciate her. When her waist-length hair got caught, tangling around that tree branch, he calmly untangled it. He could have chopped off her hair to save time, but he didn't. She knew in her heart that if she'd been at risk, he would have done so quickly and without a qualm. He did not hesitate to calm Percy's fear of horses when her cousin refused to let Garahan put him on Duncan's back. Instead of riding on the horse, Percy rode home on Garahan's back, while he held the reins, walking beside his horse, who carried herself and Phineas.

That day in the marsh, when her strength ebbed from her limbs, and she struggled to bring Percy safely back to shore, Garahan was there to pull her cousin to safety. She'd accepted that she would not make it to the bank of the pond and felt herself go under. It was a shock to be jarred back to consciousness when her stomach rid itself of the unpalatable pond water. It was that moment that sealed her fate. Whether he ever acknowledged the bond that strengthened between them that day, she would. Whether he realized it or not, she'd gifted him with her heart when he handed her over to his cousin because Killian was dry and warm, and Garahan wasn't.

Prudence would never ask of him what she knew he could not give. He'd told her of his vow to the duke, which extended to the baron and baroness—and those he rescued. A passing stranger who risked his life to help another. Garahan would run toward danger—not away from it. She was certain those he rescued would be forever grateful to him, as she would be.

He rose to his feet to refill her cup, and she heard the distinctive clank of a weapon. She noticed the scabbard on his belt. "I didn't know you carried a sword on duty."

"'Tis a saber, lass—and earned me the moniker I got protecting His Grace. *The Duke's Saber*. I haven't carried it on me rounds until recently." He returned with the water. "Have more, lass—

ye look as if ye need it."

"Thank you." She drank her fill and sighed. "I never thought I'd be able to quench my thirst again." She vowed in that moment that she would never be denied water—or food—ever again. "I need to thank Baron and Baroness Summerfield for their generosity. I promise I'll work hard to pay them back for opening their home to me, taking care of me. I will always be grateful to them." She met his gaze and looked deep into his dark brown eyes. "As soon as I am able, I will find work and make my own way, despite what my aunt and mother think I should do. I'll miss my cousins, but I won't ever go back to live with my aunt and uncle—or my parents."

THE LASS MEANT every word, and he agreed. She should not go back to the squire's home...but what of her parents? She'd alluded to something left unsaid. "What exactly did yer aunt and yer ma think ye should do, besides governessing?"

She stiffened in his arms and looked away.

"Ye'd best be telling me, as I'll not be moving from this spot—even if O'Malley, or the baron, comes to demand I return to me duties. Ye don't want that to happen, now, do ye, lass?"

She slowly turned back until he could see the haunting blue-violet of her tear-filled eyes.

"What is it, lass? Me ma always reminded me brothers and meself that holding hurtful words to our hearts only makes the hurt go deeper. Trust me, lass, ye'll feel better saying the words out loud."

She was quiet for so long that Garahan doubted she would share whatever ill-intentioned words her mother and aunt had said to her. Still, he patiently waited for her to trust him and speak. When she did, he was not prepared to hear what she had to say.

"My mother was the first to make me feel ashamed of my body, forcing me to bind my breasts so they did not embarrass her. I never questioned her dictate, though it became increasing painful in the last few years. I was reminded daily that my height and my curves were a constant embarrassment to my family. My older sisters take after my mother and aunt, slender and petite in height with blonde hair and pale blue eyes. I take after my father and his mother."

He hated the thought that she'd been forced to hide her body and been taught it shameful, instead of allowing her to accept who she was as special. He tightened his arm around her, offering his protection and comfort from past slights.

"When I refused the first offer of marriage to a man whose hands groped places that he had no right to touch, word spread that I gave my favors freely. I refused the second for the same reason... There were no other offers, as other, darker rumors spread about me."

He stiffened, and she turned her head away from him. Was she gathering her courage to tell him something more?

"That was the first time my mother told me I looked slatternly. I have no idea if my mother shared her opinions with my aunt, but when I arrived to accept the position as governess to my cousins, my aunt told me if I did not do exactly as I was instructed, the only work I would be able to find would be...on my back."

He lifted her from the bed onto his lap, cradling her to his heart. "Go ahead and let go of the evil words, lass. 'Tisn't true. Ye're a rare beauty. Yer looks go deep...all the way to the bone. The way ye risked ripping yer hair out from the roots to save Phineas showed the beauty of your determination to save him. Jumping into the marsh pond to save Percy, even though ye must have been exhausted... Going for weeks with lack of proper food... Ye trusted me with his life and were ready to sacrifice yer own. That showed yer bright and beautiful soul. The Lord decided no ordinary body would be able to protect yer soul. He created a tall, strong, curvaceous, and long-legged form. From the top of yer midnight head to yer delectable *derrière*, on down to yer toes. Lass, never, never believe any less of yerself."

He pressed his lips to her forehead to hide the tears welling in his eyes. As a rule, Garahan hid his emotions well. The last time he cried was when they'd received word of Uncle Patrick O'Malley's death.

Tucking her beneath his chin, he rocked her while she wept within the shelter of his arms. Unable to keep the truth bottled inside of him, he rasped, "I love ye, lass…every gorgeous inch of ye."

He heard the door open and then slowly close. He didn't bother to turn around to see who had been sent to remind him. Garahan knew it was past time to resume his post, but he would not leave the lass until she'd cried herself dry.

A short while later, his waistcoat and shirt were soaked clean through. Good thing he'd removed his frockcoat before sitting down. He shifted the lass in his arms, so he could wipe away the last of her tears. She murmured softly but did not waken. Unable to resist, he brushed his lips across hers. He intended to kiss her again—and often—but that would have to wait until he and his cousins brought an end to the rumor mill, and he'd spoken to O'Malley and the baron. Mayhap he'd send a missive to his brothers asking for advice. James and Aiden had been able to balance their duties to the duke with marriage, and he planned to do the same.

Then all he would have to do was to secure the lass's agreement—and have the banns read from the pulpit of the church in the village. He doubted the duke would bother to secure a special license for him.

Prudence Barstow would be his wife, and they would live happily ever after!

◆──◇◆◇◆──◇

CHAPTER EIGHTEEN

HE'D PLEDGED HIS heart to the most stubborn woman alive.

"I swear to ye, O'Malley, the woman holds me heart in her hands, and instead of falling into me arms…she's keeping her distance and squeezing every drop of blood from it."

O'Malley's uppercut lifted Garahan off his feet, but he recovered quickly.

"What in the bloody hell am I going to do about her?"

His cousin snickered. "Have ye asked her to marry ye?"

Garahan feinted to the left, avoiding his cousin's wicked left cross—and question. His jab connected soundly, and he grinned as O'Malley groaned. "Every time I start to tell the lass, she's interrupting me with plans for leaving Summerfield Chase. The thought of her leaving is burning a hole in me gut! How can she ignore me declaration of love when 'tis plain to see she feels the same for me? Did ye know she's sent off a letter to an agency to find her a position as a governess?"

Before O'Malley could answer, Garahan said, "Ye know how much she misses her cousins."

O'Malley nodded, then shifted and aimed for Garahan's shoulder and missed.

Garahan punched his cousin in the jaw. "I went to see the lads on her behalf and was told they'd been ill, and I couldn't see them." Distraught, he asked, "What else can I do to prove to the lass how much I love her?"

"Ask her to marry ye!"

His cousin's right cross surprised Garahan. Pain radiated from his chin up to his temple. He wobbled but refused to go down. Unsteady on his feet, he blinked to try to clear his vision. "Ye'll have to do better than that if ye want to get yer point across, boy-o."

His head ached, and his vision recovered in time to see two O'Malleys within striking range—a heartbeat before twin fists connected under his chin. Staggered by the blow, Garahan swung wildly, but missed by a mile, as he floated into an abyss of darkness.

⤜⟫⟫⟪⟪⤛

"WHAT IN THE bloody hell were you thinking, O'Malley?" Baron Summerfield demanded as he paced in front of the man.

O'Malley shook his head. "I've never seen the like, yer lordship. Garahan used to be able to hold his own during our weekly bare-knuckle practice bouts. And before ye think to remind me of me duties, even the duke told ye 'tis how the lot of us sharpen our skills."

Marcus stopped directly in front of O'Malley and glared. "And you know that this is a crucial time. We are battling to deflect another round of verbal attacks on my wife, my title, and yourselves! And now, from the looks of things, it appears we are going to be a man down when we need everyone we have."

O'Malley fought to swallow the snort of laughter bubbling inside of him. It wouldn't do to let the baron think he was making light of the situation—or worse, that he was not totally committed to his duty. "Yer lordship, give Garahan an hour, and he'll be right as rain. Faith, even he knows that a solid knock to the chin rattles the brain, but it clears the head. He may not be ready to admit it, but he's befuddled by the lass. She has him going every which way but sideways—talking about applying for positions when he's declared himself to her."

The baron shook his head. "Even I know when a man is unconscious. He was draped over your shoulder like a wet rag! If you didn't crack his jaw, I'll be surprised."

The knock on the door interrupted O'Malley's reply.

"Enter. Ah, Timmons, has the physician arrived?"

"Er…not as yet, your lordship."

"What is it?"

"Garahan's up and about and headed to the stables."

O'Malley grinned. "I told ye, his head was made of granite. If that's all, yer lordship, I've me duties to return to."

Baron Summerfield shoved past O'Malley and stormed out of his library. "He's not getting on a damn horse until he's been cleared for duty by Dr. Higgins!"

O'Malley swallowed his laughter as he followed behind the baron. "Me coin's on Garahan."

They arrived at the stables in time to see Garahan on Duncan, galloping in the direction of the village. "Send one of the stable lads after him," the baron ordered O'Malley.

"Aye, yer lordship." O'Malley did as he was asked, then returned to patrolling the perimeter of the estate, leaving Flaherty to guard the interior and deal with the baron's anger.

But the baron was surprised when Garahan returned from his patrol a few hours later, saying, "Faith, me head aches, but at least it's not muddled," before heading inside to assume his post guarding the interior of the baron's home.

O'Malley turned to the baron and reminded him, "Head of granite."

"I want to speak with the guard—and O'Ghill, as soon as he arrives. Have Timmons speak to the footmen who will be assuming your positions until our meeting is over."

"Aye, yer lordship. I expect O'Ghill within the hour."

Instead of the verbal reply O'Malley expected, the baron glared, gave a stiff nod, and walked away—only to pause and retrace his steps. "Did you say Garahan's declared himself to Miss Barstow? When did this happen, and why was I not informed?"

"After her fever broke the other day. I'm thinking he was waiting to speak to ye until the lass stopped being stubborn. He was honest with the lass, so she knows of his vow to the duke and yerself, yer lordship."

"It appears I'll have more to speak to Garahan about, aside from his lack of common sense."

"Anything else I can help ye with?"

"If I think of anything, I'll send for you."

"Ye know where ye can find me, yer lordship."

O'Malley sought out the butler and relayed the baron's instructions. Though he wasn't as friendly with his O'Ghill cousins as the Garahans were, he knew them to be men of their word—even if the oldest preferred to lead the life of a gypsy, rather than stay in one place long enough to sink roots.

It was time to speak to Flaherty, then to Garahan—but first he'd refill his flask. A touch of the cure may ease the pain in Garahan's thick head.

Chapter Nineteen

O'GHILL ARRIVED THREE hours later, sporting a bruise the size of a fist on his jaw and bleeding from a cut high on his forehead. His lip was swollen and split.

Garahan frowned. "Ye've been sparring without me?"

O'Ghill shrugged as he dismounted. "Ye weren't available, and I needed to let off steam."

Garahan followed his cousin into the stables, helping to remove the horse's tack. "What happened?"

O'Ghill clamped his jaw down and worked his throat, as if holding in the need to shout. Garahan wondered if he'd been successful in his search for answers or if he'd hit another wall.

"Do ye have the proof we need?"

"Not one person in the whole bloody village will reveal what they know, and I'm thinking they know good and well 'tis the squire's wife who's behind the lies. What I don't know is how she is able to hold the entire population under her thumb."

Garahan's gut churned. "When I questioned her a few days ago, the woman all but admitted that before the baron married and moved into Summerfield Chase, the squire was the man everyone looked up to and held in high regard. As his wife, she enjoyed being the *fecking* queen bee."

"'Tis what I gathered from the stingy bits and pieces of conversation the locals have told me."

Garahan struggled to rein in his temper. "We know 'tis that harpy. The lass told me everything that's happened since she walked into her aunt and uncle's home. The lads have backed up everything she has said. What more proof does the baron need for us to confront the squire about his wife?"

"The word of another adult not related to her," a deep voice said from behind him.

Garahan spun around. "We didn't see ye there, yer lordship, or we'd—"

"You'd what? Have reported immediately to me whatever information you have? You're late, O'Ghill."

The baron's voice was louder than normal, but still controlled, a fact Garahan appreciated. "O'Ghill and I were discussing other things as well, namely whose fist he ran into...repeatedly."

The baron moved closer and winced. "Best get a poultice on that bruise on your chin. Let Mrs. Green tend to those cuts. I'll not have anyone enter our home looking as if he's been beaten. My wife is a strong woman. She has recovered from the residual effects of the attack she suffered at the hands of that madman who threatened Phoebe and her family before I met her. But there are nights when I know she relives what happened. I'll have your word, men."

"Ye have it, yer lordship," Garahan answered. When his cousin remained silent, Garahan elbowed him. "His lordship's waiting for yer word, O'Ghill."

"I beg yer pardon, yer lordship. Me brainbox is still a bit fuzzy, but ye have me word. I'll see the cook first and ask her to kindly tend to me face."

The baron nodded. "When you have, I'll be in my library waiting for your full report." He turned to go, paused, and looked over his shoulder to ask, "Sparring with the blacksmith again?"

O'Ghill nodded. Garahan shook his head at his cousin. "Ye know the man will always go for a jab to the forehead to stun ye, and then the jaw to take ye down."

"I keep hoping the man will change it up a bit, like me darling cousins. I can always count on one of ye to reverse the order of yer blows—or to trip me first, then haul me to me feet before trading blows."

O'Ghill's smile had the baron shaking his head. "I've always thought the Irish were hardheaded, but never realized they were equally as stubborn as a Scotsman."

"Know many of those, do ye?" O'Ghill asked.

The baron chuckled. "If my guess is right, and my mother's prediction holds true, the eldest of my younger sisters will soon be affianced to a Scotsman—well, I'm not sure how much of his heritage is Scottish. The topic of his origins has yet to come up in any of the correspondence from home."

Garahan asked, "Would that be your sister Honoria?"

"Nay, she's Concordia's twin—they are the youngest."

"Ah, 'tis Minerva, then."

Summerfield smiled. "Aye. I hope the man knows what he is getting into—my sister is a handful, and constantly trying to emulate the Roman goddess she's been named after."

"Goddess of wisdom, isn't it?" O'Ghill asked. The baron nodded.

Garahan asked, "If her suitor is part Scots, what's the rest?"

"I believe he's Irish, God help me," the baron said. "Dark-haired and dark-eyed, and from all Mother has relayed, the description reminds me of you, Garahan."

O'Ghill snickered. "As well he should."

"I think ye owe his lordship an explanation for that comment," Garahan said. His cousin shrugged in answer. Garahan shoved him with his shoulder. "Which one is it, Angus, Lochlan, or Cormac? And when in the bloody hell were ye going to mention ye didn't leave home alone?"

Summerfield looked from one cousin to the other. "I did not realize your mother was Scottish, O'Ghill."

O'Ghill laughed. "She'd have something to say to that, yer lordship. Me ma, Anna, is the middle Garahan sister—there's three of them. The firstborn, James, is this one's da." He got in a quick jab to Garahan's ribs.

The baron seemed to digest the information. "Then who are Angus, Lochlan, and Cormac?"

"They're cousins of ours—on the Garahan side."

The baron apparently needed time to shift the bits of information they'd given him until he could make sense of it. Dealing with a large family was not a problem for Garahan. He had grown up surrounded by aunts, uncles, and cousins. He felt sorry for the baron, as it appeared he hadn't.

Turning to O'Ghill, he asked, "'Tis Lochlan, isn't it?"

"Aye," O'Ghill replied. "I convinced Lochlan and Liam to join me on me ramble. We parted ways not long after the boat docked. Lochlan stayed on in London, and Liam headed for Cornwall."

Summerfield raked a hand through his hair until it stood on end. "This cousin of yours—Lochlan—he wouldn't be Lochlan McGreevy, would he?"

Garahan and O'Ghill shared a glance. Garahan nodded, and O'Ghill answered, "Aye, Lochlan Garahan McGreevy."

"Is Liam his brother?"

"Nay, he's the youngest of our Fitzpatrick cousins," O'Ghill answered. "He's always had a desire to see the Cornish coastline—and the caves. Me aunt warned me her youngest son has a dangerous fascination with smuggling. I nearly accompanied him north, but I had a feeling in me gut that I was needed here."

Garahan knew he had providence—or was it destiny?—to thank for his cousin listening to his gut. He never would have been able to get the lads and the lass to safety quickly without O'Ghill's assistance.

O'Ghill continued, "After we heard what nearly happened to our cousin Finn O'Malley, Liam's been wanting to make the journey."

The baron reached into his waistcoat pocket, retrieved his handkerchief, and handed it to O'Ghill. "Here, this will help stanch the blood. Your head is still bleeding, and we certainly do not need Mrs. Green fainting on us." O'Ghill complied, and Summerfield added, "We'll continue this conversation after your injuries have been tended to. I find myself most curious about Lochlan McGreevy, and intend to learn as much as possible about him."

"He's led an interesting life so far, yer lordship," Garahan said.

The baron sighed. "How could he not have? He's related to you."

The cousins stood alongside one another, watching the baron stride from the stables. "Lochlan's a good man," O'Ghill said.

"Aye. How much coin do ye think he's put by?" Garahan asked.

O'Ghill snorted with laughter. "Not enough if he's set his sights on the daughter of a viscount."

"The viscount is his lordship's older brother. Their father, the earl, is still alive."

O'Ghill whistled. "How the devil do ye know so much about titles?"

"His Grace knew it would be essential knowledge for those of us in his personal guard to have. Our job has us moving about in all levels of Society. The working class, those toiling on the docks, and in the stews of London. You know as well as I do that if there's something we Irishmen know and understand, 'tis the working class, dock workers, and the stews."

O'Ghill nodded. "I'm thinking I shouldn't leave Liam to his devices too long. I'd best be heading to Cornwall first and catch up with the only O'Malley who doesn't make me teeth ache. Finn's not like the other O'Malleys."

Garahan snickered. "Me brother James said the same about the O'Malleys. Finn's married to a wonderful woman, Mollie Malloy." Remembering the time spent at Wyndmere Hall, he slowly smiled. "She's O'Malley's match in every way. Brave, trustworthy, and stubborn as a goat."

O'Ghill chuckled. "Sure and those are qualities every Irishman looks for in a wife, but how did she catch Finn's eye?"

"With her pure heart and angel's smile. They have a daughter, the spitting image of Mollie. Finn was beside himself with worry during the birthing," Garahan told his cousin.

O'Ghill's expression of disbelief was expected, as was his question: "He was there?"

"Aye, he promised Mollie that he would be. Ye can ask O'Malley when ye go inside if ye don't believe me. Thomas's brother Sean heard it from Cousin Patrick—in case ye've forgotten, Patrick's the head of the duke's guard, stationed at Wyndmere Hall, and Finn's older brother."

"*Shite*, that's a lot of information to digest when me head's aching."

Garahan brushed that aside. "Ye'll never guess what they named their daughter."

O'Ghill groaned. "Ye're not helping the pain in me head, and ye're adding one in me *arse*. Out with it, then—what's the wee babe's name?"

"Boadicea."

"Well now," O'Ghill said as they walked toward the back of the house. "The little lass will have big shoes to fill, being named after an ancient warrior queen."

Garahan agreed. "Finn told Patrick that Mollie fought like a warrior to birth their daughter, and therefore had the right to choose the name."

"Spoken like a man who's under his wife's thumb," O'Ghill murmured as they entered the hallway.

Garahan didn't bother to tell his cousin that he'd willingly do the same, if only he could get the stubborn woman who'd turned his life inside out and upside down to stop talking of leaving Summerfield Chase long enough to offer her a reason to stay.

The cook bustled toward them, motioning to the room off the pantry. "I have everything ready, as his lordship requested." They stepped aside so she could enter the room first. She washed her hands and, while she was drying them, said, "Let me see what's under that handkerchief you're pressing to your forehead, O'Ghill."

Garahan stood ready to assist Mrs. Green in case the sight of his cousin's head wound was too much for the woman. He was pleased that it wasn't required.

"His lordship was correct in that I would be using my threads to close that gash." She motioned for O'Ghill to sit down. "Now then, the threads need a few more minutes to boil. Why don't you hold this bit of linen against your split lip while I clean out that nasty cut? Afterward, I'll tend to your lip, as the poultice to bring down the swelling is still cooling."

Garahan waited until she finished cleansing the wound, had fetched the threads, and was ready to close it the wound before offering, "I'll place me hands on his shoulders while ye sew his thick head back together."

"'Tisn't as thick as yers," O'Ghill grumbled.

"Ye may be right. Why don't we wait until Mrs. Green is finished before we place that wager?"

"'Twill be too late by then—we'll know I'm right."

"I think ye're wrong," Garahan countered. He kept his cousin distracted, arguing over who was right and what to wager, until the cook tied the last knot, folded the linen into a thick square, and secured it into place by wrapping a length of linen around O'Ghill's head.

Garahan steadied his cousin and asked, "How long have the three of ye been in England?"

O'Ghill smiled. "Long enough for Lochlan to charm an earl's daughter into thinking she's in love with him."

They were laughing as they walked through the servants' door to the main part of the house. He nodded to Timmons, whose eyes lingered on the bandage before he inclined his head in greeting.

"Time to share what ye've learned, O'Ghill," Garahan reminded his cousin as they walked toward the baron's study. "Best tell his lordship everything."

"I plan to, though he may want to speak to Coleman or Vicar Chessy if he doesn't believe me."

Garahan knocked on the door and waited. "We'll see to it that he does, though I doubt he'll question yer word, O'Ghill."

The baron opened the door to admit them, motioning them to join the others. O'Malley and Flaherty waited by the fireplace. When they had, he asked, "How do you feel, O'Ghill?"

"Like I've been hit in the head during the caber toss."

Garahan snorted with laughter, falling silent when he realized the baron was not amused. "Begging yer pardon, yer lordship."

"After O'Ghill tells us what he's learned, I need to have a private word with you, Garahan."

The baron made eye contact with O'Malley and Flaherty, and their lack of expression had worry slithering into Garahan's gut. Had the baron already had a private conversation with them? Had he heard that Garahan had declared his feelings to the lass? Was the plan to boot him out?

Masking his feelings, he assumed the same position as his cousins—feet spread slightly apart with his hands behind his back—before responding, "Aye, yer lordship."

"Go ahead, O'Ghill," Summerfield said.

"The people of yer village were a bit cautious when first we met, but have become accustomed to seeing me since I've been working at the smithy," O'Ghill replied. "Though they have seemed to accept me, whenever I ask a question, I never receive a straight answer."

The baron nodded. "Go on."

"'Tis unnerving the way every blasted villager glances around before answering a question—even if it's about the weather. I'm thinking it shows they are either afraid of someone, or there's an unspoken law not to speak to newcomers."

Summerfield grunted. "There is no unwritten law about speaking to strangers, O'Ghill. As to being overheard, with all of the nasty rumors and salacious gossip being spread, I can understand those in the village being hesitant to speak when out in the open. Has the blacksmith said anything you feel is important?"

"Coleman finally trusted me enough to warn me to look about me before having a conversation in the middle of the street, and to watch what I said—and who I spoke about."

"Did he mention anyone in particular?"

O'Ghill grinned then immediately swore. The split in his lip reopened and started to bleed. "'Tis how I convinced the man to trust me enough to confide in me."

"By beating you bloody?" The baron sounded incredulous.

Garahan knew his cousin well—if he had one bruise and two cuts, the blacksmith would have similar injuries, plus one or two more.

His cousin confirmed what Garahan thought: "Hardly. I got in a solid blow to his solar plexus—may have bruised a rib or two—before I gave him two black eyes."

Garahan chuckled. "That's the cousin I know and love. Did ye hear his nose crack when ye broke it?"

O'Ghill frowned. "I was distracted by the blow to me head and must have missed it."

"Two black eyes would be a fair indication that you've broken our blacksmith's nose," Summerfield said. "I cannot say that I approve of the way you went about extracting information, O'Ghill, but let's hear what he told you before I pass judgment."

Garahan watched his cousin's face lose all expression, a bad sign that O'Ghill's temper threatened to erupt. "His lordship isn't meaning that he'd be judge and jury over yer actions," he quickly explained, "just that he'd be weighing the facts before deciding if it merited the outcome." He leaned close to add, "Baron Summerfield's only a fan of violence when *he's* the one engaged in the fight."

The baron's eyes widened before he roared with laughter. "And you would be correct in that assumption, Garahan. My brother-in-law knew what he was doing when he hired Patrick and Sean O'Malley and then asked if they had any relatives looking for work. The result is the best of the best—his sixteen-man private guard. You gather the facts, evaluate the situation, and give your advice—whether we want to hear it or not—and always speak the truth."

He nodded to O'Ghill. "If you doubt what Garahan's just said, ask O'Malley—he was assigned to protect my wife, though we weren't married at the time—when she received a ransom note for me. She got the flea-brained idea to mount a rescue effort alone, with a brass paperweight and ribbon-wrapped bundle of her hatpins as weapons!"

"From the look of ye," O'Ghill replied, "she succeeded."

Summerfield sighed. "I've never realized a man could hold enough fear in his heart to feel it in his bones. I did that day. And I'll be forever grateful hearing the sound of O'Malley's roar as he launched himself up the stairs to save Phoebe."

His interest captured, O'Ghill asked, "So her ladyship needed help after all?"

"Not much," O'Malley answered. "After I'd taken care of a few of the men, I noticed the last man standing with his back to the locked door quivering in fear."

"Well, don't stop now—tell me the rest," O'Ghill demanded.

"Yer lordship," O'Malley said, "would ye care to tell what happened next?"

Summerfield hesitated, then said, "There was a wooden door between the woman I love and what was going on. I only know what happened because you told me, O'Malley."

O'Malley nodded. "Well then, I'll tell ye what happened. Lady Phoebe had one hand against the man's chest, and the other held those damned hatpins pressed against his cheekbone—beneath his eye!"

O'Ghill's expression was one of wonder.

Garahan approved. Lady Phoebe was brave and courageous. "Ah, but 'twas what happened next that cemented the fact that his lordship enjoyed a bit of violence."

Flaherty snickered. "Tell him, yer lordship."

"I've never felt the gut-wrenching fear that grabbed me by the heart in that moment," Summerfield said. "Silence fell on the other side of the door, and I did not know what was happening. I warned Phoebe to stand back and rammed the door with my shoulder."

"Splintered the bloody thing in half and had the bugger in his hands ready to tear him apart before his eyes cleared," O'Malley continued. "He locked gazes with Lady Phoebe, and then—"

Summerfield interrupted, "No need to go into all of the details right now, O'Malley. While I appreciate the vote of confidence, and the retelling of a definitive moment in my life, I need to hear the rest of what O'Ghill has to report."

O'Ghill told them, "Coleman confided that he and Vicar Chessy had a long talk with their daughters after Garahan and the baroness left the vicarage the other day. It wasn't so much what their daughters told them as it was the timing of the events, and Garahan's involvement, that had them thinking the rumors resurfacing were tied to Garahan's rescue of the squire's governess—"

"Niece," Garahan reminded him.

"Aye," O'Ghill agreed. "Both recalled their daughters waxing poetic—'tis how the vicar explained it—about the baroness's friendly manner and kindness to everyone in the village. They made a point of telling me yer wife never had to demand they treat her with the respect she's due as the highest-ranking female in our little village. They believe she's more than earned it."

The baron's jaw clenched as his hands fisted at his sides. "I take it the squire's wife has been lording her position over the villagers as of late?"

O'Ghill started to agree, then shook his head. "If I understood the men, it has been that way for a number of years—even after ye moved here."

Summerfield relaxed his hands and his jaw. "No doubt it began after my parents spent less and less time here in Summerfield-on-Eden. They had given the estate to my older brother, but my sister-in-law is not in good health. She has improved since they moved to occupy Father's London townhouse—it's closer to her physician. Summerfield Chase was left in the care of our excellent staff until Father suggested Phoebe and I make it our home after we married."

"How often did your parents make the journey here, and how long would they have stayed on at the estate when visiting?" Garahan asked.

"Twice yearly, for a month at a time."

"That left quite a bit of time for the squire's wife to lord her position over the rest of the people in the village," Garahan suggested.

"Aye," O'Ghill said. "'Tis another thing the vicar mentioned. But he did not have the detailed information that ye have, yer lordship."

"Thank you for the information, O'Ghill," Summerfield said. "This is just what we needed. I'm sorry you had to trade blows with the blacksmith to get it. Coleman is the strongest man in Summerfield-on-Eden."

"I enjoyed it," O'Ghill replied.

Garahan chuckled. "He's met his match in O'Ghill, and more than held his own the last time he sparred with us. It's been some time—mayhap we should invite Coleman to go another few rounds."

"Later, Garahan," the baron said. "I need to send word to Standish and fill him in on what O'Ghill reported."

O'Ghill's expression was one Garahan had seen many times over the years—one of doubt. His cousin's next question confirmed it. "Do ye trust the man?"

"I have no reason not to," Summerfield answered.

"Ye have to excuse our cousin," O'Malley said. "He's only just left home, and from all that our families—the Cork O'Malleys and the Wexford O'Malleys—have told us in their letters, and what happened to me Uncle Patrick, not one of our families have reason to trust the local law."

"Aye," Flaherty said. "Me parents in Dublin have mentioned the same."

"And mine in Tipperary. 'Tis a long history of being oppressed," Garahan added.

"I've come to understand why," Summerfield said, "from conversations I have had with you—and the other members in the guard in London and Wyndmere Hall. Your experiences have added to the strong web of protection you have formed around Jared and Persephone, Edward and Aurelia, William and Calliope—and their families—and around myself and Phoebe."

He slowly made eye contact with each of the men. "My wife has yet to confide in me, but I suspect from the way she's been feeling lately that there is more than the vicious gossip that is preying on her mind. I've already consulted with Dr. Higgins, and it is his considered opinion that my wife will be sharing excellent news with me soon." Before the men could congratulate him, Summerfield held up a hand. "What I've told you is in the strictest confidence. I want my wife to believe that I do not suspect she's carrying my babe, though how she could believe I would not notice the changes in her emotions, eating habits and"—he cleared his throat—"her figure." Then he shook his head. "What is it about you men that I nearly spoke of something far too personal that I haven't even mentioned to my cousin and closest friend, Chattsworth?"

"'Tis the number of lead balls we've taken protecting yerself and Lady Phoebe," O'Malley replied.

"Nay," Flaherty countered. "'Tis the blows to the back of the head."

Garahan put a hand to his side. "The number of times we've been stabbed."

O'Ghill added, "Don't be forgetting blows to the face."

"I depend on you men to protect the most precious thing in my life—my wife," Summerfield said. "For that, I will be forever grateful. Thank you, men."

"'Tis our pleasure," O'Malley said.

"And duty," Flaherty added.

"We're happy for ye, yer lordship. Ye have our vow that we will pay special attention to Lady Phoebe," Garahan said.

"Without seeming to," O'Ghill added.

Summerfield nodded. "I'd best speak to Timmons about sending word to the constable."

When the others started to leave, Garahan spoke up. "Ye wanted to speak to me privately, yer lordship?"

"Ah, Garahan, I do. O'Malley, will you handle the message to Standish?"

"Aye, yer lordship," O'Malley replied. "Flaherty will resume his post inside, and I'll resume mine after I speak to Timmons. O'Ghill, why don't ye tag along?"

The men filed out of the room, and Garahan wondered if he'd be looking for another position come morning.

Summerfield closed the door and said, "I understand that your feelings for Miss Barstow go deep."

Garahan agreed, "She's the finest woman I know." He shook his head. "And the most stubborn. Courageous, too."

"I also understand that you have declared your feelings to her."

"I'd never force meself on a woman, if that's what ye're about to ask."

The baron looked taken aback. "That never crossed my mind. I wanted to verify that you do have feelings for her."

"Aye. If she'd stop interrupting me constantly, I'd have asked her to marry me."

Summerfield nodded. "Have you thought of what your lives would be like with your quarterly rotations between His Grace's estates?"

Garahan's mouth opened, then closed, but he could not think what to say.

"Ah, I had a similar reaction when the duke asked me what my intentions were toward his sister. You do realize there is another way to silence a woman bent on interrupting, do you not?"

Garahan grinned. "I do, and have used it once before, but with all of the rumors flying around the village, I did not want to do anything that would reflect badly on her reputation."

The baron placed his hand on Garahan's shoulder. "I know you wouldn't. I'd kiss her again—until she's putty in your hands and unable to speak—then ask her to marry you."

"Ye don't mind that I didn't speak to ye first—as I've already made a pledge to ye—and stated me intentions?"

"Not at all. I asked Phoebe before I asked His Grace's permission." The baron paused. "You aren't planning on leaving the guard, are you?"

Garahan immediately answered, "Nay. If ye didn't give me the boot, I planned to ask James and Aiden their advice on how to balance me vow to the duke and yerself with married life."

"I know you can absolutely handle both, Garahan. Now's your chance—it's your half-hour break, and I understand Miss Barstow has been waiting for you."

Garahan's heart lightened with the news. "Has she, now? Well then, I'd best not keep her waiting." He rushed to the door, yanked it open, and then paused. "Thank ye, yer lordship!"

He was a man with a purpose—and the baron's blessing. It was time to take the lass in hand and make her listen. If he had to kiss her senseless, then so be it. He would do whatever it took to get her to pay attention when he spoke from the heart and told her he would love her forever.

Garahan prayed that this time, she'd believe him.

CHAPTER TWENTY

PRUDENCE WAITED IMPATIENTLY. What was keeping Garahan? He normally stopped by right before teatime, and they would sit and talk to one another. Actually, she did most of the talking. Once her throat healed to the point where it was only a discomfort to speak—and not excruciating—she had not been able to keep from telling him her plans to seek employment now that she was no longer living with her aunt and uncle.

Of course, as she'd confided in Garahan, she fully intended to pay the baron and baroness back for their kindness. Since she had not been compensated for the governess position, she had no coin, but she had a strong back and the will to do whatever necessary to succeed. But first she intended to repay her debt to Baron and Baroness Summerfield. It was that simple.

She would offer to stay on in any capacity they needed: whether it be working in the kitchen with Mrs. Green or reporting to Mrs. Chauncey to help with the rest of the household. What a wonderful thing it would be if she could be assigned to work for Redmund, the steward—she dearly loved to be outdoors. Better still, she could help the stable master. Old Ned moved slower by the day, not that anyone mentioned the fact to the proud man. If she had to guess, she'd place his age at nearly a century—well, truth be told, mayhap only ninety.

Staring out the window that overlooked the stables, she

thought how wonderful it would be to work with the horses. She'd never had the opportunity at home. Father had instructed the stable master to send her right back to the house if she lingered, taking her time to groom her horse. Those twice-weekly rides were the only time she'd been allowed out of the house, and only if one of the stable lads accompanied her to guard her virtue.

Father and Mother had had no idea that she rode alone—every morning before dawn. Oh, how she missed riding across the open fields while the mist shrouded the deep wood on the other side of the meadow at the very edge of their property. Watching the sun break over the horizon was a joy that filled her and gave her the strength to face another day. Days filled with recriminations, harsh words, and more…the harsh treatment at the hands of her own mother. The only other person who was up and enjoying the morning air at that time was the gardener, who enjoyed the quiet of the early hour to tend Mother's gardens. He happily kept her secret, as long as she promised to only say two words to him each day: *good morning*. After she returned her horse to the stables, she'd wave goodbye, and he would smile and nod.

Though she did not miss the way her family treated her, she did miss riding, and the quiet friendship she shared with the gardener. As she recovered, and had time on her hands, she found that she missed chatting with the staff at her aunt and uncle's home. Mrs. Cabot and Gifford in particular…and then there were her cousins. She desperately missed those little boys. Each day had been filled with learning something new and exciting. They reveled in lessons about the plants, birds, and animals that lived around them. She missed their raucous, rough-and-tumble ways. Missed the way they'd wrap their arms around her waist on either side of her and hold on tightly, before resting their heads against her stomach. She'd felt needed, loved.

It had been a surprise, a sennight ago, to wake and find Garahan sitting beside her, bathing her face. She had no idea he had been caring for her while she'd been fighting a fever. She could not recall the last time she felt that she mattered to her family—

or anyone else, for that matter. Why she thought that would change when she was sent off to work for her aunt and uncle, she couldn't say. Just a hopeful feeling. Unfortunately, it had not, but what did change was that someone—make that twin someones—voluntarily hugged her. She wondered how Percy and Phineas were handling the separation.

The sound of the familiar, heavy knock on her bedchamber door was a welcome distraction from feeling sorry for herself. She drew in a deep breath and slowly exhaled. "Come in."

The handsome Irishman who'd been on her mind stood in the doorway. His broad shoulders spanned the distance, with barely an inch left on either side of him! He was resplendent in his uniform. The only spot of color was the emerald green of the word *Eire*, and the golden Celtic harp embroidered over his heart—symbols of Ireland, home to every man in the Duke of Wyndmere's guard.

She learned the duke had had the uniforms tailored to fit the broad-shouldered, deep-chested men who served him. The unrelieved black from head to toe helped them to blend in with their environment while performing their duties. She thought it called attention to their coloring. Ryan had told her that all eight of the O'Malleys—four brothers from Cork, and their four cousins from Wexford—had blond hair and varying shades of green eyes. The Flaherty brothers had auburn hair and blue eyes. And Ryan and his brothers had dark brown hair with brown eyes. His amber eyes mesmerized her with their intensity.

The expression in them now was one she hadn't seen before. It appeared as if he had been on a quest, and the object of that journey was within his reach. Her mind continued to weave stories around the man she'd dreamed of night after night, while she stared at him.

"Ye've roses in yer cheeks and a bit of sparkle to yer eyes, lass. How are ye feeling?"

She frowned, though she did not realize it. It was out of the ordinary to hear praise. Normally, she only heard criticisms. "I feel well, thank you." Prudence did not want to monopolize the conversation, as she'd only just realized she'd been doing just that since the day her fever broke. A few days of rest, and meals that filled the empty hollow of her belly, and her strength had begun to return. She had not felt this rested since—well, ever!

"Ye're thinking deep thoughts again, lass. Care to share them?"

Deciding to stick to her plan to urge him to be the one to carry the conversation today, she shook her head.

"Well then, ye can tell me later if ye wish." He walked over to where she sat, in the chair by the window, and reached for her hand. His lips were warm and firm as he pressed them to one knuckle after the other. She waited for him to turn her hand over. When he did, her breath caught. She lifted her gaze to his, and he slowly smiled. "Are ye waiting for something, lass?"

The lilt in his voice lured her closer. She shivered, unable to stop staring at his mouth. His deep chuckle should have annoyed her, but his confidence only added to his appeal. He bent his head once again and pressed a kiss to her palm, closed her hand over the kiss, and brought it to rest over his heart. "I've missed ye, lass."

So many emotions shot through her as the deep baritone of his voice wrapped around her, but it was his words that gave her something she had not had before—hope and wonder. Hope that he truly meant them. Wonder that he did not find her face and form off-putting. She craved the way he kissed her hand. Would he ever kiss her like he had that day at Summerfield Chase?

"Did ye not miss me?"

She felt her cheeks warm at his question. It wasn't that she was embarrassed; quite the opposite—she was overwhelmed. No one cared enough to ask her anything remotely relating to her emotions, thoughts, or feelings—especially the young men from her village. While her sisters had suitors calling for them by the score, she'd only had one or two. Neither one of whom she'd think of today, or else her head would begin to pound. Horrid creatures!

"Yes," she managed. "I did miss you," she whispered. "More than you can imagine."

He squatted beside her and, with his free hand, tucked a stray strand of hair behind her ear, then trailed the tip of his finger along the curve of her cheek, the line of her jaw. She trembled at his touch.

"Cold?"

She stared into those dark and dreamy eyes, eyes that she had come to know held the promise of so many things she had yet to discover. Looking into their depths, she tried to separate the emotions swirling there, and could only define a few: passion, hunger, and uncertainty. But what in the world those emotions meant, or whether they related to her, was a complete and total mystery.

"Ye're quiet today. Are ye sure ye feel well?"

"I'm sure." She felt her face flush again and dipped her head to stare at the hand in her lap—he still held her other hand to his heart. But why?

"I've been meaning to ask ye a question, lass."

"You have?"

"Aye. I've been trying for the last few days, but ye seemed to have a lot on yer mind that ye needed to share with me."

"Do forgive me," she said. "I seldom had the chance—or even the time—to have a conversation with anyone while working for my aunt and uncle, other than to receive instructions for the day…and a word or two with the cook or stable master."

"What about the lads?"

She smiled. "Except for the boys—we talked to one another all the time, about anything and everything."

"I could ask the baron if I could collect the lads and bring them over to visit with ye."

She hesitated while she fought the inner battle and finally decided to be honest with him. "I'd love to see them, but I'm afraid if I return that I'll never be allowed to leave."

"Ye have no fear of that. I'd be escorting ye over if—and only if—ye insist to go along when I pick up the lads." He put the tip of a finger beneath her chin, lifting it so their eyes met. "Nothing and no one would stop me from escorting ye home, lass."

"To my parents?"

"Nay, lass. Here."

"But I don't live here. I'm only here out of the goodness of the baron and baroness's hearts." She looked away so he wouldn't see her tears. "It's temporary, until I find work—or my parents find someone who will marry me."

The gentle brush of his fingertips had her turning to meet his gaze. He shifted so he knelt on one knee. "Ye must realize how I feel about ye, lass. I confessed what was in me heart after I rescued ye. Do ye not remember?"

HE WATCHED THE delicate flush steal across her satin-smooth cheeks again, lovely as a rosebud unfurling beneath the warmth of the sun. Her beauty captured him from the first—her blue-black hair and unusual blue-violet eyes. She was tall, with womanly curves that stayed on his mind long after he'd seen her…and those lips. He dug deep for control, and found it.

"I remember."

"Remember?" What in the bloody hell had he asked her? God, her lips would tempt a saint—and as his ma often reminded him, he was no saint!

"Everything you said," she answered, "including the part you never should have mentioned."

He slowly smiled. "Ah. How could I not, when ye were hanging right above me head? That devil of a breeze teased the hem of your gown and yer chemise. There're some things a man never forgets, lass."

"Even if I asked you to?"

He lowered the hand pressed to his heart and reached for her other one. With his gentle tug, their lips were a breath apart. She looked up and furrowed her brow. He didn't mind that she looked irritated—it was part of what drew him to her. "The sight is branded on me brain." When she didn't respond, he said, "I need ye to pay close attention, lass. I've an important question that I cannot hold on to any longer. I need to know yer answer before I drive meself over the brink into madness."

The confusion in her eyes bothered him. Was it a ruse, like the one Maggie Finney often played on the lads back home? Did the lass not feel what was between them?

"What is the question?"

"Will ye marry me, lass? I love ye."

Her mouth rounded and a puff of breath blew out, but she gave no reply. Well, at least she hadn't told him he could not love her—or that she did not love him. He would never accept either answer from her luscious lips.

"Will ye?"

She froze—as if she were statue carved of marble.

"Lass?"

She blinked.

Worry that his question had tumbled her into a state of shock filled him. But then he recalled the baron's recent advice and took matters in hand. He slipped an arm around her waist and closed the tiny gap between them. When she was flush against him, he pressed his lips to hers.

The soft sound of her sigh, as her body went slack, was music to his ears. He poured every ounce of what he felt for the lass into the kiss. Tracing the rim of her mouth with the tip of his tongue garnered a gasp that had him praising all the saints.

She trembled, and he shifted until he was sitting on the chair, with her on his lap. It allowed him to give more. His heart, his soul, everything he had, went into the kiss. But his plans to take complete control of her backfired when he felt the tip of her tongue touch his. Her shy exploration poured fuel on the fire of the passions he held in check. He could only stand the torture so long. He knew what her innocent touch meant—even if she didn't. She trusted him. God willing, she'd trust him with more than a mind-numbing kiss—and soon!

He softened the kiss and slowly ended it, leaning his forehead on hers. "I've never met a woman as courageous and giving as ye before, lass. Ye already know that yer beauty drives me to distraction. Let me be the man who loves ye, and makes love to ye, for the rest of our days. Say yes, lass."

He felt her shiver and pulled her closer to his heart, protecting her with his body. Sensing she need reassurance, he said, "I've never known a lass over the age of twelve who climbed trees—or would jump into a marsh pond to rescue a lad. Ye aren't afraid of anything, lass. Don't be afraid to let yerself love me back."

She drew in a deep breath and wiggled until he eased his hold on her. Looking down into her jewel-bright eyes, he waited. He'd said everything he'd planned to say. It was up to her to accept him—or, God help him, reject him.

"I could never be afraid of you, Ryan. You've already risked so much to save me. I'd marry you even if the only reason you asked me was your innate need to protect me from harm."

"Ye have to know that I've been speaking from me heart, *mo ghrá*."

"No one has ever loved me before. Certainly not my older sisters, and definitely not my mother. I do think my father cares for me. But no man has ever looked at me as more than someone they could grab and grope without fear of repercussions."

She cupped the sides of his face and pressed her lips to his in a soft kiss that felt like the wings of a butterfly—nay! *An angel.* "Lass…"

"Yes. I'll marry you, Ryan. Not because I'm grateful you rescued me and want to protect me, but because I think what's bursting inside of me whenever I see you, and when you hold me in your arms and kiss me…is love. I love you!"

He captured her lips in a devastating kiss that had him taut with need to make love to her. *"Mo ghrá,"* he murmured against her lips. *"Mo chroí."*

"Mo chroí is 'my heart,' isn't it?"

"Aye, and ye are, *mo ghrá.* Me love. We have the baron's blessing—do ye need yer uncle's or yer da's?"

She shook her head. "I most definitely do not need my uncle's blessing—or permission—to marry. I would like to have my father's blessing, but he'll never give it if it means disagreeing with my mother. She would never agree if she suspected, even for a moment, that I love you."

He hurt for this precious woman in his arms. How could her own family slash at her until she felt as if no one loved her? "Ye'll never want for anything, lass. Though there is one thing ye should know."

She wrapped her arms around his neck, looked into his eyes, and asked, "What do I need to know?"

"Me assignment here isn't permanent. Those of us in the duke's guard who are single rotate between the duke's estates quarterly. I'll be heading to me next assignment in two months' time. If we are married before then, I may be able to opt out of the rotation. I'd have to ask His Grace."

"Do you know where His Grace will send you?"

"Not yet. There's been a number of adjustments in the last year, as me cousins, and recently me two older brothers, have married and are no longer in the rotation."

"Wherever you go, I'll go," she promised, lifting her lips to his once more.

When he could bring himself to end the kiss, he said, "Ye won't regret yer decision to marry me, lass. I have so many things to teach ye."

"About your work for the duke and the baron?"

He stifled the urge to laugh, deciding instead to show her what he meant. He slid his hand from the nape of her neck to the base of her spine. Splaying his hand, anchoring her, he nibbled and kissed a path along the line of her jaw to the hollow at the base of her throat. He paused to dip his tongue there, tasting the sweet cream of her skin, inhaling the faint scent of lilacs that had haunted his every waking hour. "Nay, lass, about what goes on between a man and his wife."

She placed a hand to his chest and pushed against him until they were eye to eye. She shook her head as a look of sadness dimmed the light in her eyes. "I know all about that. My parents rarely have a kind word to say about one another, nor do they spend any time together. Their bedchambers are on opposite ends of the hallway." She rushed on, "I have never seen them touch the other's hand, let alone steal a kiss."

Garahan chuckled. "Ah, then they did not marry for love, as we will. I love ye, lass, and plan to spend the rest of me life teaching ye the ways two people in love can show their love without words, but with a kiss, the brush of a fingertip, or the press of their body. That's what we'll be doing every morning—and every night—for the rest of our days."

Her eyes were round with wonder and a hint of uncertainty. He pressed his advantage and kissed her until she collapsed against him. This time she cuddled closer. Nestled in his arms, she whispered, "I think I'm going to enjoy being married to you, Ryan."

Joy filled his heart. "Count on it, lass."

CHAPTER TWENTY-ONE

MRS. GREEN BUSTLED into the room a short while later, positively beaming. "You are going to make the most beautiful bride, Miss Barstow."

"Prudence," she reminded the baron's cook.

The older woman nodded. "When is the wedding?"

"I have no idea. Ryan just proposed, but he was late returning to his shift and had to leave. I hope the baron won't be angry with him."

"Don't you give it a second thought. His lordship is a fair and agreeable man. Though I am sure he will discuss the matter with Garahan, I doubt there will be any repercussions."

"Word certainly travels fast," Prudence murmured.

"Good news always does," the cook replied. "The baroness asked me to sit with you while the footmen bring your bath-water."

"Oh, but I don't want to trouble anyone. I can wash with the water one of the maids delivered earlier. I am certain it is warm enough."

"The baroness insists," Mrs. Green said. "And I concur. Now that the danger of the fever returning has passed, a hot bath is in order. It won't do any good to argue—her ladyship always gets her way."

"I'm not used to having a fuss made over me," Prudence

confessed.

"Hot bathwater is not a fuss. Did the squire's wife make you feel as if it were?"

She lifted a shoulder and let it fall. How could she tell the kindly cook that her aunt wasn't the only one who felt that requesting a hot bath was a luxury? Growing up, once her figure began to fill out, she had become invisible, ignored by her mother, sisters, and, more often than not, her father. Apparently, not seeing or hearing her amounted to extra work for the staff when she requested a hot bath.

When she did not answer immediately, the cook shook her head. "We'll have no dark thoughts from the past today. You should look forward and imagine what joys your future will hold." At the knock on the door, Mrs. Green smiled. "That will be your bathwater and the tea tray. Let's enjoy a soothing cup or two while you tell me how that handsome Irishman proposed."

The woman was a wonder, directing the footmen to fill the slipper tub in the dressing room, while pouring tea and serving the tiny, frosted cakes that were a favorite of anyone who sampled them. Percy and Phineas had probably nibbled more than their share when they stayed overnight at Summerfield Chase.

Prudence stared at the confection, wondering how difficult it would be to master the recipe. The cook her parents employed never attempted anything beyond scones—not even a butter cake. "Would I have to be proficient in the kitchen to be able to make these delicious little cakes?"

Mrs. Green paused with her teacup to her lips to answer, "Are you going to try to pry the recipe out of me?"

Prudence felt her face flush with embarrassment. "Forgive me. I had no idea—" The cook's lilting laughter had her smiling in return as her worry eased. "You were teasing."

"I couldn't help myself. I'd be happy to share some recipes with you—even Garahan's favorites."

Prudence leaned closer to ask, "Are there many, and will they be difficult to master?"

"He's mad for cream scones, berry tarts, cream tarts, and treacle tarts."

"Oh, is that all?"

The cook shook her head. "He loves these teacakes, butter cake, currant cake—"

Prudence laughed. "In other words, he loves sweet things."

Mrs. Green's eyes met hers. "He loves you, doesn't he?"

Prudence did not know what to say to that, so she lifted one shoulder in reply.

The cook took the nonverbal response in stride. "I do not believe any of his favorites are difficult to prepare, but I've spent most of my life in the kitchen. Why don't we begin tomorrow?"

Prudence was confused. "Begin?"

Mrs. Green smiled as she set her empty teacup on the table. "We'll prepare all of Garahan's favorites. The baron and baroness—as well as the duke's guard—will benefit from your lessons. And, I'll have you know, I am a very good teacher."

Prudence reached for the cook's hand and squeezed it. "You have no idea how wonderful you have been, Mrs. Green. I will always remember and be grateful for your kindness."

"Well now, since the duke's guard rotates every quarter, you'll be back. Then we will see how much your cooking and baking skills have improved since the last time you were here."

"I have so many things to be thankful for since Garahan freed me from..." She let her voice trail off. She had no intention of bringing up those horrible days she'd been locked in her attic bedchamber.

The footmen finished filling the tub and closed the door behind them on their way out. "Now then, after you undress, you can leave your things behind the screen in the dressing room," Mrs. Green said. "I'll help you into the tub—we do not need our bride-to-be to feel lightheaded from doing too much at once."

The sight of steam rising off a lilac-scented tub was a reminder of that fateful day in the marsh—only this time, she hadn't been in the pond, and was not weak from lack of food and overexerting herself in her attempts to save her cousin. As she had the last time, Mrs. Green added dried lilac blossoms to the bathwater before swirling it with her fingertips.

"Just the right temperature, and what a lovely scent." She straightened and turned to Prudence. "Now then, in you go."

She let the older woman steady her as she stepped into the tub. Prudence sighed as the water soothed aches she had been ignoring. As the heat permeated her tired limbs, she began to feel the warmth in her bones. "This feels wonderful."

"If you ask me, Prudence, you are long overdue for a bit of pampering. Between Mrs. Chauncey, the baroness, and myself, we will see to it that you are indulged. When you're ready, I'll help wash your hair. How you manage on your own with so much of it is a wonder."

"I've learned to make do. Please don't worry about me. I'm not used to the things my sisters demanded. What I haven't become accustomed to, I certainly will not miss."

The cook's only response was a deep frown.

By the time Prudence had scrubbed from head to toe, and the kindly woman helped rinse her hair—twice—she was more tired than she'd expected to be.

She was drying off when someone knocked on the door to the bedchamber. With a sharp intake of breath, she tucked the drying cloth around her and slipped behind the dressing screen while Mrs. Green answered the door. "Ah, Mrs. Chauncey, your ladyship, just in time. Prudence has finished her bath and is ready to get dressed."

"We've brought a fresh pot of tea and more sweets," Mrs. Chauncey announced. "I know how picky you are about your domain, Mrs. Green. I only touched the teakettle, tea chest, and the second platter of baked goods you pointed out earlier."

Prudence stifled a giggle at the thought of the two women invading one another's territory.

"I'm brought a chemise and gown for you to try on, Prudence," the baroness announced.

"Oh, but I am quite certain—"

"Do be quiet and just put the bloody clothes on."

A bit unnerved by the baroness's command, she fumbled her reply. "Forgive me, your ladyship. I'm not trying to be difficult—"

"Excellent," the baroness interrupted. "I'm anxious to see how the gown looks with your coloring."

Prudence did as she was told, and before she could ask, Mrs. Green was there to fasten the buttons at the back of the softest gown she'd ever worn. "It's feels like a dream." A glance down, and she fell in love with the color. "It's the loveliest shade of violet, with just a hint of blue."

"He was right," the cook told her. "It matches your eyes." Mrs. Green handed her a pristine pair of silk stockings and scarlet ribbon garters.

Prudence remembered Ryan's description of his first sight of her and felt a flutter inside. He never should have seen her like that! But he had, and now that she was to be his wife, he would see quite a bit more of her than her stocking-clad legs and bottom. She sat and pulled on the stockings, securing them with the ribbon garters. She had so much to thank him for.

"We're waiting!" the baroness announced from the other room.

The cook produced a new pair of half boots—quite dainty, and the opposite of the pair Prudence owned. "Oh, but I do not need new boots."

"Have you seen the state of yours after their dunking in the pond?"

"Er, no. I haven't."

"Trust me—trust Garahan and accept the rest of his gift. It's high time you replaced those boots."

"They still have a sole on them—don't they?"

The cook laughed softly. "Aye. But you are not to even think of wearing them with this gorgeous gown. Garahan mentioned you saving your old pair for outdoor romps with your cousins."

She smiled. "He is so generous. Garahan's going to ask my uncle if the twins can visit me. When they do, we'll go mucking about!"

The cook's smile dimmed for a brief moment, then brightened once again. "Well now, that sounds like a lovely idea." She handed Prudence the boots. "Do you need help putting them on?"

"No thank you." Prudence slipped them on, smoothing her hands over the butter-soft leather, she remarked, "I won't dare wear these outside for fear of ruining them."

"Prudence?"

At the sound of the baroness's voice, Mrs. Green winked. "We'd best not keep her ladyship waiting."

Prudence hugged the woman and stepped back. "Do I look all right?"

"You are a vision." Mrs. Green gently tugged Prudence's arm and led her into the bedchamber, where the baroness and the housekeeper waited for them at the small table.

Unsure of herself, she let her arms fall to her sides and waited.

Lady Phoebe circled her, mumbling beneath her breath, but Prudence could not quite make out the words. Finally, the baroness stepped back and beamed. "You look stunning. The color is the exact shade of your eyes and complements your fair complexion and blue-black hair." She tipped her head back and laughed. "Garahan is going to swallow his tongue when he sees you."

"Oh, but I thought to save this lovely dress for the day we marry. Isn't it customary to have the banns read in church three weeks in a row? I don't mind waiting."

"This is a gift from your intended, to be worn today. You came to us with the clothes on your back," the baroness reminded her. "When I sent one of the footmen to retrieve the rest of your belongings, I was dismayed to discover they would not fill a hatbox!"

"The fault is my own—you see, I was not careful enough

with the three gowns I brought with me. The boys were always asking to go on outings and, more often than not when we did, managed to get stuck, requiring me to fetch them down or pull them free. Well, except for the times Garahan came to the rescue. I fear the gown I wore to the marsh is in sorry shape."

The baroness slid her arm around Prudence's waist and led her over to the table where Mrs. Chauncey poured tea. Mrs. Green served tiny sandwiches, and more of the delectable teacakes. "Only three gowns? What were your parents thinking?"

"At least they were not too very worn when they gave them to me."

"They were not made specifically for you?" the baroness asked.

"I cannot remember ever being fitted by the modiste, though my sisters were on a regular basis. They are so beautiful and in demand at local functions, so it was expected."

"Why would your parents not insist you be fitted, too?"

Sharing her circumstances with Garahan had nearly shredded what was left of her self-worth. Prudence could not bear to tell the baroness. She shrugged in answer.

Mrs. Chauncey handed her a teacup, while Mrs. Green passed a plate to her. She thanked them and sipped from her cup. The tea tasted wonderful. "I haven't had tea this strong in some time. It is absolutely delicious."

The baroness smiled and nodded. "There is more in the pot, and once we empty it, we will send for another."

"Oh, no thank you. This is such a treat for me. I cannot thank you and the baron enough for opening your home to me. Taking care of me must have added to your staff's already busy day."

Lady Phoebe slowly smiled. "You do realize that a large portion of the tending was done by Garahan?"

Prudence's teacup rattled on the saucer as she set it on the table. "I...uh, wondered. That is to say..." She cleared her throat. "Really?"

"He insisted," the baroness told her. "Haven't you noticed the dark circles beneath his eyes are almost the same shade as his eyes?"

"I haven't. I should have paid more attention, but that is no excuse for not properly thanking Ryan. I will when he arrives after the next shift change. And I would like to do something in return to thank you. As I have no coin, would you accept an offer of my help with the household chores, or mayhap the kitchen? I used to ride in the mornings, and took very good care of the horse I rode. I'd be happy to lend a hand in the stables—the gardens, too." When the baroness remained silent, Prudence added, "Please?"

"We shall think of something. Won't you pass Mrs. Chauncey your cup? She'll refill it for you." Turning to the cook, the baroness said, "And another of your delicious, frosted cakes, if you don't mind, Mrs. Green."

Teacup in hand, dessert plate piled with teacakes in front of her, Prudence had to pinch herself. "Ouch!" Lady Phoebe's snort of laughter had the others joining in. "I thought I was dreaming."

"Enjoy yourself—soon enough, you'll be a married woman and responsible for taking care of Garahan's every need."

She noticed the baroness stressed the word *every*. "Is there more that I will be responsible for than feeding him and seeing that our room and his clothes are clean?"

"Room?" Mrs. Chauncey asked.

"Feeding him?" Mrs. Green asked at the same time.

Lady Phoebe reached for Prudence's hand and gave it a gentle squeeze. Releasing it, she said, "I daresay you shall have a cottage—and will not be living in one of the upstairs rooms. But it takes time to construct one. Before you say a word, this is our gift to you and Garahan, with every wish for your happiness."

Prudence was speechless in the face of the baroness's generosity.

Lady Phoebe leveled a glance at the housekeeper and her cook before turning back to Prudence. "Has your mother spoken to you about the marriage bed?"

Prudence felt her face heat with embarrassment. "Er…there was no need. After all, who would marry… That is to say… No."

The baroness sighed. "Well, we cannot have you feeling like a lamb led to slaughter on your wedding night, can we, ladies?"

The older women agreed, and the three of them shared the intricacies of what it meant to seal one's marriage vows.

Prudence listened but was not quite sure that what they explained was possible. As she had no experience, she paid attention, gathering the facts, hoping she was brave enough to undress in front of her husband-to-be, let alone do what they described in detail. Through the telling, Mrs. Green held one of her hands, and the baroness held the other. She blinked more than once and was fairly certain her mouth opened a time or two to emit a squeak of shock.

When they'd explained about the pain—and possibility of her bleeding the first time her husband made love to her—it felt as if the top of her head lifted off. She couldn't feel it. A firm pat to her cheek had her paying attention again.

"Now that you understand what will happen physically, you need to know that you will feel pleasure, too," the baroness told her. "I have a feeling Garahan knows what he is about in that regard."

"I cannot seem to catch my breath," Prudence replied.

"Yes, you can," Mrs. Chauncey insisted.

"Close your mouth and place your hands over your mouth and nose, like this." Mrs. Green demonstrated with her cupped hands.

"And then breathe in slowly, deliberately," the baroness ordered her. "Now then, you will take slightly deeper breaths, and slow down as you begin to breathe normally."

When she had herself under control, Prudence immediately said, "Forgive me. It's just that I was remembering what Ryan had said about making love and having so much to teach me."

"If Garahan is half the man I believe him to be," the baroness said, "there will be joy and wonder on the part of the teacher as well as the student."

"I'm afraid I'm not ready for any more detail. I haven't fully digested all you have already told me." As soon as Prudence said the words, a feeling of warmth and gratitude filled her. "I will never be able to thank you enough for taking the time to explain what to expect. I am quite certain that I would have been shocked and frightened out of my wits otherwise."

One by one, the women rose from their seats. Lady Phoebe hugged Prudence and smiled. "I believe I shall see what my darling husband is up to."

The cook quickly followed, reminding Prudence, "Rest now, and don't let all that we've told you muddle your thoughts."

The housekeeper nodded as she tugged on the bellpull. "Trust in your husband to know what to do, and be patient in the teaching."

When the footmen arrived a few moments later, instructions for emptying the tub and removing the tray were given and soon followed.

A short while later, Prudence was alone once again, with thoughts of her wedding night alternately delighting and terrifying her. Every time she felt a bit of panic take hold, she whispered, "I trust you, Ryan."

Exhausted, she finally closed her eyes and drifted off to sleep.

CHAPTER TWENTY-TWO

AFTER HE PROPOSED to the lass, Garahan concentrated on his duties. Patrolling the paths along the edge of the baron's holding, he kept his gaze trained on his surroundings. His thoughts were never far from the worry that the proof they had obtained so far would not be enough to confront the squire and his wife. Though he and the men were in agreement that the squire was not responsible for continuing the verbal attacks on the baron and baroness, the duke's guard, and mayhap, inadvertently, the duke, they all agreed that the man had to have known what his wife was up to.

Torn between wanting to storm over to their home, grab the squire by his cravat, and demand he spill his guts, and following orders, Garahan continued to patrol the perimeter of Summerfield Chase. If that first attack on the duke and his family at Wyndmere Hall a couple of years ago hadn't prepared him to be ready for anything, nothing would.

At the end of his shift, he reined in his horse and turned him over to the stable master. Old Ned crooned to the horse, and Garahan chuckled. "Duncan adores ye."

"He's a fine gelding and knows it. He revels in the attention he receives, and the way he reacts to it is his way of letting you know he will continue to do whatever you ask of him."

Garahan had to agree. "Duncan has never let me down when

on duty—or when we hear a cry for help. Half the time, he senses the danger a heartbeat before I do."

"As I said, he's a fine gelding. Don't worry, I'll take care of Duncan for you." Gifford nodded toward the door. "Best be on your way, Garahan. I understand someone has been waiting to see you."

The delighted smile on the old man's face had Garahan eagerly anticipating his next visit with the lass. As he crossed the expanse between the stables and the rear entrance to the building, his heart began to pick up. The heady thought of pressing his lips to hers, sipping more of her sweetness, filled him as he took the servants' staircase to the second floor and strode toward her bedchamber.

He was surprised to find the door open, and immediately dismayed to find Mrs. Chauncey sitting with the lass. There'd be no passionate kissing tonight.

"We were just speaking of you, Garahan," the housekeeper said. With a nod toward the lass, she asked, "Doesn't Prudence look well rested?"

His gaze riveted on the lass, and the blood rushed from his head to his feet. She was a vision in the blue-violet gown he'd asked the village seamstress to create. It was more than worth the coin spent. 'Twas an elegant gown without froth and frippery added to detract from the simplicity of the gown—or her beauty. The color was what he hoped it would be, and mirrored her jewel-bright eyes.

As he quietly studied her, she blushed, and a delicate hint of rose tinged her cheeks. "Ye look lovely, lass."

Her smile bloomed. "Thank you for thinking of me, Ryan." She smoothed the gown and lifted her gaze to meet his. "You should not have gone to the expense of having a gown made for me. It might give the baron and baroness the wrong impression."

He coughed to cover his laughter. "I've spoken with his lordship, and I've heard ye have spoken to her ladyship. They knew of me intentions, and yer acceptance of me proposal. There is no wrong impression here." He glanced at the housekeeper and said, "Now, if Mrs. Chauncey was to do me a favor and leave us alone for a bit—"

"Shame on you for thinking I'd leave the two of you unchaperoned. Whether you have asked for her hand or not, Miss Barstow's reputation will not suffer further because you cannot keep your lips to yourself."

Garahan strode over to the housekeeper, lifted her off her feet, and swung her around. "Faith, ye remind me of me ma!" He set her on her feet, kissed her cheek, and added, "I'm in yer debt for not boxing me ears, Mrs. Chauncey."

The housekeeper lifted a hand to her hair, tucking in a few stray hairpins. "I do not believe in violence, although I may be tempted if you think you will charm me into leaving this room."

"Ye wound me, if that's truly what ye think. Me intentions are honorable, and me respect for the lass knows no bounds."

The housekeeper inclined her head. "Well then…"

He winked. "'Tis me lips and me heart that have other ideas." He walked over to where the lass stood, eyes wide, with a hand to her throat. "They've tasted paradise and crave another sip." He lifted her free hand to his lips and pressed a kiss to the back of it— kissed each knuckle before turning her hand over and pressing a swift kiss to her palm. As he had before, he wrapped her hand around the kiss. "Think of me when ye open yer hand, and know that if not for your staunch chaperone, I'd be kissing the breath out of ye, lass." She wavered on her feet, and he caught her to him, pressing his lips to the top of her head. "Ye don't know what ye do to me, lass. Me brains are scrambled, and me heart's fit to pound right out of me chest."

The sound of a throat clearing broke through his ardor, bringing him back to his senses.

"Forgive me, lass. I did not mean to muddle yer senses, nor did I intend any harm to ye. 'Tis the sight of ye that grabbed me by the heart and pulled me to ye. Me heart recognized ye as its other half the first moment I saw ye."

A heavy sigh warned him that either O'Malley or Flaherty was behind him. He eased the lass back into the chair, turned around, and nearly groaned. The raised brow and silent question on Baron Summerfield's face had him thinking he may have some fast talking to do.

Before he could offer an explanation, the baron said, "I have received a response from His Grace."

Garahan jolted. Was the baron implying that he'd written to the duke about him? "Good news or bad?"

Baron Summerfield motioned for Garahan to follow him, but then paused in the doorway to say, "Forgive me for interrupting your visit, Miss Barstow. I have an urgent message to deliver to Garahan."

Garahan's eyes met hers over the baron's shoulder, but before he could tell her not to worry, the baron nudged him further into the hallway and closed the door. "Not a word until we are in my upstairs study."

Garahan knew then his time with the duke's guard had ended. He followed the baron, fully prepared to hear that because his heart would not be denied, he would no longer be one of the men the duke trusted with his family.

Had he embarrassed either the housekeeper or the lass with the innocent kissing of her hand? He had not compromised the lass's reputation, nor had he broken his vow to the duke. Mrs. Chauncey was in the room the entire time. That would be a small comfort when he'd be looking for a way to support the woman he planned to wed.

Garahan was so deep in thought that when the baron stopped to open the study door, he plowed into the man. "Forgive me, yer lordship, I—"

"Was obviously thinking about the vision in blue-violet you left behind." Before Garahan could respond, the baron held up a hand and walked into the room.

"Yer lordship—"

The baron shook his head. "You will have a chance to speak

after I read His Grace's response to my missive."

Garahan stood at attention, waiting for the duke's decision, without paying attention to the baron. He already knew what His Grace would say.

"...special license."

His eyes met the baron's. "Did ye say license?"

Summerfield chuckled. "Aye, Garahan. Phoebe was the first to note how protective you were of Miss Barstow. O'Malley later confirmed what I suspected. Having been blinded to all else but Phoebe from the moment she threw her arms around me, I understand the challenge you have been dealing with—separating your duty from your desire."

Garahan squared his shoulders. "I would never shirk me duty, nor compromise the lass."

The baron placed a hand on Garahan's shoulder. "I know that, and so does O'Malley—and my wife for that matter. But, at the moment, with the threat of another attack looming over our heads, we have to be circumspect in our actions and our words. Should someone who does not know how deep your promise to my brother-in-law and our family goes hear or observe the direction of your interest, we run the risk of sinking even deeper into the mire of lies and innuendo that hang over us."

Garahan nodded. "I never meant for ye or the others to think I'd forsake me vow."

"Neither myself, nor the rest of the guard, would think that of you. For that matter, neither would the duke, which is why he was more than happy to respond to my request and immediately secure a special license for you." Summerfield reached into his waistcoat pocket, withdrew the sealed document, and handed it to Garahan.

He broke the seal, opened it, and exclaimed, "It has me name on it!" He kept reading. "And the lass's as well."

Summerfield shook his head. "I should hope so, as she is the woman you proposed to. Now you will not have to wait for the banns to be read. I've already spoken to Vicar Chessy, who has agreed to marry you this evening."

Garahan's hand tightened around the document. "I need to ask the lass—what if she's not ready?"

"According to my darling wife, Miss Barstow is indeed looking forward to pledging her life to you. Phoebe will have spoken to her by now. If you'd like to take a few moments to gather yourself—and mayhap change your shirt—I expect the vicar will be arriving in within the hour."

Garahan's heart soared at the realization that tonight he'd be a married man—sharing the marriage bed with the woman who had him by the *bollocks* from the first. He rushed from the room, then leaned back in to say thank you, before sprinting down the hallway.

Everything he dreamed of was falling into place. His perfect mate would be his from this day forward. He could not wait to begin their first lesson in making love.

PRUDENCE COULD NOT look away from the man standing beside her, devouring her with his eyes. She fought to conceal the way her body trembled at the thought of what lay ahead of them tonight, but her hands gave her away.

Ryan gave them a gentle squeeze as he repeated the vicar's words, promising his life to her until he breathed his last.

She did the same, and watched the way his expression softened from intense passion and desire to one she was coming to recognize as love. Love for *her*!

"You may kiss your bride."

Ryan pulled her close and kissed her until her eyes crossed and she could no longer feel her feet. Her head felt light, and she swayed.

"This is the first time I have performed a marriage ceremony where the bride fainted when the groom kissed her."

GARAHAN VAGUELY HEARD O'Malley say something about an Irishman's prowess, but was busy kissing his bride—who had yet to untangle her tongue from his. Finally, when he could no longer feel the top of his head—but did feel the need for his wife stirring to the point of embarrassment—she set him free and tucked her head beneath his chin. He was grateful he had to scoop her into his arms—it would save him from his cousins' comments about his aroused state.

He met the vicar's expectant expression with one of gratitude. "Thank ye for marrying us, Vicar Chessy. I'm grateful to ye, and to the baron and baroness for their foresight in asking the duke to obtain the special license. Thank ye all!"

"I never thought to marry," Prudence told the vicar. "Since coming to Summerfield Chase, I have learned that I am worthy of love and friendship and not to be hidden away behind locked doors." She blinked away the tears welling in her eyes and turned to the baron and his wife. "I will always be grateful to you for sheltering me in my time of need and for making it possible for Ryan and me to wed." She tightened her arms around her husband's neck and confessed, "I doubt either of us would have been able to wait for the banns to be read."

There was a moment of silence before joyful laughter erupted behind them. Garahan felt as if he were about to burst as he strode from the room. Not wanting to cause more talk in the household, he whispered of the caresses and succulent kisses he planned to bestow on his wife…head to toe.

He'd made it halfway up the stairs when she asked, "Is it permissible for a wife to kiss a path from her husband's neckbone to his knees?"

Garahan stumbled, but caught himself, before they fell backward down the stairs. "Minx! Aye," he answered. "'Tis more than possible, and could be yer second lesson. But there's a more important lesson to start with. Why don't we start there once I get ye behind closed doors?"

In answer, she yanked on his hair and pulled his mouth to hers.

◆◇◆

CHAPTER TWENTY-THREE

PRUDENCE FELT HER entire body quiver when Ryan set her on her feet and ran his hands from her shoulders to her wrists and back.

"Do ye have any idea how much I love ye, lass?"

Unsure if she should blurt out all of her knowledge at once, or wait until he started to undress her, she shook her head.

He pulled her into his embrace. "Let me show ye." He tipped her head back and kissed her tenderly, exploring the contours of her mouth, while his hands moved over her curves, caressing parts of her that she only touched when bathing!

She trembled, and he soothed her, whispering of desires, promising delights if she would trust him.

"I do."

He swept her off her feet and carried her over to the bed, where he set her on her feet again. "Turn around. I'll unfasten your buttons."

She complied. This time, she did not bother to hide her shivers.

"Cold?"

She shook her head.

"Afraid?"

Again, she shook her head.

"I would not want ye to be cold, or afraid of me, lass. I'll go slowly as I warm ye up. Let me help ye off with her gown and chemise."

The fluttering low in her belly intensified as he brushed the sides of her breasts when he lifted the gown over her head. Her chemise quickly followed, and she tried to cover herself, but he stayed her hands, holding them out to her sides as his gaze swept from her head to her toes.

She could not meet his eyes. No one had mentioned how it would feel to stand before her husband clad only in her stockings, garters, and half boots.

As if she had said that last aloud, Ryan murmured, "Yer boots will have to go." He sat on the edge of the bed and pulled her onto his lap, drugging her with one of his mind-bending kisses. He must have removed her boots when he kissed her, because she wasn't wearing them when he set her in the middle of the bed. As soon as his warmth was gone, worry filled her. What if she did not respond as he expected? How could she possibly be expected to? She had never done this before.

He removed his cravat, frockcoat, and waistcoat, holding her gaze the entire time. The expression on his face, and the desire in his eyes, took the frantic edge off her worry. He knelt on the bed and pressed his lips to hers. This time, he plundered her, showing her without words that he was ready to begin his tutelage. When he ended the kiss, he rasped, "Ye taste of honey and an indefinable sweetness, lass. I wonder if ye taste as sweet elsewhere."

He eased off the bed and removed his shirt, then unbuttoned the placket on his trousers, but did not take them off. As if he sensed her uncertainty, he said, "I'll not harm ye, lass, I'm after a taste of the milk and honey yer skin reminds me of. Will ye let me?"

She couldn't seem to form the words to answer, but she managed to nod.

He covered her body with his, and she was immediately aware that although she was tall, and not slight by any means, her husband was broader through the chest and shoulders than she suspected—the proof was posed above her, watching her like a hawk.

Why was it that she suddenly felt like his prey? His eyes darkened, and his nostrils flared, as he bent his head. Warm, firm lips caressed the side of her neck, before tracing a path along her collarbone.

She closed her eyes and felt the warmth of his breath at her ear.

"I need ye to look at me while I'm teaching ye, lass."

"Teaching me?"

"Aye. I'll be sampling yer bounty. Ye can either say aye, or nay, if me caresses are not making ye burn for more."

It suddenly became clear what the baroness and the ladies had spoken of. His lips blazed a path from the base of her throat to her breastbone. He wasn't actually going to put his mouth on her breast, was he?

Heat, bold and powerful, had her crying out as his tongue teased her nipple. He swirled it over the tight bud until she thought she'd go mad. When he drew her breast into his mouth and suckled her, her heart stopped...and then began to pound as she writhed beneath him.

Mindless to everything except the feel of his mouth on one breast, while his fingers worked their magic on the other, she gripped his shoulders and held on while he worshiped her breasts.

When he lifted his head, the intensity of his desire added to the heat spiraling inside of her. "Promise me ye'll never again bind yer beautiful, bounteous breasts, lass."

That part of her had been called many things in the past, but never bounteous or beautiful. "I promise."

He shifted off her, shed his trousers, and returned to the bed. This time his mouth was not angled over her mouth or breasts— it hovered over her belly. She was about to ask what he was about when he rasped, "Trust me to pleasure ye, lass. If ye say stop, I'll stop."

His lips and tongue circled her belly, testing a path toward the top of her thighs. He masterfully teased and nibbled until he reached the juncture of her thighs. She tensed and waited to see what he would do, ready to say nay at any time. When the heat of his mouth claimed her, she trusted her husband not to hurt her. Giving herself over to him completely, she was rewarded when he thrust his tongue inside of her, driving her toward something she did not understand.

His fingers worked their magic as he stretched her. She knew and waited for the pain. But it didn't come as he continued to ply her with his lips and tongue. The tension inside of her built to a crescendo. She gripped his shoulders and held on, until she was mindless to anything but his touch. She tensed, then screamed his name, as the coil burst, and he took her beyond herself to a place she hadn't known existed… Paradise!

"Ye're ready for me, lass."

"Ready?"

He rubbed his magnificent body over hers as he positioned himself between her thighs and bent to kiss her. Shock filled her at the erotic combination of the familiar taste of his mouth and her essence. He lifted his head, his gaze fierce as he rasped, "Now and forever, lass." She lifted her hips, but he shook his head. "Say the words back to me, lass."

"Now and forever, lass."

His face had a tortured expression as a snort of laughter exploded. "Close enough." He plunged into her. She surrendered to the pain, thereby easing it, as the promised pleasure soon took its place.

SHE WRAPPED HER arms around him as he thrust into her again and again. Her gasps of pleasure and pants of exertion had him plunging into her wet warmth until he was fitted to the hilt. Her legs clamped around him, and he wondered if loving the lass was going to be the death of him. He thrust into her one last time. He felt her passage tighten around him. She tensed and gasped as he tossed them over the peak into the heavens beyond.

He stirred first, marveling that the innocent woman in his arms gave herself over to him, trusting him completely. He traced the arch of one brow and then the other, pressing his lips where the tips of his fingers had been. She did not move when he stroked a hand over her silken hair. He planned to convince her to wrap around it them—without any discomfort to her—the next time they made love.

He sighed at the image the idea conjured, and she snuggled closer. "Me life changed for the better the day I found ye dangling from that tree branch."

Garahan was surprised when he heard her whispered reply. "It was all part of my plan to get your attention, taking the boys to the tree and teaching them to climb it. Tangling my hair in that branch was difficult, but I knew it would be worth it when you just happened to ride by and hear Percy's cry for help."

He chuckled. They were still locked together as he rolled over until she was on top, and he could see her expression—that of a woman who'd been well loved. Though he knew she was untutored in the art of lovemaking, she'd had his head in a spin from the moment she stood before him wearing those scarlet garters. "I've a mind to keep ye in silken stockings and scarlet ribbons, lass."

Her smile belied the blush staining her face. He knew she had to be embarrassed and shy, though she overcame it quickly enough once he let his lips convince her to concentrate on the pleasure they could provide.

"How is it that ye weren't afraid of making love to me, when yer face lost every ounce of color after I proposed to ye?"

"It did?"

"Aye. I was having trouble waiting for yer answer and re-member asking ye to let me be the man to love ye, and make love to ye, for the rest of our days."

She squirmed on top of him and gasped. He cupped the back of her neck and kissed her lavishly. "Have ye forgotten the question, lass?" When she stared at him, he chuckled. "How is it that ye weren't afraid of making love to me?"

She licked her lips and finally answered, "The baroness, Mrs. Chauncey, and Mrs. Green shared a pot of tea and a tea tray full of Mrs. Green's frosted teacakes while they explained what to expect in the marriage bed."

"Did yer ma not tell ye when ye were younger?"

"She didn't think I would ever need to know," she whispered, hiding her face from him.

He cupped her face and waited for her eyes to meet his. "'Tis her loss, lass. Ye're a brave, talented, intelligent woman whose beauty nearly cut me off at the knees the first time I saw ye."

She rolled her eyes at him. "Hanging on to that branch."

To remind her, he tensed his buttocks and lifted them off the bed. Buried so deep inside of her, he knew he had her full, if dazed, attention. "That was the first time I observed the lovely curve of yer sweet *arse*." Her hand covered his mouth, and he nipped her palm. She immediately removed her hand. "I've a mind to have of bite of it."

She frowned at him. "My hand?"

He could not keep his laughter inside of him. It was a marvel to be joined with the woman he loved—and laughing. "Nay, lass, yer *arse*."

"You're joking."

He rolled them over until she was tucked beneath him. Slowly pulling out until he was poised at the entrance to her warmth, he waited for her to ask him to stop. She had to be sore, but his need to make love to her again had him by the throat. When he nudged her, she lifted her hips, and he slowly slid home. "I'd never joke about a yer delectable *arse*."

They were laughing when he eased out of her, gasping when he plunged deep. This time he knew just where to stroke her and how much pressure to use to bring her to fulfilment. He urged her higher, but held himself back, waiting for her to come apart in his arms. When he felt her stiffen and arch up beneath him, he thrust into her, pinning her to the bed. While tremors of pleasure rocked her, he let go of the stranglehold on his control and poured his seed inside of her.

He slid a possessive hand beneath her bottom and held her captive against him, giving his seed time to take hold. When their heartbeats slowed and their breathing returned to normal, he rolled them onto their sides, tucking the bed linens around them, holding the lass to his heart.

They lay quiet for a long time, as he dozed lightly. He felt her shudder and rubbed a hand up and down her spine. "Are ye chilled?"

"I'm sorry. I seem to have lost control of my body as well as my senses."

"I noticed, lass, and am not complaining, as the same happened to me."

"Ryan?"

"Aye, lass?"

"Would you send me away if—"

"If?"

"I… Well, that is to say…"

"Whoever said I'd send ye away is daft. Ye captured me heart from the moment our eyes met. Don't be believing I'd feel otherwise."

Blue-violet eyes searched his face for a sign that he meant what he said. Finally, she whispered, "You wouldn't send me away?"

"Nay, lass. Why would I?"

"Because of my daughter. *She* said you would send us to a convent."

He buried the shock of the charge against him deep enough to tease his wife, "Faith, I could be wrong, but I'm thinking I'm the first man to plumb yer delectable depths. How could ye already have a daughter?"

"I do not have a daughter!" She tried to push him off her, but she was no match for his strength.

"Give it up, lass. I'll move when I'm ready to. I wasn't after condemning ye. I was teasing ye. Have ye never been teased before?" When she shook her head and tears welled up, he kissed them away and held her to his heart. "Lass, I would never send ye—nor any babe of ours—away. Whether our lovemaking produced a lass or lad. How could I? It would be a bit of yerself and a bit of me. Didn't anyone ever tell ye that children are the Lord's gifts to us, and are to be treasured?"

He felt her shake her head and eased back to watch her eyes. He needed to see her expression when he said, "I know it wasn't Lady Phoebe, Mrs. Green, or Mrs. Chauncey who would tell ye a lie like that." He didn't want to ask, but had to know, in order to begin to help her realize the truth of his words. He would never let her or any babe she bore him leave. He suspected it was another wicked slash from her upbringing. "Was it someone close to ye?" She closed her eyes, and he warned, "Keep yer eyes on me, lass. Look into me eyes and tell me the truth now. Was it yer ma?"

Tears filled her eyes, but she didn't seem to notice, so he wiped them away without mentioning the fact that she was crying.

"Yes. She told me that if I was ever fortunate enough to find a man fool enough to look past my flaws, and produce a babe, I would have a daughter built just like me."

From the way her body stiffened, he knew there was more vitriol she needed to get off her chest. "What else did she say, lass? Ye can tell me. I'm not about to let ye out of me sight, nor will I ever let another man touch ye. We're bound together forever, *mo ghrá*. Remember you repeated the words exactly as I said them—*Now and forever, lass.*"

"I didn't repeat them like that. Did I?"

"That ye did, and 'twas the first time I laughed making love. I'm thinking it won't be the last, because our love is wrapped with strands of joy. I've waited long enough. Tell me what else yer ma said to ye."

She drew in a deep, steadying breath and slowly let it out. "That my husband would either leave me or send us away…" Her voice trailed off, and she fell silent for a few moments. "For fear our daughter would grow up to be as gangly and homely as me, with the same overblown figure that would mark her as it marked me—as a slattern—for the rest of her life."

"I'm thinking we owe yer darling ma a visit."

The horrified expression on her face had him holding back his laughter, especially when she told him, "I don't think so."

"Oh, but I want to thank the woman—and yer da—for raising such a loving, giving, intelligent woman who is as beautiful inside as she is outside. I think I'll bring along O'Ghill. He'll back me up, as he was tempted to offer for ye himself." He couldn't resist kissing the breath out of her when her mouth rounded in a perfect *O*. "That's from O'Ghill—not that I'll be telling him I finally gave ye the kiss he's been hounding me to pass along."

When her lips curved into a smile, and the lines of strain on her face relaxed, he knew they'd passed the crisis her ma had caused. He'd been tempted to offer to sew the harpy's lips together, but was unsure if the lass held more of an affection for her ma than he realized. Best to keep that offer to himself until it was needed.

He kissed her softly, tenderly, and settled her in his arms, pulling her back against his chest. He drew in a deep breath and the scent of lilacs. When he felt her relax, he whispered, "I wouldn't give yerself or our babe up, even if she were a change-ling."

"Do you know for the first ten years of my life, my mother called *me* a changeling? Only when my father was not around. I always wondered why, until my Grandmother Barstow came to visit. She was tall—and curvy with it—and had blue-black hair and my color eyes. All of the women on Mother's side of the family are petite with light hair and pale blue eyes."

"Watery blue."

She giggled. "Pale blue—like the sky when there's a thin layer of clouds."

"Not nearly as entrancing as me darling wife's blue-violet eyes."

"Ryan?"

"Aye?"

"In case I wake up in the morning and scream because I forget we're married, please remember I love you."

He was laughing when he kissed her senseless.

CHAPTER TWENTY-FOUR

A FEW DAYS later, Garahan was wondering if he'd underesti-mated how stubborn his wife could be. "If ye need anything, all ye have to do is ask. I'm wanting yer word not to leave Summerfield Chase without a proper escort."

"I promise—unless my cousins send word that they need me. You know how worried I am about them."

He frowned at her and repeated, "Ye'll give me yer word not to leave, or I'll ask the baron to post a guard around ye! We've footmen enough to see to the task."

"You wouldn't dare!"

"*Mo chroí*, I would give me life for ye." He pulled her into his embrace. "'Tis a small thing to ask that until matters are fully settled that ye stay where I know ye'll be safe while I'm on patrol."

She mumbled something unintelligible against his chest. He nudged her chin up and pressed a whisper-soft kiss to her lips. When she tightened her arms around him, he deepened the kiss to a more satisfying level before ending it.

"Unless I have a proper escort, I won't leave."

"There's a lass. I'll be holding ye to yer word."

MRS. HONEYCUTT WAS angry and letting her husband know it. "I cannot believe you have not confronted the baron demanding he return our niece!"

The squire could not believe his wife was still harping on the situation he felt had been settled when word reached them Garahan had married Prudence. He had yet to inform his brother-in-law, her father, unsure of how to explain the events leading up to the marriage without implicating his wife—and himself—in the matter.

"Prudence is married to one of the duke's guard! We do not have any rights as far as she is concerned—and nor do your sister or our brother-in-law."

His wife grabbed the sleeve of his frockcoat and yanked on it. "My sister will go along with whatever we decide to do. Can you ignore the letter we just received, thanking us for housing her while they selected a husband for her?"

The squire felt his patience snap. "Have your wits gone begging? She is married—there's naught to be done!" He twisted out of her hold and walked away from her.

"I have a plan," she said, rushing after him. "We know the name of the man my dear sister and her husband selected. We can earn double the coin my sister promised to send for sheltering our darling niece. If we send word to the gentleman that his intended has been held against her will, he may feel obliged to reward us."

He could not resist the lure she dangled. Thinking of the hounds he planned to add to his pack, and the fine hunter he lusted after, he paused in the doorway. "Tell me the rest of your plan."

PERCY GRABBED PHINEAS by the arm and dragged him along the hallway until they were well away from the sitting room, where they'd overheard their mum's plans for their cousin.

Samuels raised an eyebrow at the twins as they raced past him and slipped in through the doorway to the servants' side of the house.

"In here," Phineas whispered. He nearly tripped over his brother as they dove into the pantry. Percy scooted further into the room as his brother opened the large cabinet in the corner and they ducked inside. "What if Mum finds us in here?"

"She won't," Percy told his brother. "You know she always looks for us in the schoolroom first."

Phineas winced. "Did you read a chapter like we were supposed to?"

"It's no fun without Prudence reading with us," Percy said. "She made history come alive, with tales I've never heard before."

"I miss acting out the part of our ancestors," Phineas said. "We were really good at fending off the marauding Normans who wanted to take our land!"

The brothers scooted closer together in the dark of the cabinet. "We can't let anyone steal Prudence!" Percy said.

"We're going to save her," Phineas promised.

"How?" Percy wailed.

His brother clapped a hand over Percy's mouth and whispered, "Garahan married her. I heard Mrs. Cabot and Gifford talking about it. He'll protect her."

Percy agreed, "He'll save her from the marauder that Mum and our aunt are going to pay to kidnap her. Isn't that what you're supposed to do when someone steals your wife, save them?"

"If we ask Garahan and get his promise, he'll do it," Phineas said. "A vow's a promise, just like the one he made to the duke."

"And Prudence," Percy was quick to add. "He spoke vows when he married her."

"She made them back," Phineas reminded his brother.

"So, if he rescues her…" Percy said slowly, working it out in his head. "Then if someone steals Garahan, she'd rescue him, too! Just like she tried to rescue us."

"Yeah, but she needed Garahan's help," Phineas said. "He's bigger and stronger."

"She's pretty strong."

"Maybe she'll fight the marauder off, and he won't steal her away."

They sat in silence for a little while. While they hid, they talked over different ways to get word to Garahan, and finally they decided they would be brave—like Garahan had told them they were the day he busted down the attic door when Mum had locked their cousin away.

"I think we should go now," Percy said. He stuck his head out of their hiding place and then sat back. "I don't see anyone."

"Let's go," Phineas said. "If we ask Gifford not to tell anyone we left, he won't."

"Wait! How are we going to get to the baron's house?"

Phineas shrugged. They sat with their heads in their hands, dangling their feet out of the open cabinet door, thinking.

"I know!" Percy said. "We run toward the village and hope somebody will see us and give us a ride to the baron's house."

Phineas elbowed his brother in the ribs. "That'll take too long. You know what you have to do, Percy."

Percy's eyes widened, and for a moment he didn't move. Then, as if he'd just decided, he nodded. "We'll ask Gifford to saddle Honey for us. Prudence always said she was a gentle mare."

"I'm proud of you, Percy," Phineas exclaimed. "I know you're afraid of horses. We'll both be brave and risk punishment, borrowing a horse without permission, and riding all the way to the baron's house to tell Garahan."

They quietly closed the cabinet door behind them and looked both ways before slipping into the hallway. The brothers ran out of the back door before anyone was the wiser. When they reached the stables, the boys were frantic, until they saw Gifford coming in through the side door.

"What are you two up to?" the stable master asked.

"We've got to save her!" Percy said.

"We have to tell Garahan!" Phineas said at the same time.

"Hold on, just a minute—" Gifford began, only to be interrupted by Percy. "We can't!"

"They're going to pay someone to steal her," Phineas said. "What if the man hurts her?"

It only took a few minutes for the stable master to decipher what the twins were trying to say. "Miss Barstow…er Mrs. Garahan is in danger?"

"Yes!" the boys shouted simultaneously. "Can you please saddle Honey for us?" Percy asked. "We have to warn Garahan."

Gifford's jaw dropped at the question. "But you're afraid of horses, Percy."

"I can't help it," the boy whined.

"We're both going to be brave," Phineas added. "'Cause we have to help Cousin Prudence."

"Wait right here, boys. I'll get the tack, and you can help me saddle Honey."

A few minutes later, Gifford returned leading the docile mare over to where the boys waited. He let them help, then boosted Phineas up onto her back first—he would be holding the reins—and Percy second.

"Whatever you do, keep Honey to a fast walk," Gifford warned. "Though you boys are brave, it's not safe for the two of you to be riding double and galloping all the way over to Summerfield Chase." The boys agreed as Gifford handed Phineas the reins, cautioning Percy to hold tight to his brother. "Are you ready?"

The brothers were quick to assure the stable master they were. He led them out of the stables, checking in all directions before letting go of Honey's bridle. "Be careful," he said. "Be safe!"

As soon as the boys reached the road that would lead them to the baron's house, Phineas hollered, "Hang on, Percy! We're gonna ride like the wind!"

Percy clung to his brother's back as the mare obliged and picked up the pace until they were racing over the road, clinging like a pair of burs to the horse and each other.

They were within sight of the baron's home when they heard a horse coming up fast behind them. Afraid their father had sent one of the footman after them, they urged more speed from Honey, until they heard a deep voice call out, "Ye'll break yer fool necks if ye don't slow down!"

"Garahan?" Phineas said.

He caught up with the boys and urged the mare to slow down, before grabbing hold of her halter. "What in blazes were ye two chasing after, and why are ye out when yer ma told me just two days ago that ye had a stomach ailment and couldn't visit with yer cousin?"

"Prudence wants to see us?" Phineas asked.

"She didn't scale that oak, and get caught in the branches, because she was after taking in the view, lad."

"But Mum told us she never wanted to see us again," Percy said.

Garahan frowned. "She wouldn't have jumped into the pond after ye if she never wanted to see ye again, lad."

"Mum doesn't always tell the truth," Phineas confided.

"'Specially about Prudence," his brother added.

"Where are ye headed, lads?"

"To warn you," Phineas replied.

"Yeah," Percy added, "we heard Mum telling Father about her plan to pay someone to steal Prudence from you."

"We don't want anyone to take her away," Phineas said. "You'll protect her."

"Won't you?" Percy asked.

"I will. Ye have me word, lads." Letting go of their horse, Garahan told Phineas to follow him to Summerfield Chase. "Me wife should be in the kitchen with Mrs. Green right about now.

She'll be practicing baking me favorites. Ye'll stay for tea then, lads. Won't ye?"

"Will there be teacakes or scones?" Percy asked.

Garahan chuckled. "Both, I imagine. Let's find out."

A short time later, they arrived. Garahan dismounted, handed his reins to the stable master, and turned to help the boys down. "Ye remember the baron's stable master, lads. Old Ned will ye take good care of—what's yer mare's name again, lads?"

"Honey!" the twins replied.

"She looks sweet as can be," the stable master said with a grin. "I'll take good care of her for you."

Garahan and the boys had started to walk away, when Old Ned called out to Garahan, "I just remembered—your wife rode into town with one of the maids. She said it was urgent, to tell you she had an escort, and they'd be back in time for tea."

GARAHAN'S HEART FELT as if it slammed against his rib cage. He rubbed at the deep ache. *She'd given her word not to leave.* "A maid is not a proper escort!"

The stable master nodded. "Your wife insisted that I remind you the matter was urgent, Garahan, and that she didn't go alone."

Garahan ground his teeth together, accepting that she hadn't ignored his dictate entirely. He bent down and told the boys, "Go into the kitchen and fetch whoever ye see first, O'Malley, Flaherty, or his lordship!"

"What do we tell him?" Percy asked.

"What ye've told me—hurry, lads!" Garahan urged as he turned to the stable master. "Let me have Duncan's reins. We haven't ridden far or hard yet today." He held the sides of his horse's face in his hands. "Have we, lad? But ye'll give it all ye've got so we can find me wife, won't ye?"

Duncan lifted his head and snorted.

"There's a lad," Garahan said, mounting his horse. "Did me wife say what they were after in the village?"

"Another rumor and a visit with the blacksmith's daughter and the vicar's daughter," Old Ned replied.

Garahan thanked the stable master, pressed his thighs against his horse's sides, leaned close to his ear, and commanded, "Give it all ye've got, lad!"

Horse and rider took off like a shot, with Duncan's long, strong legs eating up the distance between Summerfield Chase and the village. Garahan's training kicked in, as he cleared his mind of worry and focused on finding his wife. Praying he'd find her sitting in the parlor at the vicarage, or in the blacksmith's home, he let go of the fear curdling in his gut.

CHAPTER TWENTY-FIVE

BY THE TIME he reached the vicarage, all thoughts of finding his wife cozily chatting with the young women evaporated. The blacksmith and the vicar ran toward him.

"Our girls!" the vicar said.

"They've stolen our girls and your wife!" the blacksmith told him.

Garahan clenched his jaw to keep from shouting and quietly asked, "Tell me what happened—one at a time."

The blacksmith spoke first. "A large carriage drove into the village, stopping at the inn. My Olivia and the vicar's daughter were going to meet your wife at the inn and walk back here to have tea with Mrs. Chessy."

The vicar nodded. "When the hour grew late, I told my wife not to worry, that I'd take a walk down to the inn to see what was keeping them, and that's where I ran into Coleman."

"The carriage was gone by then, wasn't it?" Garahan asked.

"Aye," the blacksmith answered. "But I can tell you there were four matched grays pulling that carriage. They looked as if they'd ridden a fair distance and could use the rest."

Garahan's spirits lifted. He could catch up to them at the inn in the nearby village, a short distance away. "Did anyone notice the direction they drove off in?"

The vicar shook his head.

"They were headed south," Coleman told Garahan. "I was about to ride out after them."

"How long ago did they leave?"

"Not more than half an hour ago," the blacksmith replied. "I'm going with you."

"I will too," the vicar said.

Garahan locked gazes with the blacksmith. "Coleman, I need ye to stay behind and tell the others what happened and which direction I've gone in."

The blacksmith hesitated, then agreed.

"Vicar, I'll need ye to stay behind to calm yer wife, and the lads, if they don't listen and come looking for their cousin."

Vicar Chessy's worried look changed to one of determination and purpose. "I will see to it they do not follow you. Is anyone else accompanying you?"

"Faith, it's yer lucky day, Garahan," O'Ghill said as he rode up. "Seems I'll be saving yer *arse* once again."

Relief filled Garahan. "I'll be grateful later. They've taken Olivia Coleman, Melanie Chessy, and my wife." He turned to the blacksmith. "Did anyone see them being forced into the carriage?"

Coleman shook his head. "Nay. The girls and your wife rushed over to the carriage. The hostler said they appeared worried about whoever was inside."

"No cries for help after they were inside the carriage?"

"None."

O'Ghill spoke up. "They were silenced. Had to be at least three men inside the coach to keep the women from crying out."

Garahan thought it over. "A weapon pointed at one of the women might also guarantee their silence. We'll see when we catch up to them. We're heading south, O'Ghill."

"I've got yer back," his cousin promised.

The two men rode like the devil was nipping at their heels. "We've got to gain as much ground as possible," Garahan shouted. "Watch for signs that the carriage turned off when we get to the crossroads."

"Ye've done this before," O'Ghill said.

"Too many times to count," Garahan replied.

They were silent as they rode in the direction the carriage was last seen traveling.

The trail was easy to follow. It had rained the night before. Garahan broke the silence. "There's another inn not far from here."

"I know if it, as I stayed there before arriving in time to aid me favorite cousin perform a rescue—the first time," O'Ghill said. "What do ye know about the captors?"

"They could be had for a bag of coin," Garahan answered. "I'm not sure who they are, or where the squire's wife found them. The lads rode double to track me down, telling me they overheard their parents talking about paying someone to steal me wife!"

"Bloody, buggering bastards!"

Garahan nodded at his cousin. "Me thoughts exactly. Why would they have taken the young ladies, too?"

"The possibility of demanding more coin for their safe return?" O'Ghill said, before falling silent. He urged more speed out of his horse, alerting Garahan that his cousin had thought of something dire.

"What are ye thinking?"

"They might not be after coin as much as the fair-faced lasses they stole, along with yer beautiful wife."

"They'd best not have laid one hand on me wife's head, or I'll cut out the bastard's black heart!"

They slowed to a fast trot as they approached the village and headed toward the inn. O'Ghill glanced at the saber his cousin wore and said, "It'd be quicker just to run him through."

"Not nearly as satisfying as making the bloody blackguard pay for stealing me wife and those two young lasses. Ye probably know them better than I do, having spent time in the village working as Coleman's apprentice."

"They're fresh-faced, young lasses," O'Ghill told him. "Both just six and ten. They have their whole lives ahead of them, yet in the last month have had their reputations shredded—and now this."

"Aye," Garahan agreed. "If the information we've gathered is correct, it was by someone who used to claim to be the cream of the local society—the jealous, bloody witch! The talk will linger long after we've proven the rumors to be lies. Tainted by that woman's lies, how will either of their das be able to arrange a marriage for them?"

O'Ghill didn't answer right away. He reined in his mount alongside Garahan's as they arrived at the inn. "Who knows what the Lord has planned for the lasses? Let's see what we can find out—" He stopped cold when Garahan's hand gripped his arm.

"There's four matched grays being rubbed down over there." Garahan pointed to the large barn at the back of the inn yard. "Do ye see the stable lads changing horses?"

The men saw the carriage at the same time. With a slight nod, Garahan indicated he'd approach from the left, while O'Ghill approached from the right.

With a whispered word, and a bit of coin, the hostler told them the coachman and a gentleman had told him to change the horses and have the carriage ready to leave in half an hour. "Where are the ladies traveling with them?" Garahan asked.

"I thought the man traveled alone," the hostler answered. "Why do you want to know?" Garahan reached into his waistcoat pocket, but the man stopped him. "I recognize the Celtic harp over your heart—it's the insignia of the duke's guard. You work for the Duke of Wyndmere. He's traveled through here more than once. Honest man."

"Aye. Then ye know the only reason I'd be asking after the ladies is if they were in danger."

The hostler nodded and pulled the blunderbuss from his waistband, signaling to two men, who rushed over at the sight of the weapon. "Trouble, Marks?" one asked.

"Aye, we may need your assistance. Stand ready, men."

Garahan led the way over to the carriage, surprised when he heard a loud thud and watched the carriage sway. "Lass, are ye in there?"

The muffled cry had him yanking open the carriage door. He reached inside and grabbed hold of the first man's throat, tossing him on the ground. "Get yer bloody hands off me wife!" he roared as a second man groped the lass while the two younger women's muffled sobs echoed within the confines of the coach.

O'Ghill pulled open the door on the opposite side, yanked the man's head back, and held a knife to the man's throat. "Ye'll listen to me cousin and let go of his wife, or I'll be forced to slit yer throat from ear to ear." With a nod to the lasses, he advised, "Ye'll be wanting to turn yer heads and close yer eyes."

"What in the bloody hell are you men doing in my private coach!" a deep voice demanded.

The hostler pointed his blunderbuss at the man's face and ordered him, "Don't move, or I'll be forced to shoot."

"Do you know who I am?" the man asked.

At that moment, the hostler's stable hands grabbed hold of the man, one on either side. "Nay, but I do know you'll want to explain why you are transporting these women against their will," the hostler said.

Garahan untied his wife's gag and the ropes that bound her hands behind her. The world stood still while he held her against his pounding heart, whispering a prayer of thanks that he'd reached her before she suffered more at the hands of her captors.

"I knew you'd find me," she said as she hugged him, then pushed against his hold. "Olivia and Melanie have already been through so much. They should not have been abducted along with me, but wanted to help the poor woman we were told was ailing inside the carriage."

Prudence untied the gag and the bonds holding the vicar's daughter, while Garahan did the same for the blacksmith's. Garahan looked over his shoulder in time to see his cousin's fist plow into the face of the man he'd threatened with his knife. O'Ghill looked up and nodded. "I'll have him trussed up like a goose in a moment. We can toss him in the empty stall with the one ye knocked out when ye tossed him out of the carriage on his head."

"He's lucky I didn't follow through with me intention." Garahan turned to the hostler and asked, "Do ye have a private room at the back of the inn, Marks? I'd rather not subject the women to any gossip while they collect themselves. I'll be needing to bring the man yer men have subdued, and the others, with us to Summerfield Chase to remand them into the custody of Constable Standish—after we question him."

"You and O'Ghill?" Marks asked.

"We'll be asking some of the questions," Garahan said. "Though I'll be leaving the bulk of it to his lordship, Baron Summerfield, and O'Malley, head of the Duke of Wyndmere's guard stationed at Summerfield Chase. I'm certain Standish will have questions of his own."

"I demand you thugs release me!"

No one paid attention to the owner of the carriage. The hostler nodded to Garahan. "You'll need to speak to our local constable—Frampton—to make those arrangements. I can help you with the room. Follow me." He paused and looked at the bedraggled state of the women. "Can they walk?"

"I can," Prudence said, with more gumption than Garahan had thought his wife would have after being kidnapped. Her voice sounded clear and unworried when she added, "I think Olivia hurt her foot when she kicked the man you tossed out of the carriage, Ryan. You might need to carry her."

"Ye kicked him, Olivia?"

The blacksmith's daughter nodded. "He already tied my hands behind my back, and then tied that nasty gag around my mouth." Her eyes filled as she told Garahan, "I kicked him when he grabbed Melanie by the front of her gown."

"I'll deal with him later," Garahan promised as he lifted Olivia in his arms. "What about you, Miss Chessy—can ye walk?"

Instead of answering as his wife and Olivia had, Melanie burst into tears, and would have crumbled into a heap if O'Ghill hadn't scooped her up in time. "Easy, lass, I've got ye. Ye have me word, on me cousin Garahan's thick head, that I'll not harm ye."

Following Marks, Garahan was relieved to see his wife walking as if she'd gone for a ride in the park, instead of in a carriage, against her will, after being abducted. He could not wait until they were alone and he could ply the truth of the ordeal from her. He knew she was putting on a brave face for the other lasses' sake. He could not have been prouder.

CHAPTER TWENTY-SIX

"COLEMAN TO SEE you, your lordship." Timmons stepped back to admit the blacksmith.

Summerfield rose and offered his hand to the man. "It's been a while, Coleman. What can I do for you today?"

The big man crushed his cap in his hands. "Garahan wanted me to tell you what happened and where he's gone."

The baron bellowed, "O'Malley!"

The head of his guard nearly collided with Summerfield when he stepped outside of his study. "I saw the blacksmith arrive and had a feeling it had to do with me cousin. What's happened?"

THEY HAD JUST closed the door when Lady Phoebe bolted down the staircase, her maid Beth right behind her. "I cannot believe my husband just shouted for O'Malley, and then closed the door without telling me what is happening!"

Wisely, her maid did not say a word.

"Does he think to keep important news to himself because he is a man, and I am a woman?" Phoebe demanded.

"I, um…have no idea."

She was incensed that, once again, one of the men in her life was trying to protect her—there had been a time when she had let them, after being held at knifepoint, but that was then. But this was now, and she would not tolerate it! "Wait here, Beth."

"You cannot just barge into his lordship's study. You will remember to knock, won't you?"

Phoebe's smile was overbright. She had no intention of barging anywhere. She'd get to the bottom of whatever was going on, with or without her husband's agreement!

Her footfalls did not make a sound as she crept up to the door. With great care, she placed her hands, and then her ear, on the door.

"Garahan's wife, my daughter, and the vicar's daughter were pulled into a black town coach—similar to yours, your lordship."

"Oh my Lord!" Phoebe turned to her maid and whispered, "Someone abducted Garahan's wife and the blacksmith and vicar's daughters!" She pulled away from the door. She had heard enough. She knew who was behind this atrocity, and was through being the solicitous Baroness Summerfield!

She grabbed Beth by the arm and pulled her toward the door to the servants' side of the house. She opened the door, tugged her maid across the threshold, then closed the door behind them.

"Where are we going?" Beth asked.

"Shush!" Phoebe hissed, dragging Beth past the kitchen and the rooms off the long hallway, then out the back door. When they were outside, she grabbed hold of Beth's shoulders and rasped, "If I have not returned in two hours' time, send O'Malley after me."

"But where are you going, your ladyship?"

"To end this once and for all!"

Her maid's eyes were round with fear. "End what?"

Phoebe struggled to remain calm, but the tale one of the scullery maids brought back from the village had been the truth: the squire's wife tried to get rid of her niece, had nearly let her die from the fever—and now this! "I'm going to confront that social-climbing excuse for a woman! If she thinks she's good *ton*, she has attics to let!"

"The squire's wife?"

"Yes! Don't you see? It all makes sense. There has been rumor after rumor since Marcus and I moved into Summerfield Chase. We've tried to rise above them, and ignore them, continuing our good works for our tenant farmers and those who live in the village. Yet the innuendo that began just a few months ago involving my dear friends and the duke's guard, and Marcus and me, was resurrected...and hit a new low. It was despicable, salacious gossip."

"I thought His Grace and his contacts put an end to the verbal attacks," Beth remarked.

"He did, and we thought that would be an end to it. But the rumors started up again—right here in Summerfield-on-Eden. I will not stand by idly while Garahan's wife—a woman I admire— and two innocent young women from our village are abducted!" Phoebe squared her shoulders and lifted her chin, vowing, "Heads will roll, Beth. Mark my words, that strumpet will pay for what she's done!"

"Your ladyship, wait! I'll go with you."

"No," Phoebe told her. "I need you to stay and tell O'Malley where I've gone. He'll remember the last time he had to follow me—I needed his help rescuing Marcus that time. I may need his help again."

The maid nodded, and Phoebe ran to the stables. A few moments later, she rode out on his lordship's beast of a stallion.

"Your ladyship!" Old Ned chased after her. "Wait!"

Marcus and O'Malley burst through the door behind the maid in time to see Phoebe tearing down the road. "Is that my wife riding St. George?" Marcus demanded.

Old Ned's shoulders slumped. "Lady Phoebe said she had your permission to ride the stallion, your lordship."

The baron ignored the stable master, asking the maid, "Where is she going?"

Beth wrung her hands and glanced from the baron to

O'Malley and back. "She said I was to tell O'Malley—"

"Answer the bloody question!"

The maid took a step back. "To confront the squire's wife."

Summerfield barked, "Saddle my hor—Bloody hell, she *took* my horse. Saddle one of the geldings. O'Malley, you come with me. Where's Flaherty?"

"'Tis his shift riding the perimeter. He should be returning any min—He's right over there!"

O'Malley whistled, and Flaherty leaned low over his horse, galloping toward them. He dismounted on the fly, asking, "What's happened?"

"His lordship and I are going after her ladyship," O'Malley replied.

The baron told the blacksmith, "I need you to stand guard with Flaherty until we return, Coleman. Trust that Garahan will return with Olivia, Melanie, and his wife."

Coleman nodded. "Before Garahan left with O'Ghill, he asked the vicar to stay at the vicarage in case he was needed, and asked me to ride out here to tell you and the others what happened."

Summerfield laid his hand on Coleman's shoulder. "Thank you. I'll wager we'll see Garahan in a few hours."

"He should have caught up to the carriage by now," the blacksmith said. "He and O'Ghill were on horseback."

The stable master approached with their mounts. Summerfield and O'Malley mounted and took off.

Flaherty frowned. "They're headed to the squire's home, aren't they?"

"Aye. Apparently, her ladyship borrowed his lordship's stallion."

"St. George?" Flaherty asked. "She'll be hearing an earful when the baron catches up to her. Fill me in, Coleman. We may need to send one of the footman for the constable."

The blacksmith wasted no time in relaying what he knew.

Flaherty sighed. "Her ladyship taking off on her own will no doubt remind his lordship about that time she received the ransom note."

"Ransom note?" Coleman asked.

"'Tis a long story for another time—after we settle matters here. Constable Standish was following another lead, but he should have returned by now. With the information he was tracking down, we should have enough damning evidence to confront the person behind the attack on the baron and baroness. We'd best have Timmons send one of the footmen to the village. Standish will expect us to keep him informed."

Coleman offered to stand guard outside while Flaherty spoke to the butler, but Flaherty had other ideas. "Beth, lass, will ye fetch Timmons for us?"

"Yes, of course," the maid replied. "I hope her ladyship doesn't come to harm."

Flaherty asked, "Did she have her brass paperweight or ribbon-wrapped hatpins with her?"

The maid shook her head.

"Ribbon-wrapped hatpins?"

"Another long story," Flaherty told Coleman. "Fetch the butler. Hurry, lass."

Beth rushed into the house, and they could hear her shouting for Timmons. A few moments later, three footmen were charged with standing guard, while Timmons sent a fourth to fetch the constable.

Flaherty armed the footmen and sent the men to guard the perimeter. He and Coleman would remain by the stables that faced the road leading to the squire's home. "I hope her ladyship doesn't resort to violence."

The blacksmith whipped his head around to face Flaherty. "But she's such a tender-hearted, soft-spoken lady. How could you even think that?"

Flaherty snorted. "Ye don't know her ladyship like I do. Threaten her husband, one of the family, or her friends, and she'll go for yer throat. 'Tis an honor to be assigned to guard the baron and baroness." Coleman's expression had Flaherty nodding. "Ye understand, then, why his lordship and O'Malley rode out of here ready to avert disaster."

The other man nodded. "I'll have to stop judging a person by their appearance."

"'Twas one of the first lessons I learned after joining the duke's guard. Every one of the Lippincott men—and those related with Lippincott blood from their mother's side—married a strong woman who would fight to the death to guard their husband's back."

"Admirable trait in a wife," the blacksmith admitted. "My wife was like that."

"Then ye know and appreciate that sometimes 'tis more work to guard one of their wives than their lordships."

Coleman had a faraway look in his eyes. "Aye, but I wouldn't have had it any other way."

Flaherty inclined his head. "Neither would His Grace or their lordships."

CHAPTER TWENTY-SEVEN

PHOEBE RODE STRAIGHT up to the front steps of the squire's home, dismounted, and pounded on the front door.

Samuels opened the door with a frown on his face. "What is the meaning—Oh, do forgive me, your ladyship. I had no idea it would be you banging on the door."

"I'm here to inform the squire's wife that we have all of the proof we need she is the one recirculating old rumors with the intent to discredit my husband's reputation and my own."

The butler's face drained of all color. "Won't you come in? I'm quite certain Mrs. Honeycutt, or the squire, would wish to speak to you."

"I'll not set foot in this den of iniquity! Tell her that we know she arranged to have Mrs. Garahan abducted, along with Miss Coleman and Miss Chessy! I want to see her face when she boldly denies any knowledge of the heinous crime!"

The butler disappeared inside, and she turned to stroke the stallion's blaze. "I won't stop you if you want to take a little nip out of her." When she turned around, the squire was glaring at her. "Oh, good. You'll want to hear this too, squire. By now my husband has sent for the constable. With the proof the duke's guard has gathered, and the conversations that have been shared with us, we have more than enough proof to charge your wife."

"With what?" the squire demanded.

Phoebe smiled. "Verbal assault against an upstanding member of the *ton*, who happens to be related to the Duke of Wyndmere, along with the abduction of the wife of one of the duke's personal guard and with two young women from our village."

She had the distinct pleasure of seeing the squire's face flush crimson. His mouth opened and closed, reminding her of a well-fed trout. An odd gurgling sound emerged until he snapped his mouth shut. He closed the distance between them, bellowing, "Get out of my house!"

Unaffected by his anger—or his intimidation tactics—she tilted her chin up and met his glare with one of her own. "I am not *in* your house."

"Get off my steps! Leave my property at once!"

She would later swear she saw steam coming out of his ears as he lifted his arm. Unease slithered through her. Did the bacon-brained squire intend to push her? St. George reared up on his hind legs and let out an ear-piercing shriek.

The squire stumbled backward, ending up on his backside. Phoebe kissed the horse between his eyes. "My hero. Thank you, St. George."

Her mistake was turning her back on the man. The blow to the back of her head stunned her—but not the stallion. He struck out at the squire with his front hooves, and the man's high-pitched scream had the stable master, two footmen, and the butler trying to grab hold of the horse's reins.

Phoebe thought she heard Marcus whistle the three-note call he always used to summon St. George, but her vision started to gray as the pounding pain at the base of her skull made itself known.

She felt as if she were floating, and then something wrapped around her, keeping her prisoner. She tried to fight her bonds, but the gray shifted to black as darkness pulled her under.

MARCUS HELD HIS wife against his heart and shouted, "Who in the bloody hell struck my wife?"

The squire grabbed hold of the fireplace poker his wife held. "Good God, Hortencia, what have you done?"

His wife glared at him, refusing to answer.

O'Malley reached past the baron and lifted the overweight man by the throat. "Did ye hand that poker to yer wife after ye struck her ladyship?"

The squire finally tore his gaze away from his wife, meeting O'Malley's eyes, but he, too, refused to answer.

"Ye'd best be answering the baron before ye meet yer maker, though I doubt he'll have ye or yer black soul."

Samuels stepped forward and placed a hand on O'Malley's arm. "You won't kill the squire. With all of these witnesses, even the duke would not be able to save you."

The squire was struggling to breathe, clawing at O'Malley's hand squeezing his throat.

"I'm thinking the squire has a few minutes left on this earth. We can wait for the guilty party to step forward."

No one spoke, though more than one of the servants dared a glance at the squire's wife, confirming O'Malley's suspicions. He reached into his waistcoat pocket and handed his handkerchief to the baron. "This'll help stanch the blood, yer lordship."

The baron seemed to snap out of the trance he was in, holding his bleeding wife in his arms. "Good God," Summerfield rasped, "what if she loses our babe?" He handed his wife to O'Malley, who waited for the baron to mount his horse before carefully handing Lady Phoebe to him. "Leave these two to the constable," he said. "He'll be charging the squire and his wife with attempted murder. If she loses the babe, it will be a double murder!"

O'Malley stared at one staff member after another. "Anyone

willing to speak up and tell the truth will not be implicated in the crime." Then he mounted his horse, quickly catching up to the baron. "I'll ride ahead and let Mrs. Chauncey and Mrs. Green know what happened. Trust them to take care of Lady Phoebe until I return with Dr. Higgins."

Summerfield glanced down at the woman in his arms. "They will pay for striking my wife. I'll strangle the squire myself if she loses our babe."

"And I'd be standing at yer side as yer witness, proclaiming that justice has been served, yer lordship," O'Malley replied.

BY THE TIME O'Malley returned with the physician, Phoebe was sitting on her husband's lap at the kitchen table.

"Well now," O'Malley said as he entered the kitchen. "I can see that her ladyship had us worried for naught. How do ye feel, yer ladyship?"

"Like someone bashed the back of my head with a lead pipe."

"I'm sorry we didn't arrive sooner," O'Malley apologized.

"If my wife hadn't taken it upon herself to ride out unprotected, against my strictest rule, and taken St. George to boot," the baron said, "we would not be sitting here waiting for the good doctor to sew her head back together."

Lady Phoebe snorted. "Our positions would be reversed, and Dr. Higgins would be about to sew your head back together."

"I'm thinking it would be me own hard head that would be in need of a cold cloth," O'Malley said. "Faith, if the squire or his wife clocked me on the back of the head, I'd have a lump—not a gash."

"If you think for one minute—*Mmmpfh.*"

The baron ended the conversation by kissing his wife. "Now then, wife, do be quiet." He glanced over his shoulder at Dr. Higgins. "Please excuse the upheaval. My wife has been in high dudgeon since she opened her eyes."

"How long was she unconscious?" the doctor asked.

"A few moments, no more than that."

The physician nodded. "That will count in her favor. Now then, your lordship. We need to clear the room, leaving either Mrs. Chauncey or Mrs. Green to lend a hand."

The baron nodded to those gathered. "Thank you for coming to lend a hand. My wife and I are in your debt for acting so quickly."

One by one, the staff left to return to their posts. As Timmons was leaving, the baron asked, "Would you please check on Beth, Percy, and Phineas? I don't want them to know what happened at their home, and I bloody well do not want them to return there until matters have been settled. I do not trust the squire's wife not to take out her anger on her twins."

"Of course, your lordship. I will see to it that the boys do not end up in the middle of—"

The kitchen door swung open, and Percy and Phineas landed at the baron's feet. "We're sorry, Baron Summerfield. We didn't mean to listen, but we heard the raised voices when you came in and thought it was our cousin who was hurt. We're so sorry it was you, Lady Phoebe," Percy said.

"Did our mum really strike you?" Phineas asked.

"My back was turned, and I'm afraid I don't know who hit me. Thank you for worrying about me, boys," Phoebe replied.

The boys were about to rush over to the baroness when Flaherty placed one hand on Phineas's shoulder and the other on Percy's. "Now then, lads. We need to let the doctor patch up Lady Phoebe. Why don't ye come with me, and I'll take ye to speak to the hero of the day."

"But the baron's right here," Percy said.

"So is O'Malley," Phineas added.

"'Tisn't his lordship or me cousin O'Malley that is the true hero of the day—'tis St. George."

Both boys fell silent as their eyes rounded with wonder. "His lordship's horse?" Percy asked.

"Aye. We heard the high-pitched battle cry St. George makes whenever he stands on his hind legs," the baron said.

"My husband's brave stallion thought he was protecting me," Phoebe added.

Before the boys could ask any more questions, Dr. Higgins said, "Everyone cease talking. The kitchen must be cleared. Her ladyship is far too pale to suit me."

"Yes, doctor," the boys said at the same time.

Flaherty nodded to O'Malley, who followed as Flaherty whisked the boys out of the way, then out the back door. "Well now," he said as he closed the door behind them. "I'm thinking St. George is waiting for his reward."

"For what?" Flaherty asked.

"For saving her ladyship. What do ye think, lads—should we give him a carrot or an apple?"

"Carrot," Percy said.

Phineas frowned at his brother. "An apple!"

"Mayhap he'd like it if you feed him a carrot, Percy. Then Phineas can feed him his dessert—the apple."

O'Malley waited until they were out of hearing range before returning to stand guard in the doorway to the kitchen. He resumed his position just inside the room in time to hear the physician ask Lady Phoebe if she felt any cramping.

"No. As a matter of fact, I haven't in quite some time. Why, do you—" She grabbed hold of her husband. "Marcus, do you think… I've been wondering… Is it possible?"

Summerfield brushed a lock of hair out of her eyes and pressed his lips to her forehead. "Aye, my love, given how we've been spending our evenings. I've been waiting for you to share your news with me. Now I understand why you haven't."

She leaned her forehead against her husband's shoulder as the doctor examined the wound at the back of her head. "Should I feel cramping so early on, Dr. Higgins?"

The physician asked for a pair of scissors before replying, "A greater number of my patients have not experienced any, but there are those that have. I need you to understand that I am not predicting what will happen, only apprising you of what may happen, your ladyship."

O'Malley clenched his fists as a tear trickled down Lady Phoebe's cheek. He sent up a silent prayer that their babe was unharmed.

"But I have been feeling twinges off and on for the last few days, which is why I had not considered that I may be carrying our babe." She shifted when the physician asked her to.

"I'll need to trim the hair away from the wound. Your ladyship has such thick hair, no one will notice." Working quickly, he began to cleanse the area he uncovered. "As to any twinges, as you have called them, I'm instructing you to remain in bed for at least a sennight. If, by the Grace of God, you have as strong a constitution as I believe you do, I will rescind that order and allow you to get up. But," he added, "if you do not follow my orders, you run the risk of losing your babe."

Tears filled her eyes, but she blinked them away. "I promise to do exactly as you say, Dr. Higgins. Is there anything else I should not do?"

"Complete bed rest," the physician said before meeting the baron's gaze. "Alone."

"No. I'll not let my wife lie awake through the night worrying that the worst will happen."

"But what if—" she began, only to be interrupted by her husband.

"Given that we are not alone in the room, Dr. Higgins is being circumspect and trying not to embarrass you. In a roundabout way, he is advising no intimacy between us until he feels you are out of danger of losing our babe. Isn't that right, doctor?"

"Thank you for explaining, your lordship," the physician said. "Now, if you would please hold your wife's head still for me, I'll add a few stitches. The gash is not as deep as we feared, but still needs to be closed."

A short while later, the physician departed, and the baron carried his wife upstairs. Flaherty returned with the lads, who bravely accepted the news they would be staying the night, with her ladyship's maid to watch over them.

O'Malley and Flaherty stood guard with the other footmen, waiting for Garahan's return.

CHAPTER TWENTY-EIGHT

GARAHAN IGNORED THE pain slicing through his gut and the pounding at the base of his skull to stare at their captives. The lass was safe. The blackguard's attempt to abduct his wife had failed. They'd garnered a bit more information after the innkeeper advised them that an Elliott Anderson had reserved a room at the inn a fortnight ago. The plan had been in place before Garahan married the lass! That it had been carried out after they'd wed was even more nefarious.

"Now then, Anderson, let's start again. This time without prevaricating. Admit ye forced me wife and two innocent lasses from our village into yer carriage."

"It is Lord Anderson, and I did not force the women. They voluntarily entered the carriage."

Garahan's heightened senses detected the faint scent of lilacs, and he knew his wife had entered the room behind him before he felt her hand on his forearm.

His wife moved to stand beside him and immediately contradicted the prisoner. "That's a lie. We heard what sounded like a woman hysterically sobbing inside his carriage, and we came to offer assistance."

"That's—"

O'Ghill had the man by the throat, cutting off his reply. "Ye'll not want to be casting aspersions on me cousin's wife—nor will ye be lying to me cousin. I might let him gut ye if ye do."

The man blinked as his face grayed. He looked from Garahan to O'Ghill and back. "I won't get paid if I reveal—"

Garahan reacted as if he'd been struck by lightning. He tucked his wife behind him and dove over the table, leading with his fist. *Coin?* The bloody bugger was worried about *payment?*

He didn't even feel the impact of the blows he pummeled Anderson with until O'Ghill pulled him off their prisoner, warning, "Ye can't kill the bugger until we get the information we need."

"Ryan, please listen to Killian," his wife implored. "We need to know who paid him to abduct me, and those other poor young women. I'm still in shock that what we thought was a woman in that carriage was actually a man with a high-pitched voice." When he did not answer, she added, "I'm very interested in hearing what the rest of the plan was."

"No, ye aren't, because there's some things best left unsaid. Besides, Anderson won't be speaking after I punch his teeth down his bloody throat."

The lass moved quickly—he had to give her that. She scooted in front of him, wrapped her arms around him, and whispered, "We need the information so you can take me home and hold me until the sun rises."

"*Mo ghrá*, I'd be doing far more than holding ye."

She brushed a kiss to his cheek. "I certainly hope so."

When she reached up and cupped the side of his cheek in her hand, his anger began to ebb. He looked into the depths of her eyes and saw his love for her reflected back at him. "Do ye remember the question ye asked me the night we were wed?"

Her face flushed a delightful shade of pink.

"We'll attend to that when we get home." He lifted her hand and kissed the back of it, lingering over each knuckle, pressing his lips to each one. Her sharp intake of breath pleased him, reminding him of the pleasures that awaited them. He turned her hand over, kissed her palm, and closed it. "Hang on to that kiss and return it to me once O'Ghill and I have finished here."

"I love you, Ryan."

"Faith, I depend upon it, lass, and love ye back." He nodded to the innkeeper, who stepped forward. "Please escort me wife back to the room where the lasses are waiting. She's given us the details we need for their side of the story."

"My pleasure. After you, Mrs. Garahan."

He waited until they left, then turned and stared at the disheveled man in front of him. Dark pleasure filled him as he noted the man's cravat was stained with blood from his broken nose, and one of his sleeves had been ripped off and now hung near his elbow. But what had him smiling was the trio of bruises along the man's jaw. "Ye'll tell me who offered ye coin, or ye'll be swallowing yer teeth."

O'Ghill mimicked Garahan's stance—arms crossed, feet spread, glaring at the man.

"Hortencia."

"Do she go by one name only?" Garahan asked.

"Honeycutt."

Garahan and O'Ghill leaned toward the man from opposite sides, as Garahan asked, "Squire Honeycutt's wife?"

Anderson nodded. "She'll never pay me the rest now."

Red dots danced before Garahan's eyes as the lid blew off his temper. He growled and lunged for the man, but O'Ghill intercepted him. "We have his confession, and the name of the mastermind behind the kidnapping of yer wife. I'm thinking the man's an *eedjit* and has no idea of your connection to His Grace."

"He'll be a dead man if ye move to the side, O'Ghill."

"You know a duke?" Anderson asked.

Garahan scoffed. "Saved His Grace's life—and that of his family—more than once. I'm one of the Duke of Wyndmere's trusted personal guard. So, aye, ye could say I know His Grace."

Anderson slumped forward until his head hung a few inches above the table.

"I take it this is news to ye," O'Ghill said.

Their prisoner's head shot up, and anger blazed in his eyes. "She never once mentioned that the chit was married—nor did her mother. Neither of them mentioned a connection to the duke."

"That's Mrs. Garahan to ye. What's this about her mother?" Garahan asked. "Best tell us all ye know—it'll save time and questioning once the constable arrives, and when you're facing his lordship and the head of the duke's guard at Summerfield Chase. 'Twill be up to our Constable Standish how quickly ye make the journey from Summerfield-on-Eden to London."

"Apparently, Mrs. Barstow's father was a baronet of some importance." Anderson met Garahan's gaze and said, "Mrs. Barstow has aspirations of obtaining social standing through her other daughters. Hence the plan she and her sister, Mrs. Honeycutt, hatched to have Miss Barstow—"

"That's me wife," Garahan reminded him.

"You were not married when the arrangements were made."

"Give us the details, Anderson," O'Ghill ordered the prisoner.

"I was to coerce—or kidnap—her youngest daughter, Prudence, and marry her over the anvil in Scotland."

"In Gretna Green?" O'Ghill asked, and the man inclined his head.

Garahan curled his hands into fists. The need to beat the man ate away at his control. He stared at Anderson until the man's fear began to show. Garahan capitalized on that fear, asking, "She wasn't supposed to arrive in Scotland with her virtue intact, was she? Was it part of the plan to leave her there after ye denied that ye violated her?"

Anderson hesitated before he said, "I changed my mind once I saw her."

"Ye filthy, lying—"

O'Ghill shouldered Garahan aside. "Shut yer gob. I'll take it from here. What did ye plan to do with Mrs. Garahan?"

"Her beauty ensnared me," Anderson confessed. "I planned to make her my mistress. Mrs. Honeycutt and Mrs. Barstow would never have found out. They would have paid me double for compromising her, and—"

O'Ghill grunted as he was shoved aside. Garahan planted his fist beneath Anderson's chin, lifting him out of the chair and into the wall behind the table.

The door opened, and a deep voice proclaimed, "I see you've finished questioning Lord Anderson."

Garahan cracked his knuckles and sighed. "I have. Constable Frampton?" The man nodded, and Garahan said, "He's all yours, constable."

"Normally I would hold you for questioning, as it appears you have beaten an upstanding member of society into uncon-sciousness. However, after receiving an urgent missive from Baron Summerfield, I'm inclined to listen to his advice, as there is a connection here to a more serious matter."

"What could me more important than the abduction of me wife and two young women from Summerfield-on-Eden?"

"The attempted murder of Baroness Summerfield."

Shock reverberated through Garahan. "What's happened? How is Lady Phoebe?"

"I'll relay everything I was told, but am to assure you she will make a full recovery."

Garahan raked a hand through his hair. "As I've been assigned by the duke to protect his sister and brother-in-law, I need to know what happened."

"Apparently, she was struck from behind. The guilty party has not confessed, but the baron has been informed by a few witnesses that it was Mrs. Honeycutt."

"How badly was she injured?" O'Ghill asked.

"Compared to some head wounds I've seen over the years, relatively minor. From what the baron indicated, they will not lose their babe. O'Ghill, how are you involved in all of this?"

"Babe? O'Ghill, we have to leave now!" Garahan interrupted. "I'll never forgive meself that Lady Phoebe was injured in my absence."

Frampton moved to block the doorway. "Not so fast. You will answer my questions, then you may leave."

"I'm visiting me cousins Garahan, O'Malley, and Flaherty," O'Ghill told him.

Anderson stirred, and the constable walked over and pulled him to his feet. "I had planned to keep you overnight, Anderson, and leave for London in the morning. However, Garahan has convinced me that you are to be questioned by Baron Summerfield and the head of the duke's guard at his home. Constable Standish will be escorting you to London."

Frampton nodded to Garahan and O'Ghill. "I'll join you and the ladies in the back room to hear what occurred earlier, after I secure this man with the others in the stable. My men will guard him while we eat. The innkeeper's wife makes the tastiest mutton stew."

"We'll accompany ye and fill ye in," Garahan said.

"Tell me what happened."

Garahan relayed the events, with O'Ghill filling in any blanks.

Anderson bellowed Garahan's name.

Garahan turned around. "What do ye want?" The knife Anderson had buried in his side burned like a son of a bitch. "Ye bloody bugger!"

Frampton's men held Anderson while O'Ghill ripped off his coat and folded it up to press it against Garahan's side after removing the weapon. The prisoner was bound hand and foot—and gagged—and then tossed into the empty stall.

"How bad is it, Killian?" Garahan asked.

His cousin didn't hesitate to answer, "'Tis a paltry flesh wound. Nothing to worry over." He pressed harder. "Why don't ye lean on me? Yer darling wife will be wondering what's keeping us from dining with them."

"Ye make it sound as if we're traveling together and have stopped to eat."

O'Ghill chuckled and replied, his voice sounding strained, "That we have, ridden side by side all the way from Summerfield

Chase." When Garahan's legs gave out due to blood loss, O'Ghill tossed him over his shoulder. With one hand pressed to his cousin's wound and the other to his back to keep him from slipping out of his grip, O'Ghill sprinted toward the back of the inn.

"The physician is likely still here," the constable told him. "Take Garahan to the room two doors down from the women."

"Get that doctor in here now!" O'Ghill swept his arm across the large table in the room before laying his cousin out on it. "Garahan, open yer eyes!" His cousin moaned. "Ryan, lad, yer wife will be here any minute. Open yer eyes to tell her yer wound isn't serious."

"Ye're irritating the *shite* out of me, O'Ghill. Don't let me wife in here until ye tell me the truth. I've lost an important chunk of me innards, haven't I?"

O'Ghill was laughing when the door burst open, but it wasn't the physician standing in the doorway.

⤞⤜

"WHAT'S GOING ON in here?" Prudence demanded, pinning her husband with a determination that wavered at the sight of his blood. Dear Lord, it was everywhere! "Does he have any left, Killian?"

"Any what?" the man asked, keeping the pressure on Ryan's side.

"Blood! What happened to him?"

"I can speak for meself," Ryan rasped.

Prudence hiked up her skirts and ripped the bottom off her chemise. Folding it until it was thick enough, she rushed to her husband's side, makeshift bandage in her hands, and whispered to Killian, "We'll need more bandages."

He hesitated only a moment to lift his own makeshift bandage aside so that she could press the material to her husband's side. At Ryan's sharp intake of breath, she apologized, "I'm so sorry if this hurts, *mo ghrá*, but we have to stop the bleeding."

"I'll be right back," Killian promised.

"Ryan, can you hear me?" she asked.

"Aye, lass," Ryan replied.

"Don't you dare bleed to death on me! I'm not finished with you!"

He snorted and immediately groaned. "Have pity on me, lass, and don't make me laugh—it hurts too much."

"How deep is the knife wound?" the physician asked, entering the room with the constable.

Prudence shook her head. "I only had enough time to take O'Ghill's place, keeping pressure on my husband's wound." Blowing a strand of hair out of her eyes, she added, "I think it's slowing down." She ignored the pain in her belly as she glanced at her blood-covered hands pressed against Ryan's side. "O'Ghill is fetching more linens for bandages." Tears welled in her eyes and spilled over. "I'm so happy you are still here, Dr. Lumington. I'll do whatever you need—except leave the room."

Killian returned with a stack of clean linen strips in time to observe the physician wash and dry his hands and approach Ryan with a thick wad of linen in his hand. "When I tell you to move, do so quickly, Mrs. Garahan."

"Of course."

"Move!"

Prudence got out of the way, and only left Ryan's side long enough to wash and dry her hands. She noticed a flask on the table near the washstand and picked it up. When Killian looked her way, she nodded to him, relieved that her prediction held true—the bleeding had slowed considerably. There had been so much blood, she worried that the knife had hit something vital.

She locked her knees when they started to give out, resolving not to fall into a heap now, promising herself she could weep later—after the physician cleansed and closed the wound.

"Lass?"

"I'm right here, Ryan."

Anticipating his promise not to leave, she brushed her fingertips across his brow.

"Be sure to close the door behind ye on yer way out."

"I am not leaving!"

"Lass, I've been stabbed before, and know when a wound is serious. I'll not have ye smacking yer lovely face on the side of the table when ye faint at me feet."

"I am not weak, and I am not leaving!"

Ryan closed his eyes. "O'Ghill, toss the lass over yer shoulder if ye have to, but I'll not have her back in here until me hide's been sewn back together."

"Me pleasure, boy-o."

Prudence lifted her chin and stood her ground. Killian wouldn't dare pick her up and throw her over his shoulder, would he?

O'Ghill grinned. "Faith, Garahan, ye've snagged yerself a woman worth keeping!"

"I'll have you know that I—Ooompf!" She could not believe Killian did what her husband asked him to do.

"Tell the lasses I'm fit and fine and will be ready to leave in an hour."

Killian chuckled until he closed the door behind them and set Prudence on her feet. Steadying her, he said, "Me cousin's a proud man, and is in considerable pain, lass. He'll not want ye to witness when they give him a bit of wood or leather strap to bite down on while the physician sews that gash closed. From how he bled, 'tis deep. Let him salvage his pride. 'Tis important to him, so it should be important to you."

Instead of arguing with him, Prudence flung her arms around Killian, buried her face against his chest, and sobbed.

"Ah, lass, don't worry about Garahan—he's been injured worse than this and pulled through."

She sniffed and loosened her hold, confessing, "We've only been married a few days. How am I going to survive if he gets hurt again?"

Killian wiped the tears from her face. "Ye will because ye love him, and ye'll understand 'tis because of his vow to the duke that he will stand strong no matter if he's faced with a saber, rifle, pistol, knife, lead pipe, or a blasted plank of wood. 'Tis part and parcel of what we're made of, lass."

"I can't live without him," she rasped.

"Well now, don't be burying the man before he's dead. Find the backbone I know ye possess and go wash the tears from yer face. Have a cup of tea, and ask for a wee bit of whiskey in it. It'll calm yer nerves so when ye return to yer husband's side, he'll see yer strong, beautiful self—and not the worried woman having a good cry."

"I'm not worried," she protested.

"Ah, that's better. Go wash up and have that tea."

She laid a hand on his arm and looked into his eyes. "I'm so glad you were here, Killian. I think I've finally found a family that will accept me for who and what I am."

He bent and pressed a swift kiss to her lips. "Count on it, lass. Now shut yer gob and wash yer face!"

She was laughing as she hurried to do as he asked. Gauging how long it might take to cut Ryan's clothes away, clean the wound, and stitch him back together, she realized she did not have to worry—or rush. Her husband was in good hands. It was important to clean up and return to apprise Olivia and Melanie of what had happened. They'd be worried otherwise.

As she reached for the round of lavender-scented soap, she sent up a prayer of thanks for her husband, his cousin, and the physician who would be saving Ryan's life.

Olivia and Melanie rushed over to her as she entered the room where they waited.

"Ryan was hurt, but he'll be fine, and insisted we be ready to leave in an hour, but I think it'll be a bit longer. O'Ghill suggested we add whiskey to our tea. I borrowed a flask I found on the side table in the room with Ryan."

As she joined the young women at the table, she asked, "One drop or two?"

They were laughing when Killian returned.

CHAPTER TWENTY-NINE

GARAHAN FELT LIKE he'd been run over by the duke's town coach. Dr. Lumington assured him that although the knife had gone deep, it missed any vital organs. He further explained the pain and difficulty drawing in a breath were due to two cracked ribs.

"Courtesy of O'Ghill," Garahan muttered. "He just had to toss me over his shoulder."

"And saved your life by applying pressure and moving you inside onto a clean surface instead of leaving you lying on the straw-covered floor of the stables," the doctor reminded him.

The bandages covering the wound and the ones to bind his ribs required Garahan to stand perfectly straight. A bit more difficult than he remembered.

The sound of boisterous laughter reached his ears as he reached for the door. He'd expected silence, maybe the sound of someone crying—his lovely wife, or one of the lasses who should have been worried about him.

He yanked the door open to bedlam. "What in the bloody hell is going on in here?"

Prudence rushed to his side and wrapped her arms around him before he could warn her not to press against his injury. He moaned, and she immediately let go. "Oh, Ryan! Forgive me. I'm so sorry. I was just so happy to see you standing, let alone walking without aid, that I lost my head."

He frowned, leaned close, and sniffed. "Have ye been drinking?"

She smiled and pressed her mouth to his. His brain scrambled at the intense and lavish kiss. He finally managed to untangle his tongue when his cousin remarked, "'Tisn't the lass's fault. I encouraged her to have a wee bit of whiskey in her tea." Olivia and Melanie giggled when O'Ghill stared at them. "I never meant for her to add it to *their* tea—they're only six and ten! What'll their fathers have to say when we bring them home?"

"That'll be on yer head, O'Ghill. Ye're the one who suggested the whiskey. I was occupied gritting me teeth while the physician jabbed me with a needle and thread, tugging one side of the knife wound to the other, sewing it shut."

O'Ghill was quick on his feet to catch the vicar's daughter when she gasped and floated toward the floor. "If ye hadn't nearly bled out, I'd be telling ye what a *fecking* pain in the *arse* ye are!"

Prudence's eyes brimmed with laughter. "Um…Killian, you just did."

He placed Melanie on a chair and started patting her hand. "Quit laughing, lass, and lend me a hand. 'Tis yer fault she's in such a state."

Garahan slowly smiled. "I'm thinking 'twas yers. Ye run at the mouth like a horse's *arse* when ye're rattled."

His cousin glared at him, and then Prudence, but she waved him away and sat beside the vicar's daughter.

"I've half a mind to leave ye to escort the women home. I've another cousin waiting for me to arrive in the Lake District—one who appreciates me."

"Please don't leave, Killian," the lass pleaded. "I'm worried about Ryan—what if something happens on the ride home?"

O'Ghill stared at Garahan. "'Tis all yer fault! Ye had to go and find the perfect woman to marry, and then draw me into the rest of yer troubles! I didn't ask for any of it!"

Garahan sighed. His cousin felt cornered. He knew what that

was like, as he'd been there more than once himself. "I could not have managed without ye, O'Ghill. We both know it. Forgive me temper. Dr. Lumington took me flask. I was looking for it, otherwise I'd have been here before now."

O'Ghill stared at Prudence. "I think I know where it ended up."

She giggled, and Garahan scrubbed a hand over his face. "If I hadn't given me vow to the duke—and another to me wife—I'd leave the lot of ye here with O'Ghill! 'Tis a bloody shame me own wife doesn't have an ounce of pity for what I've been through in the last two hours. Draining me flask and sharing it with two young ladies who, I'll wager, have never touched a drop of the cure in their lives."

O'Ghill strode over to stand beside him. "Ready to leave when ye are. We can send one of the baron's footmen to collect the ladies tomorrow when they are sober."

"We only had a few drops in our tea," Prudence insisted.

"How many cups of tea have ye had, then, wife?" Garahan asked.

She frowned. "From the first pot—or the second?"

Garahan rolled his eyes, ignoring the pain shooting up his side. "I can't leave the lot of ye here. God only knows what kind of trouble ye'll get into."

"We haven't caused any trouble, have we, Melanie?"

The vicar's daughter stopped staring at O'Ghill long enough to blink. "Not one bit."

"There, you see, darling? We've behaved like ladies."

The endearment smoothed the ruffles of his pride, and the jealousy he felt hearing his wife's laughter when she should have been by his side. He beckoned her to him, remembering he had asked her to stay with the women while the physician took care of him. "I'll have yer promise not to have one more drop of whiskey, nor will ye give any to the lasses."

"I wouldn't dream of it."

The sincerity in her gaze and the wisp of passion swirling in the depths of her blue-violet eyes had him sighing. "Ye'll be the death of me, lass."

She slid a hand around his neck and brought his lips to hers. "Not if I can help it."

He let his wife have her way, waiting for the tip of her tongue to seek his. He let his pent-up worry and desire free as he kissed her with the promise of the passion they would share... If he could just get her alone...in a room...with a key. They wouldn't need a bloody bed, as long as they could lock the world out for a few hours. He'd take her against the door—twice. Once with her back to the door and her hands above her head. Then a second time with her bounteous breasts pressed against the door, and her delightful *derrière* begging him to take a bite out of it, before he buried himself to the hilt, touching her womb as he thrust into her over and over.

He couldn't wait to teach his wife the delights of making love to her from behind. Just thinking of how deep he could go had him hard as stone. He swiftly ended the kiss before he embarrassed her in front of the young women and his cousin.

When he met his cousin's gaze over the lass's head, he nodded. O'Ghill's broad back had afforded them a few moments of privacy, shielding the younger women from a passion he doubted they were ready to observe. "'Tis not a long ride, but given the amount of tea ye ladies imbibed, I'm thinking ye best visit the necessary before we leave."

O'Ghill snorted at the indignant gasps from the lasses, saying, "'Tis a bodily function, lasses. Ye'll find that we Irish aren't so namby-pamby as ye English."

O'GHILL AND THE women were ready and waiting when Garahan and Constable Frampton approached, with the prisoners behind him. The constable directed the loading of his prisoners into an open wagon, positioning one of his guard on the bench and one in the back with the bound and gagged prisoners.

Garahan told the ladies, "Constable Frampton has sent an

urgent missive to his lordship and yer fathers, lasses. They will know ye're safe with O'Ghill and meself. Once ye're inside the carriage, ye can close yer eyes and rest all the way home."

Olivia and Melanie thanked the constable. Instead of walking away, Frampton approached Garahan. "I'll leave two of my men in charge until we get back. Given your recent injury, I have decided to ride along with another two of my men." He climbed onto the wagon and laid his rifle across his lap. "We'll follow you, Garahan."

"As soon as they arrive, Jakes and Rafferty will be driving. O'Ghill and I will be riding alongside the carriage."

As soon as the words were out of his mouth, Melanie and Olivia rushed over to Garahan and kissed his cheek, before kissing O'Ghill. "We are so grateful that you rescued us. If Prudence hadn't been with us..." Melanie said, then fell silent.

Olivia finished what her friend intended to say. "We would not have been as brave. Her courage strengthened ours. Thank you, Prudence."

Melanie nodded. "Thank you."

"Let's be on our way," Garahan said. "The innkeeper has offered two of the stable hands to accompany us. They will drop us at our destination, stay the night, and then drive the carriage back in the morning."

The hostler walked toward their group flanked by two wiry men who were holding the reins to Garahan and O'Ghill's geldings. "Jakes and Rafferty volunteered to drive the carriage after witnessing what happened earlier." The men handed the reins over to Garahan and O'Ghill, shook their hands, and nodded to the women.

"Thank ye, Marks," Garahan said. "Please tell the innkeeper we appreciate the loan of yer stable hands. 'Twill be an uneventful journey. We'll feed them and give them a place to sleep before sending them off in the morning."

"After they have a fine breakfast," his wife added.

"Aye. Mrs. Green has a way with scones that'll add a lift to yer day." Garahan pulled his wife close for a quick kiss before helping her and the young women into the carriage. He closed the door, leaned in, and warned, "No whiskey!"

The musical sound of his wife's laughter lightened his heart and took a bit of the edge off the pain shooting up his side. He knew a fever was common with a knife wound but hoped to avoid that possibility.

He and O'Ghill flanked the carriage, weapons at the ready, should they meet with any brigands on the road back to Summerfield-on-Eden.

By the time they reached the village, he was bone-weary, but strove not to show it. Their first stop was to deliver the prisoners to Constable Standish, where they would spend the night behind bars. The constable greeted the other lawman and frowned at the way Garahan was favoring one side. "Who shot you?"

"No one."

Standish stared at him. "Stabbed."

"Aye."

"Stitches?"

Garahan drew in a deep breath and forgot about his ribs. Holding a hand to his side, he answered, "A few."

"Probably cracked a rib or two."

"Two. Now leave off with the questions. I'm wanting to deliver the lasses to their families, go home, and—"

Prudence chose that moment to interrupt, "You have to excuse my husband, Constable Standish. I'm afraid Ryan's flask is empty, and I think he's looking forward to having a glass of whiskey when we arrive at Summerfield Chase."

Standish reached into his waistcoat pocket and pulled out his own flask. "Take mine. I won't need it tonight. I'll be guarding these men until you return with the baron and O'Malley in the morning."

"Thank ye, Standish," Garahan replied.

"If you ever find yourself tiring of getting shot at or stabbed, I could use a man like you."

Prudence wrinkled her nose and asked, "Wouldn't he run the risk of similar injuries working for you, Constable Standish?"

The constable was laughing as Garahan urged her back inside the carriage. "Let's take these poor lasses home."

His flask—having been emptied by his wife—was no longer on his mind. The weight of the constable's flask against his uninjured side would take the edge off the pain when he finally got his wife behind closed doors.

He sighed. That was another thing he had to address—their living situation. As a married man, he didn't want his wife sleeping with his cousins in their quarters in the stables. She deserved more than a room in the baron's home—although it was a grand room, to be sure. The lass had told him the baroness mentioned something about patience and waiting for a cottage to be built. He'd ask about it in the morning.

They pulled up in front of the blacksmith's house and were greeted by Coleman's booming laughter as his daughter launched herself into his arms.

He held her tight to him as he looked over her shoulder to Garahan and O'Ghill. "I'll never be able to thank you."

"Returning yer daughter to ye, safe and sound, is thanks enough," Garahan told him.

"Mayhap if ye could see yer way to keeping me on a few more days," O'Ghill said, "I'd be obliged to ye."

Coleman grinned. "I'll see you in the morning."

Their next stop was the vicarage. The vicar must have heard them coming, because he was waiting on the front steps, his lantern held high to dispel the dark. "Melanie?"

"Papa!" The vicar's daughter stumbled but caught herself as she rushed to her father's arms.

"We prayed that you would be unharmed."

The vicar looked at Garahan and O'Ghill for confirmation. Garahan nodded to Prudence. "Ye can thank me wife—she's the reason yer daughter and the blacksmith's daughter are unharmed. She kept their spirits up and, according to yer daughter, kept at their captors to focus the attention on her instead of the lasses."

"Thank you, Mrs. Garahan. From the bottom of my heart."

"I'm so sorry this happened in the first place," Prudence replied.

The tinge of guilt he heard in the lass's words hurt his heart. He wanted to help alleviate it, but the vicar spoke first. "Do not take on the guilt of another's actions," Chessy advised her. "I'm grateful you were there."

"Melanie!" Mrs. Chessy rushed out of the vicarage to embrace their daughter. Through her tears, she thanked the men and ushered her daughter and husband inside.

"Our next stop is Summerfield Chase," O'Ghill told the men driving the coach.

"Do you think we might have a bit of bread and something to wash it down with before we bed down for the night?" Jakes asked.

Rafferty snickered. "I'm hoping for a bit more than bread, but would be just as happy with a glass of whiskey."

Garahan chuckled. "I'll wager Mrs. Green will have prepared either a hearty stew or some of her meat pies for ye. I'll be happy to supply the whiskey. I have a small stash in the stables, where me cousins and I have our quarters."

"You work for the duke, are assigned to guard the baron and his wife, and you sleep in the stables?" Rafferty asked. "Doesn't seem like they appreciate you."

Garahan mounted his horse and started riding before he answered, "Me cousins—not O'Ghill here; he's only just arrived from home recently—O'Malley, Flaherty, and I choose to stay in the stables. We have four-hour shifts and rotate them daily. 'Tis easier all around to have quick access to our weapons, ammunition, and our horses."

"Well then, that makes sense. Let's move out," Jakes said before releasing the brake and clicking to the horses.

THOUGH THE HOUR was late, light flickered inside the baron's home, and the lanterns were still lit by the stables and barn. Garahan led the way, dismounting outside the stables. Rafferty set the carriage brake and hopped down. "We'll see to the horses first, then—"

"Past time you were home, Garahan. Let's put your horses to bed," Old Ned remarked while coming out of the door to the stables.

"Ye're back!" O'Malley strode over to where they stood. "Where's the lass?" Garahan winced as he reached for the carriage door, and O'Malley sighed. "Shot?"

Prudence stepped out of the carriage and wrapped her arm around her husband. "Stabbed. Let me help you to the kitchen, Ryan. I'm sure Mrs. Green has the herbs to reduce a fever handy."

Garahan stiffened. "I don't need any bloody herbs, lass, or help walking. You're the one who was forced against yer will into that bloody bugger's carriage! I should be assisting *ye* to our room."

From her expression, he realized he'd injured her feelings. The lass looked tired, and he suspected her head ached from too many splashes of whiskey in her tea.

Her reply confirmed it, as did the irritation in her voice. "Well, I'll leave you to your duties, then, shall I?" She spun around and rushed into the house.

Garahan started after her, but O'Ghill stepped in front of him. "After all yer wife has been through at Anderson's hands, ye show her the edge of yer temper instead of patience and understanding? If ye didn't take a blade to the side, I'd be knocking ye on yer *arse!*"

"What's this?" Flaherty asked, approaching his cousins. "Isn't it a bit late for a round of bare-knuckle?"

"Garahan's *bollocks* are in a twist over his getting stabbed," O'Ghill said. "He's taking it out on his wife."

"Why didn't ye escort her inside?" Flaherty asked.

"Because me *eedjit* cousins keep demanding answers to their *fecking* questions!" Garahan shoved O'Ghill and Flaherty out of his way and stormed after his wife.

CHAPTER THIRTY

HE BURST INTO the kitchen, holding on to his side, and asked, "Have ye seen me wife?"

The cook frowned at him and pointed to the door to the servants' staircase.

Knowing he needed to apologize, but wishing Prudence hadn't tried to coddle him in front of his cousins, he took the steps two at a time, wincing with each step. Reaching the top, he paused, wondering if the lass would try to see Lady Phoebe first, or head straight to the room they'd been using for the last few days.

He cocked his head to one side, listening for the sound of feminine voices. He heard them coming from the direction of the baron and baroness's bedchamber. Swallowing his pride, he strode toward the door, only to be forced to take a step back when Summerfield emerged.

"Garahan? I got the impression you'd be tied up for a while seeing that men from the inn received a hot meal and a place to bed down for the night. I take it Old Ned stabled the horses?"

"Aye, the stable master and both men were headed into the stables with our horses and the carriage team. O'Malley will ensure the men have a meal, while the others will stand guard. How is Lady Phoebe?"

The baron's shoulders slumped. "She's suffering from the

blow to the back of her head, but my darling wife won't admit it. As to the matter of our babe, she's been consigned to bedrest for a sennight."

Garahan nodded, wondering how the baron appeared so calm. If their roles were reversed, he'd be demanding immediate justice.

"Prudence did not mention her ordeal at all," the baron told him. "She's more interested in my wife's welfare. Your wife is lucky to have escaped harm after being abducted—as are Olivia and Melanie."

"Aye, though to hear the young lasses tell it, my wife kept her head and helped keep their panic at bay. She's a strong woman—but I'm wondering if she has not had the chance to allow herself time to absorb what happened."

"If your wife is as strong willed as mine, I suspect you'll not find out until the middle of the night, when she'll relive what happened as she sleeps. My best advice is to remember that she won't wake knowing she is safe in your arms—she may try to strike you."

"'Tis a sound notion, yer lordship. Thank ye for mentioning it. The lass is strong, and I'd prefer not to appear before the others sporting a black eye in the morning."

The two men stood silent for a moment listening to the soft voices on the other side of the door. When it seemed as if the women would be chatting for a while, Summerfield said, "It may be too soon to ask, and I would not if not for my wife's injury and delicate condition, but do you think Prudence would mind sitting with Phoebe during the day? It would ease my mind—and yours—if they were both resting, keeping one another company. It might do the both of them a world of good if they were able to talk to one another about their ordeals."

"Knowing me wife, she may have already offered. What of the lads? Are they still here?"

Summerfield nodded. "I did not want to send them home until we knew who struck my wife. I couldn't take the chance that their mother might take out her anger on the twins. We're hoping one or two more of their servants will add to the already damning evidence against Mrs. Honeycutt. Did you know that their cook and stable master spoke to Standish?"

Relief filled Garahan. "They are the two staff members I was hoping to speak to once I returned with me wife and the lasses—safe and sound. Mrs. Cabot in particular, as she alluded to a conversation she'd overheard." A sharp pain had him sucking in a breath.

The baron stared at him. "Have you had whatever wound you received taken care of yet?"

"Aye." Garahan appreciated that the baron didn't treat him like an invalid. "The physician who attended me wife and the lasses at the inn was still there and was able to stitch me back together."

Summerfield shook his head. "I had no idea guarding the duke would be such a perilous job, nor that being related to him held the same danger."

"But ye wouldn't change yer circumstances for the world."

The baron nodded. "You have the right of it. I was blessed the day Phoebe hurtled herself into my arms, mistaking me for my cousin."

"I'm thinking Viscount Chattsworth had a good laugh at yer expense. I know I would have if it had been one of me cousins—O'Ghill in particular."

Summerfield chuckled. "It's good to have you back. I'm relieved to hear that Prudence was not injured."

"She had the lasses to look after and still feels responsible that they were kidnapped with her, but the vicar reiterated that it was not her fault."

"After she has a short visit with my wife, I'll send her to your bedchamber."

"Thank ye, yer lordship—the sooner the better. I...uh seem to have injured her feelings," Garahan confessed.

The baron clapped him on the back. "I'm afraid, if you are

like me, it may not be the last time. If I've learned anything being married to Phoebe, it's that all women have tender feelings. Just when you think you have them figured out, they do something else to baffle you."

"I'll keep that in mind. Thank ye for the advice."

"Did you drop off the prisoners?"

"Aye. Constable Frampton and his men drove the wagon with the prisoners. He decided to stay the night and assist Constable Standish keeping guard over the prisoners."

The baron's frown intensified. "The damning evidence is piling up against the squire and his wife."

"And the lass's own mother! What of the lads? Where will Percy and Phineas go? The wheels of justice are often slow to move."

"Phoebe and I spoke about it earlier. We'll offer them a home until matters are settled with their parents."

"And if the squire and his wife end up behind bars?" Garahan asked. "Given that the lass's own mother instigated the plan—and paid to have her daughter abducted—no court would appoint her as guardian to her nephews."

"I daresay she will be receiving a call from the local constabulary in their village by morning. Have faith that these wrongs done to your wife will be righted and justice will be served."

"As will the constant verbal attacks on yerself and her ladyship."

Summerfield agreed. "Getting back to the subject of the twins, Phoebe and I will have two rambunctious young boys to look after. I've been praying that Phoebe and our babe are unharmed. If our prayers are answered, we realize that she may not be able to handle the rowdy boys on her own in her condition. Do you think Prudence would be amenable to taking over their care, as she had been doing before you brought her here?"

"Ye can count on it. She loves the lads like brothers and has been missing them. Have ye asked her yet?"

"Phoebe and I wanted to ask you first. After all, you are newly married."

"Aye, and mucking things up with me wife already. Would ye mind if I mention it to her first? Not because I think she'd refuse. I know for a fact she won't, but because it may ease her temper at bit after I apologize to her."

"Not at all. I'll send Prudence out in a few minutes."

"Thank ye, yer lordship."

"Good luck."

Garahan stared at the closed door and muttered, "I'll need all the luck I can get."

A few minutes later, his wife opened the door and stopped to stare at him. Her eyes were wet and red-rimmed.

"Lass! Are ye feeling poorly? What's happened since ye stormed away from me?"

She sighed as they walked toward their bedchamber. "I was talking to the baroness. She could have been killed! I don't know how she bounced back so quickly. After speaking with her, I realized how much I have to be grateful for. I'm sorry I lost my temper with you, Ryan, but you need to understand that I was worried about you. I've never known anyone whose been stabbed before—let alone shot, whacked over the head, or any of the other injuries you have suffered working for the duke and his family."

"'Tis I who should be apologizing for snapping at ye. Me pride got the better of me—when ye were trying to coddle me in front of me cousins. They'll never let me live it down."

"I see that we both have a bit more to learn about the other's feelings and temperament." She pressed a kiss to his cheek. "I'm awfully tired—would you mind if I went to bed?"

He opened their door and held it for her. "As long as ye don't mind that I go with ye."

She walked into their room. "I don't think I could bear to be alone tonight. My imagination will be providing endless what-ifs the moment I close my eyes. I keep reliving the moment when I entered that carriage and realized it was not a woman we heard crying—but a man. He clapped his hand over my mouth before I could warn Olivia and Melanie not to climb into the coach!"

He closed the door and locked it. "Fret not, lass. Ye're safe, and the lasses are home again with their families doting on them. Let me do the same for ye." He closed the distance between them. "Do ye need help undressing?"

She laughed. "I should be asking you that."

He shrugged. "I still have one arm that isn't hampered by a few cracked ribs and threads that have been pulling since the doctor stitched me up."

"You must be in considerable pain. Should I ring for something to ease it?"

He pulled her into the shelter of his embrace. "Ye're all the comfort I need tonight, lass." His lips met hers, and the pain in his side faded as her love flowed over him, comforting him.

They undressed one another and slipped into bed, with Prudence pressing her breasts against his back as she wrapped herself around him. Her softness eased the tension in his back, while her whispered words of comfort lulled him to a state of relaxation.

The whisper-soft kisses to his back had him groaning. "Lass, ye're killing me."

"I'm sorry. I'll stop."

"Nay," he said, pulling her on top of him and shifting onto his back. "Don't stop, lass."

"I know you must be in terrible pain, but I cannot let go of the thought that I'd never see you again. Never touch your face or kiss your mouth…or kiss you from your neck to your knees."

Ignoring the twinge in his side, he lifted his hips, but she surprised him by inching up until her lips were brushing against his, softly, tenderly. He felt his need for her growing, but tamped it down as she pressed her lips to the hollow of his throat. "Lass—"

"It's my turn to pleasure you. Don't interrupt!"

He groaned when her lips left a trail of heat along his breastbone.

Halfway to his stomach, she paused. "I'm so sorry you were

injured. As soon as the physician allows you to remove the bandages, I'll kiss every inch that I have to skip over for now." She swirled the tip of her tongue over him, then nipped where her tongue had been as she blazed a trail, drawing ever closer to the part of him that ached for her, burned for her.

He nearly swallowed his own tongue when his innocent wife began to explore the length and breadth of him with her mouth.

"God in Heaven, lass. Ye need to stop."

"I didn't tell *you* to stop. Don't you want me to—"

"Aye, lass, too much. I'll explain later, trust me."

She sighed. "As long as I haven't done something you didn't like."

After he shifted so he had her where he wanted her, she sighed and opened for him. He lifted his hips and filled her, then slowly pulled out. Over and over, he thrust then retreated, until he heard her breathing change and knew she was ready to fly. He gripped her hips and levered them up off the bed with the power of his thrusts, sending them into the heavens and beyond.

When she was limp, he shifted her to his good side and pressed a kiss to her temple. "I thought I'd never have the chance to make love to ye again. 'Tis the only time I feel whole, lass."

"I didn't want you to know how scared I was, because I knew you would worry."

"I nearly lost me mind."

"Could I ask you a favor, Ryan?"

"Aye, anything."

"I know you're hurt, and I hate to ask, but would you hold me until I fall asleep?"

He tipped her chin up and kissed her softly, lingering when he tasted a hint of himself on her lips. "Me pleasure, lass."

Exhaustion took its toll, and they drifted to sleep, safely locked in one another's arms.

WHEN SHE CRIED out the first time, he soothed her with whispered words of love until she calmed again. The third time she woke him from a deep sleep, he knew then the lass buried her fears deeply. If it took a lifetime, he'd coax each and every worry from the depths of her soul, and replace them with love and light.

He watched the sky outside their window lighten as dawn approached. Though his ribs ached where she pressed against them, he did not move for fear he'd wake her. She'd finally quieted about an hour ago. It wasn't a hardship at all with the weight of the woman he loved pressed against his heart, her legs tangled with his. A reminder of their lovemaking.

When she began to stir, he pressed a kiss behind her ear. When she sighed, he traced the rim of her mouth with the tip of his tongue. When she moaned, he kissed her with the passion he'd held in check during the long hours spent watching her sleep.

As the sun's rays filled the room, he made slow, sweet love to her with his words, his mouth, his body.

PRUDENCE WOKE SLOWLY with a delicious feeling of having been well loved the night before and sometime just after dawn. The deep, rhythmic breathing had her turning so she could trace the line of her love's jaw. When he did not waken, she boldly kissed where her fingertips had been. Still he slept—deeply.

Unsure if it was permissible for a wife to explore her husband while he slept, she slowly pushed the covers aside to take in the glory of his broad shoulders and his heavily muscled chest. Scooting up in bed, she leaned over him and studied what she'd ignored the night before—his nipples. They were flat and smooth and fascinated her. Would it arouse him if she flicked them with her tongue?

Thinking she should ask permission, she tried to rouse him. "Ryan?"

His breathing did not change, so she called his name again.

Her husband must be exhausted—and all things considered, he should be. She wasn't, but she had not been stabbed. She tried one last time. When he did not waken, she took matters in her own hands—rather into her mouth.

He jolted on the bed and wrapped his arms around her. "I wondered what ye were up to, minx. Planning to have yer way with me while I was unconscious?"

She wrinkled her nose and frowned. "But you weren't, were you?"

"I didn't want to frighten ye, lass." He slowly smiled. "Given yer explorations last night, I was hoping ye might kiss yer way down me chest again. I've a mind to teach ye a few things, if ye're willing."

"I'm a fast learner."

"Any faster, lass, and you'd be giving me a fine wake this morning." When her lips brushed the edge of his collarbone, he warned, "Mind ye don't use yer teeth, lass."

She plied her lips and tongue along the same path as last night, but this time he didn't stop her until he was ready to explode.

He rolled over, pinning her beneath him. She wrapped her arms around his neck and her legs around his waist, glorying in the weight of him as he plunged into her again and again, bringing her to the brink of madness. The flick of his tongue on her breast, and his guttural cry of completion, shot her to peak and over.

When her heart finally calmed down and she caught her breath, she snuggled into the crook of his arm, marveling that he made her feel as if she were normal, and not some giant woman to be cast aside because of her height and her curves. She didn't want to press him with the questions swirling in her mind, but she would one of these days...

"What has ye frowning, lass, after we pleasured one another into near oblivion?"

"Oh, it wasn't anything to do with our lovemaking," she

assured him. "It's just…"

"Out with it, lass. Don't hold it inside where it'll fester."

"You make me feel normal, like I'm not a behemoth."

His anger was palpable when he demanded, "Who in the bloody hell ever called ye that?"

"It isn't important now," she replied. "What is important is that you make me feel different, and when I'm with you, no one makes fun of my size or my figure."

He skimmed a hand over and around her curves, titillating her with the brush of his fingertips here, and the press of his hand there.

She moaned his name. "You make me feel—"

"How do I make ye feel, lass?"

"Loved."

"Well now, *mo ghrá*, 'tis because ye are. I love ye with me heart, me soul, me body, and me mind." He slid his hand down to cover her belly. "Lord willing, in nine months, proof of our love will come into the world screaming at the top of his—or her—lungs."

"Promise you won't turn away from me when I grow fat with your child."

"Lass, the image that brings to mind has me craving another taste of ye, but I've already used up me strength. Why don't we ring for a bit of breakfast?" When she giggled, he amended, "Lunch, then. And while we're at it, hot water to fill the tub in the dressing room for our bath."

"Our?"

"Aye, lass, there's a lesson I've a mind to share with ye about making love in the tub."

"What about your stitches?"

"I'll let ye put some of Mrs. Green's healing ointment on them and bandage me up after our bath."

"And it won't hurt your ribs to, er…"

"To sit in a tub and wash yer tender bits that I've no doubt used and mayhap abused last night and this morning? Nay, lass.

Let me take care of ye. Then it'll be yer turn to doctor me so ye don't hound me about healing salves and herbs."

"I said I was sorry to have angered you."

"And I apologized and explained a bit about me cousins. Though by now, they'll be thinking I'm a hero."

"Because of how you saved us?"

He leaned close until they were a breath away. "Nay, lass. Because of how many times I made ye cry out me name making love to ye."

She covered her mouth with her hands, and he roared with laughter. "Don't worry, lass—'tis all a part of living together as man and wife in a household filled with other people and their servants."

"Does everyone know how we spent the night?"

"Aye, and this morning. Ye've a fine set of lungs on ye, lass."

"You're joking, aren't you?"

He shook his head and grinned. "I wouldn't worry yer pretty head about it. If anyone says anything, just smile at me and pretend ye didn't hear the question."

"Wouldn't that be ludicrous if what you said is true and everyone could hear me?"

His smile broadened. "Not one person would dare mention it to our faces. They are ladies and gentlemen—staff included. Besides, 'twill be worth it, as me cousins won't be giving me any lip for the foreseeable future. Well…at least until our first babe is born."

"First babe?"

"We'll have an even dozen, I'm thinking."

He was laughing when she collapsed in his arms. "I've got ye now lass, and I'll never let ye go."

"Twelve?"

"All right, ye win, lass—thirteen, but that's me final offer."

"Ryan?"

"Aye, *mo ghrá*?"

"You're full of *shite*."

"Faith, I knew ye were the lass for the moment I saw yer delectable *derrière* above me head."

They were laughing when their lips met in a kiss that promised a lifetime of love and happiness.

❖❖❖

EPILOGUE

THE HOUR BEFORE dawn was Garahan's favorite time of day. He spent that hour watching his wife sleep while he memorized the curve of her cheek, the tilt of her lips, and the womanly curves that distracted him to no end. This was their time—before he reported to his first shift working for the baron, and before the lass slipped from their bed when their son would let out his lusty cry of hunger.

She stirred, and he pressed his lips to hers, waking her with a kiss. She turned to him, wrapping herself around him as he slid home into her welcoming warmth. They made love as the sun broke over the horizon.

Replete, he tucked her head beneath his chin and sighed. "I have to leave our bed soon."

She snuggled closer. "I know. Just hold me for a few more minutes."

How could he refuse the love of his life? "Only a few minutes more, lass, else neither of us will leave this bed till noon." Their babe making the snuffling sounds that were a prelude to his first demand to be fed had them laughing. "Time and our babe's empty belly wait for no man."

He jumped out of bed, scooped up their son, and gently handed him to his wife. With awe, he watched the little one root around to find the comfort he sought, suckling at his ma's breast.

Unable to stop himself, Garahan traced the tip of his finger along her collarbone and then down to her other breast, marveling that a woman's body could not only give pleasure, but sustenance.

"Ye're a remarkable woman, lass. The longer I know ye, the more I'm convinced the Lord fashioned ye just for me."

She smiled as she stroked the downy-soft hair on their babe's head.

Needing her attention focused on him, for just one moment more, Garahan said, "I'm thinking I'm ready to start on the second of our thirteen children."

"Don't even suggest such a thing when I'm still feeding our firstborn and haven't lost the weight from carrying him."

"Ye don't need to lose any of the weight on my account. Yer body is a banquet, lass, where I'll happily sup for the rest of me life."

"And that is my cue to rustle up something for my darling husband before he heads out of our cottage to report for his first shift of the day. Will you be guarding the perimeter, or are you on patrol riding into the village?"

"Neither—me first post of the day is guarding the interior."

"Please give everyone my best and ask the baroness if she'd like to have tea midday. We have the second cradle you insisted we needed when you thought I was large enough to be carrying twins. She'll have a place for their babe to sleep while we visit."

"What do I know of the changes a woman's body goes through while she's carrying?"

She frowned at him. "Hopefully a lot more. If, and when, the Lord blesses us with another babe, you won't make the same comments."

"Haven't I apologized more than once over the past few months?"

"You have."

"Haven't ye told me ye forgive me?"

"Yes, I did, my dear husband, but that does not mean that I will forget!"

"Faith, but ye remind me of me ma more and more each day."

"Thank you for the compliment, Ryan. You know how much I've enjoyed exchanging letters with your mother."

"She hasn't been filling yer head with so-called tales from me youth, has she?"

Prudence smiled as she placed their son to her shoulder and gently rubbed his back until he burped. "Only the one about you climbing to the top of the ruins near their farm and screaming until your da climbed up and carried you down. You were twelve summers, weren't you?"

"I was five! I had no idea ye were an evil woman, Prudence Garahan!"

"Faith, but ye love me anyway," she said, mimicking his brogue to perfection.

Their laughter filled the cottage as he pressed his lips to hers.

About the Author

Historical & Contemporary Romance "Warm…Charming…Fun…"

C.H. was born in Aiken, South Carolina, but her parents moved back to northern New Jersey where she grew up.

She believes in fate, destiny, and love at first sight. C.H. fell in love at first sight when she was seventeen. She was married for 41 wonderful years until her husband lost his battle with cancer. Soul mates, their hearts will be joined forever.

They have three grown children—one son-in-law, two grand-sons, two rescue dogs, and two rescue grand-cats.

Her characters rarely follow the synopsis she outlines for them…but C.H. has learned to listen to her characters! Her heroes always have a few of her husband's best qualities: his honesty, his integrity, his compassion for those in need, and his killer broad shoulders. C.H. writes about the things she loves most: Family, her Irish and English Ancestry, Baking and Gardening.

C.H.'s Social Media Links:
Website: www.chadmirand.com
Amazon: amazon.com/stores/C.-H.-
Admirand/author/B001JPBUMC
BookBub: bookbub.com/authors/c-h-admirand
Facebook Author Page: facebook.com/CHAdmirandAuthor
Facebook Private Reader's Page ~ C.H. Reader's Nook:
facebook.com/groups/714796299746980
GoodReads:
goodreads.com/author/show/212657.C_H_Admirand
Instagram: c.h.admirand
Twitter: @AdmirandH
Youtube:
youtube.com/channel/UCRSXBeqEY52VV3mHdtg5fXw

www.ingramcontent.com/pod-product-compliance
Lightning Source LLC
Chambersburg PA
CBHW060342310726
48976CB00003B/682